WHACK A MOLE

CHRIS GRABENSTEIN

CARROLL & GRAF PUBLISHERS

New York

Whack-A-Mole

Carroll & Graf Publishers
An Imprint of Avalon Publishing Group, Inc.
245 West 17th Street
11th Floor
New York, NY 10011

AVALON
publishing group incorporated

ISBN-13: 978-0-78671-818-4
ISBN-10: 0-7867-1818-8

9 8 7 6 5 4 3 2 1

Interior book design by Jamie McNeely

Printed in the United States of America
Distributed by Publishers Group West

For Buster and Fred.
One man's best four-legged writing partners.

The dogs on Main Street howl
'cause they understand
If I could take one moment into my hands
Mister I ain't a boy, no I'm a man
And I believe in a promised land

—Bruce Springsteen
"The Promised Land"

ONE

I've never been what you might call an "overachiever" but at age twenty-five I've already done the worst thing any human being can possibly do.

John Ceepak, my partner, tells me I should let it all out. Get it off my chest. Make what the priests used to call a full and complete confession.

Fine.

I'll do like Ceepak suggests.

It all starts with this stupid ring he found.

TWO

L ast Sunday. Six fifty-five A.M.

Bruce Springsteen is on the radio reciting my most recent résumé: *"I had a job, I had a girl, I had something going, mister, in this world. . . ."*

I'm sitting in The Bagel Lagoon waiting for Ceepak. He lives here. Not in the restaurant with the bagels—upstairs in the apartment on the second floor.

"She said Joe, I gotta go, we had it once, we ain't got it any more. She packed her bags, left me behind. . . ."

The Boss is laying it on thicker than a slab of walnut cream cheese. Says he feels like he's *"a rider on a down-bound train."*

I can relate.

Katie's gone.

She said, "Danny, I gotta go." Okay, it doesn't rhyme as good as it might've if my name was Joe like the guy in Bruce's song. Katie, my ex-girlfriend, moved to California. Grad school. Left town in March.

I hope California is as nice as Sea Haven—this eighteen-mile-long strip of sand-in-your-shoes paradise down the Jersey Shore. I hope it has boardwalks and miniature golf and fresh-cut fries and a fudge forecast that's always smooth and creamy like it has been at Pudgy's Fudgery for the past seventy-five years, at least according to the sign flapping out on their sidewalk near the Quick Pick Fudge Cart.

On the radio, Bruce is done singing the blues.

Me, too.

At exactly seven A.M. every Sunday, the Reverend Billy Trumble shoves all rock 'n' roll off the air. He's been doing seven A.M. Sundays on WAVY for nearly thirty years.

"Friends, do you think it is early?" his smooth voice purrs. "Trust me—it is later than you think. Judgment Day is nigh. . . ."

"Turn it off," hollers Joe Coglianese from the back of the shop. He and his brother Jim run The Bagel Lagoon. Joe's in charge of stirring the pot where the bagels bob in boiling water. Jim mans the counter. It's the middle of July and already 80 degrees outside. It feels hotter if you factor in the humidity, plus the steam rising up from that humongous bagel vat. No wonder Joe is the grouchier of the two Coglianese brothers.

Jim snaps off the radio.

I tear another bite out of my bagel.

Ceepak should be joining me any minute. We're both cops with the Sea Haven P.D. and, even though it's our day off, today we are men on a mission.

Ceepak, who's like this 6 '2", thirty-six-year-old Eagle-Scout-slash-Jarhead, found something he thinks is valuable buried on the beach while he was sweeping the sand with his metal detector.

This is what Ceepak does for fun when there are no *Forensic Files* or *CSI* reruns on TV. He's even in this club: The Sea Haven Treasure Hunter Society. It's mostly geeks and geezers, guys who strap on headphones and walk the beach like the minesweeper soldier in every bag of green plastic Army men—who, come to think of it, are now chocolate-chip-camo-brown because they've been to Iraq and back, just like Ceepak. They hunt for Spanish doubloons, abandoned Rolexes, rusty subway tokens, discarded paper clips—anything that makes their detectors go beepity-beep.

Anyway, a week ago, Ceepak dug up a ring from P. J. Johnson High School up in Edison. Class of 1983. Inside the ring he found an inscription: B. Kladko. Ceepak being Ceepak, he investigated further and came up with a Brian Kladko who, indeed, graduated from PJJHS in 1983 and still lives somewhere nearby. We're going up there today to take his class ring back to him.

After Katie split, I fill my weekends as best I can.

While I wait, I check out the early-morning crowd. It's mostly tourists from New York and Philadelphia, making them experts on both bagels and cream cheese. They swarm into The Lagoon ordering their favorite combos, forgetting they came down here to try new stuff, like Jersey blueberries or Taylor Pork Roll.

The door opens and all of a sudden it's like somebody walked in with a load of last week's lox in their shorts. A lot of noses suddenly crinkle, mine included. Phew.

"Something's fishy around here," says the big guy who's just come in. "Look no further. It's me!"

"Me" being Cap'n Pete Mullen. He runs one of the deep-sea fishing boats over by the public marina, and he's been taking tourists out after tuna and fluke for so long his clothes all smell like they've been washed with Low Tide-Scented Tide.

"Whataya need, Pete?" asks Jim, the bagel brother behind the counter.

"Baker's dozen. Got a charter going out this morning."

Cap'n Pete has a walrus mustache that wiggles like a worm on a hook. He grins at a kid who's staring at him, watching the lip hair twitch. "I'm Cap'n Pete, laddie. But you can call me Stinky. Stinky Pete."

The boy laughs. So do his folks.

"You run a fishing boat?" asks the dad.

"Sure do."

Pete is good. He comes in to buy breakfast and ends up hooking and booking more clients. I'm sure before their week in Sea Haven is over this fine family of four will be strapping on life vests and heading out to sea on the *Reel Fun*—Cap'n Pete's forty-seven-foot Sportfish.

Jim scoops up an assortment of bagels from the bins and hands the bag to Cap'n Pete.

"Well, I best be shoving off." He chops a salute off the brim of his admiral's cap to the little kid. He sort of looks like the Skipper from *Gilligan's Island.*

Now he shoots me a wave.

Grins.

"Hey, Danny—have Johnny give me a holler. I missed the last meeting."

I'm in midchew so I nod and wave. To hear Ceepak tell it, Pete is the unluckiest of all his treasure-hunting buddies. The guy's never found anything under the sand, although occasionally he manages to reel in an interesting boot or tire on his fishing lines.

I chomp off another bite of bagel and eyeball the couple that just stormed in. Studying people is a habit I've picked up working with Ceepak. He's always sizing folks up, trying to decipher their *real* story, the one they're trying to hide.

The fiftysomething guy is wearing what I call *preppy nautical:* untucked polo shirt, khaki slacks, Docksiders without socks.

His slightly younger wife has on a wide-brimmed straw hat anchored with a scarf strapped tight under her chin. Her coffee can–size sunglasses make her look like she has gigantic ant eyes. I figure she's trying to hide from the world. She also seems to be having trouble with the menu. Keeps staring up at the chalkboard, where things aren't all that complicated. The Bagel Lagoon? Basically, it's about bagels.

"Honey?" The husband is hoping to nudge his wife toward a decision.

"Do you have toast?" she asks.

"No," says Jim. "Bagels."

"Eggs?"

"She'll have a raisin bagel," says the husband.

"I don't like raisins."

"Fine. Make it a plain."

"I don't like plain, either."

"Well what *do* you like?"

Obviously, these folks came down the shore to put a little sizzle back in their marriage. I'm glad things are working out so well for them.

"If you paid more attention, you'd know what I like!" The wife steps closer to the counter, farther away from her husband.

"I'll have a poppy," she finally says.

"Anything on it?" asks Jim.

Her eyes go back to the menu board. There are six different kinds of cream cheese and four kinds of butter, if you include peanut. This could go on for hours.

I turn and stare out the window.

Well, well, well.

Here comes Rita. Down the side-of-the-building staircase from Ceepak's apartment.

Over the past year, my partner has struck up a romance with a lovely local lady named Rita Lapczynski. She's a single mom, about thirty-five, who has this huge swoop of blonde hair, which, if my detective's instincts do not deceive me, currently features a pillow dent on the left.

Interesting.

Rita comes into the bagelry.

"Morning, Jim."

"Rita! How you doin'?"

"Yo, Rita!" Joe in the back gives her a big wave of the wooden paddle.

"The usual?" asks Jim.

"Yes, thank you."

"One Salty with a schmear. Coffee light."

"Excuse me. My wife was next," says the preppy husband.

"I'm sorry," says Rita.

"Honey?" says the husband. His voice sounds patient. His eyes, however, are in a hurry. "We are on a schedule. . . ."

"Do not rush me, Theodore!"

Jim goes ahead and fixes Rita her bagel.

Rita is humming to herself. A little smile crosses her face. I guess she spent the night upstairs because her son T. J. is on vacation—up in New York City, staying with an aunt who lives out in Queens. In fact, I know Ceepak paid for the bus tickets. My partner's running a reverse version of The Fresh Air Fund—sending a shore kid up to the polluted city.

Jim takes Rita's cash, keys the register, and hands her back her change, which she drops into the tip cup. Rita waitresses over at Morgan's Surf and Turf. Those who live by tips are always the best tippers.

Finally, she sees me.

"Hey, Danny."

"Hey, Rita. How's it goin'?"

"Fantastic. Looking forward to hearing about your adventures up in Edison."

"Okay."

"Take care now. Have a great day!"

"Sure."

I watch her head toward her car. Then I count to five.

Right on cue, Ceepak comes through the door. So that's how it works: she slips out first, he sneaks down a minute later. Clever.

Now an important thing to know about John Ceepak is that he lives by this very strict, very rigid moral code. It's easier to explain than to follow. Ceepak will not lie, cheat, or steal, nor tolerate those who do. It's a holdover from his fourteen years in the Army. The West Point Honor Code. This morning, I plan to use it against him. Big time.

The wife in the insectoid sunglasses decides she doesn't really want anything for breakfast—except maybe a new husband—and hurries out the door fumbling with a pack of cigarettes. Hubby follows.

"Good morning, Danny," Ceepak now greets me. He's as bright and chipper as usual. The dimples in his cheeks seem a little more animated this morning, but his hair reveals no pillow wrinkles. Then again, his buzz cut is way too short to dent.

"Have you been waiting long?" he asks.

I smirk. "Long enough."   •

"You had breakfast?"

"Yeah."

"Awesome."

Here comes the fun part. "So—did Rita spend the night?"

"Yes."

I act *amazed*.

"Really?"

"Yes. Ready to roll?" Ceepak's still smiling. No guilt. No shame. No bullshit or cover-up. Just the simple, unvarnished truth.

Apparently, it really does set one free.

Two hours later we're at the food court of the Menlo Park Mall outside Edison, New Jersey. We're sitting in plastic chairs at a table near the Cinnabon counter. The scent of warm dough and cinnamon swirls through the air like invisible frosting—it smells even better than sticking your face inside a box of Cinnamon Toast Crunch cereal. Trust me. I know. I've done this.

Ceepak puts a little clear plastic bag on the table. The ring.

"I can't believe you found it!" says Brian Kladko.

It's your standard high-school ring. Big cut stone in the middle of a gold band. The school's coat of arms inscribed on one side, Latin words nobody still alive can translate on the other.

"Where'd you guys say you were from?"

"Sea Haven," says Ceepak.

Kladko doesn't pick up the ring. He drums the cellophane window on his big Cinnabon box. Take-out breakfast for his family.

"Where exactly is that?" he asks. "Sea Haven?"

"Down the shore," I say.

He nods. Smiles. Fidgets with the box flaps. "Okay. Sure. Near Asbury Park, right?"

"Further south."

"Okay."

He looks at his watch. The ring with its big red rock is still sitting there, all alone in its tiny plastic pouch, stranded like the pimply girl nobody wants to dance with at the prom.

"Well, thanks for driving all the way up here and all."

He stands.

"Sir?" says Ceepak, pointing to the table. "Your ring?"

"Oh. Right. Duh."

"We hope you'll come visit us in Sea Haven again," says Ceepak.

"Yeah. Why not? Be nice to see it."

"You've never been?"

"No. Don't think so." His voice sounds a little shaky.

"Interesting," says Ceepak. "Then I wonder how your ring wound up buried on our beach?"

"Guess you'd have to ask Lisa."

"Lisa?"

"My old girlfriend. I gave the ring to her. A long, long time ago."

THREE

Sir, I wonder if I might ask you a few questions?" says Ceepak.

"Sorry. I really need to. . . ."

"This will only take another minute. Please." Ceepak gestures toward the chair, politely commanding Mr. Brian Kladko to sit his butt back down.

"What? Are you guys private detectives or something?"

"We're with the Sea Haven Police Department."

Kladko sits.

"Unh-hunh." Kladko keeps his eyes on Ceepak, the man with the muscles and close-cropped hair—the guy who always looks like he's in charge, even without saying it.

"I'm curious about the ring's provenance," says Ceepak. "Its history."

"So, is this an official investigation?"

"No. More like a hobby."

Kladko thinks about that. "What? Oh, I get it. You have one of those metal detectors or something."

Ceepak nods. Kladko relaxes.

"Interesting," he says. I don't think he means it.

"I find it to be so," says Ceepak.

"Well, like I said. I gave the ring to Lisa."

"Does Lisa have a last name?"

"Yeah. De-something. DeSoto. DeMarco. That's it. Lisa DeMarco."

"And she was your girlfriend?"

Kladko grins. Shrugs. His message is clear. She was no big deal.

I watch Ceepak watching Kladko.

"Since she had your ring, I assume you two were going steady."

"Yeah. I guess. Sure." I can see Kladko start to wonder where this is going.

"What happened?"

Kladko shrugs. "We broke up."

"But she kept your ring?"

"Yeah."

"You didn't ask for it back?"

Kladko tries to look bored. "Nope. Never got the chance."

"Why not?"

"She left. A month after I gave her the ring, she was gone."

"When was this?"

"Summer of '83."

"Did Ms. DeMarco attend P. J. Johnson High School?"

"I think so. I forget where we met. It was a long time ago. Hey—I guess I can wear my ring to the twenty-fifth reunion in 2008, huh?"

The three of us just sit there, inhaling the cinnamon-scented air.

"Are we almost done? I've got some very hungry kids at home."

"Any idea where Ms. DeMarco went?"

Kladko gives us another shrug. "Sea Haven, I guess. I suppose she went down there to have some fun. Hang out. She liked to party, you know what I mean?"

Ceepak ignores the not-so-subtle hint.

"Frankly, I'd forgotten all about Lisa till you guys showed up. DeFranco."

"Excuse me?" says Ceepak.

"DeFranco. That was her name. Lisa DeFranco. I think her mom still lives around here. I see her sometimes at the A&P over on Amboy Avenue."

"Shopping?"

"No. She works one of the registers up front. That's how I knew it was her. The nametag."

Ceepak nods. "Thank you, Mr. Kladko."

"That's it?"

"Thank you for your time."

"Hey, no problem. . . ."

He tucks the plastic bag with the ring in it into the front pocket of his khakis the same way you might stuff away one of those curling gas-pump receipts the machine spits out after you fill up on your credit card. Apparently, it holds very little sentimental value.

"I wonder if Mrs. DeFranco is working at the A&P this morning," says Ceepak as we watch Kladko hustle down the escalator.

I have a hunch we'll soon find out.

On the ride over to the A&P, Ceepak explains.

"Mr. Kladko is hiding something."

"Yeah. I figured as much."

"'Everybody's got a secret, Sonny. Something they just can't face.'"

Ceepak isn't calling me "Sonny" because he forgot my name. He's quoting Springsteen. "Darkness on the Edge of Town." It's something we do with each other because we both love The Boss, the poet laureate of the Jersey Shore. However, when it comes to actually having lyrics memorized, Ceepak wins, hands down. I'm better at the sing-along parts. The *sha-la-la-la's*.

"Don't you find it curious that Mr. Kladko chose to meet us at a mall?" Ceepak now asks.

"I guess it was his turn to get the kids their Sunday morning Cinnabon fix. Kill two birds with one stone and all that."

"Perhaps. Or, maybe he didn't want us bringing the ring and any questions it might raise into his home."

"Questions from Mrs. Kladko?"

Ceepak nods.

"He had to agree to see us. Showing reluctance would have seemed odd. However, he immediately assumed we were private investigators. Our very presence made him nervous."

It never occurs to Ceepak that simply talking to him about the weather can make someone nervous.

Especially someone with a guilty conscience.

FOUR

I pray that when my mom is sixty-five she isn't bagging groceries on the 12-ITEMS-OR-LESS line at the A&P. This is what we see Mrs. DeFranco doing when the store manager points her out to us.

"She has her break at ten."

"We'll wait," says Ceepak.

It's nine fifty-eight. The manager folds his beefy arms across his chest—it's clear that nobody in his little kingdom ever sneaks off early.

Mind you, neither Ceepak nor I are wasting our two minutes of waiting time. We're both observing Mrs. DeFranco. Ceepak probably sees more than I do—but I notice some stuff, too.

Like the way the she jams the bread into the bag on top of the bananas and then adds the sixty-four-ounce Hawaiian Punch can so she can simultaneously smoosh somebody's food and ruin their day, just like all her days started being ruined years ago.

She looks tired. Haggard. On her feet for too long—twenty years too long. She looks like an old cloth left out in the sun, one you used to clean your car, then dropped on the driveway where it baked until the cotton started to crack.

Long story short, I'm guessing Mrs. DeFranco is going to be a real laugh-a-minute when we talk to her.

"Where the hell is Sea Heaven?"

"Down the shore," I answer, not bothering to correct her.

We're standing in the humid shade out front of the A&P. Mrs. DeFranco is sucking hard on a Marlboro—one of the real long ones so it'll last her the whole break. We had to flash our badges to get her to talk to us. Actually, we had to flash them to get her to quit saying, "Leave me the fuck alone," in front of all the little kids buying gumballs from the machines near the sliding doors.

"We'd like to ask you a few questions about your daughter," says Ceepak.

"Who?"

"Lisa."

"You seen her? She in Sea Heaven?"

"No. Not that we're. . . ."

"What'd she do? She kill somebody or some shit like that?"

"No, ma'am. In fact, we have no idea where she might be."

"Well, that makes two of us. I ain't seen or heard from her in twenty-four years."

"I don't understand. . . ."

"She ran away!" Narrowing her eyes, she takes another hot drag off the cigarette. I can hear the paper broil. "She hit the highway. Never told me where she was going. Never called—not even once. No postcards, neither."

It's hard to tell what she's feeling. The Marlboro seems to interest her more than her daughter.

Ceepak, as always, wants to help. "Maybe Lisa is still in our area. We could look for her. Initiate a search."

Now she laughs. "Fine. Knock yourself out."

"She'd be what?" says Ceepak. "Forty-two? Forty-three?"

"Something like that," says Mrs. DeFranco. She sends out a steady stream of smoke. "Check all the whorehouses first."

"Ma'am?"

"The whorehouses. That's where she'd be, the fucking little slut."

Okay. We definitely have some of those Dr. Phil-type mother-daughter issues going on here.

"Your daughter was promiscuous?" asks Ceepak.

"She was a fucking tramp. I heard about it. Heard what she did under those bleachers and out in the parking lot with all them boys."

"Back in 1983, when she first disappeared, did you file a missing person report?"

"Why? She wasn't missing. She *ran away*. Besides, I was busy. Had my own shit to take care of. Ronny said I was doing the right thing. . . ."

"Ronny?"

"This guy I was seeing back then."

"Do you have a photograph of your daughter? It might help us find her if . . ."

"I threw all her pictures in the trash."

"Did your daughter go steady with any particular boy?"

She laughs. Smoke comes out her nose. "Why buy a cow when the milk's free? That's what she was. A fat fucking cow. Ate too much junk food. Guess that's my fault, too, hunh?"

"Didn't her father intercede with these young men?"

"Her father? Hah! That bastard left before Lisa was even born. It was just her and me—and then, when I'm finally getting my own shit together again, she takes off and Ronny dumps me."

"I apologize if we've stirred up painful memories, ma'am."

Ceepak sounds totally bummed. Not the end he'd imagined for our mission to Edison. I'm bummed, too. For him.

But Mrs. DeFranco isn't done yet.

"When she left town, she was even fatter."

"Ma'am?" asks Ceepak.

"Jesus. How stupid are you? Lisa was knocked up, okay? She was fat because she was pregnant."

"Are you certain?"

"I found a positive EPT in the trash next to the toilet, didn't I?"

We wait. She still looks like she has something more to say.

"And then?" Ceepak encourages her.

"She packed her shit, took off in the middle of the night, and I never saw her again. She was gone. Fine, I said. She doesn't want to come home, that's her fucking choice."

Ceepak looks sad.

"Anything else you can tell us, ma'am?"

"Before she left, she showed me a ring. A present from her boyfriend. Oh, she was so fucking proud. But it wasn't no engagement ring and it sure as shit wouldn't pay for no abortion, neither. They don't give you jackshit when you hock those things. I know. And I told her so, too."

FIVE

E xit 80 on the Garden State Parkway.

That's when Ceepak finally says something.

"Can you drop me off at the animal shelter?"

"Sure."

"Rita is meeting me there. Fourteen hundred hours."

"No problem."

Two weeks ago we collared this dog. A stray. You might be surprised how many families come down the shore with their four-legged friends, decide they're sick and tired of scooping up poop, and set their beloved pets free.

Of course, it's against the posted regulations and all sorts of municipal ordinances to have doggy scavengers running around loose on the beach, begging at every umbrella for Pringles or the last licks on a Fudgsicle. Eventually, somebody notices and calls the cops. With the help of a long, looped pole, we eventually nab the perp.

Ceepak, however, is the only cop who actually visits his prisoners at the South Shore Animal Shelter in Avondale. He even gave this one particular pooch a name: Barkley. He said it's a classic. Maybe. I thought Fido was the only classic dog name. Or Rover.

Anyhow, before we left the A&P in Edison, Ceepak had gone back inside to buy a foil pouch of Pupperonis. I figure he's thinking about Barkley the Dog right now so he can stop thinking about Lisa the Runaway and her miserable-excuse-for-a-mother who couldn't be bothered with filling out a missing person report on her only child because she was busy with her "own shit." Ceepak can actually help the stray dog. It's doubtful whether he or anybody else can help Lisa DeFranco, who must be fortysomething years old by now and is probably living someplace in Florida or Texas.

I ease on the brakes. We're inching closer to the shore exits, so the Garden State Parkway automatically turns into a two-lane parking lot. Suddenly we're not moving.

"A/C good?" I ask.

"Fine."

I used to drive around in a white minivan that I purchased secondhand from my mom. (She cut me an okay deal on it when she and Dad retired to Arizona, but I had to haggle.) Once I started pulling down a regular paycheck, I decided it was time to trade up. Now I've got a used Jeep Wrangler. It's a good beach vehicle. Not that I've ever driven it on one. That would be against the law, and since I'm now a cop, I'd have to write myself a ticket.

The traffic starts moving again. We're doing at least five, maybe ten miles per hour.

"Next weekend will be worse." This from Ceepak.

"Yup," I agree. Because of the sand castle contest.

"We can handle it."

"Yeah," I say. "I hear the pro team from San Diego's going to build the Sphinx."

Bizarre but true.

There are actually sand professionals who tour the country competing against each other for cash prizes in "sand carving" contests. This summer, Sea Haven is sponsoring its first one ever. Next weekend. The town fathers hope it'll bump up business in the middle of July, which happens to be when business is already insane. In a beach resort, you make ninety percent of your money in June, July, and August. So you need to keep coming up with new schemes for cashing in while the sun still shines, because after Labor Day the kids go back to school and their parents stay home with the ATM cards.

We finally pull into the shelter lot at 3:30—an hour and a half behind schedule. The lovely Rita is waiting for us.

Ceepak sees her and smiles.

She's got on the white blouse and black pants she wears to work the Sunday brunch shift at Morgan's Surf and Turf. It's a five-days-a-week gig for her. Weekdays, she works at a bank. She holds down the two jobs because she's had to raise her son, T. J., all by herself.

T. J., now sixteen, helps out with their finances. He works on the boardwalk and at Burger King. This Ceepak-financed two-week trip to his aunt's is the longest vacation the kid's ever had.

"Say 'hi' to Barkley for me," I say.

"Will do. See you tomorrow."

"Sorry how the trip turned out."

He looks at me. Nods.

"Me, too."

"Hey, Danny!" Rita hollers and waves.

"Hey!" I holler back. "You guys have fun. Pet a dog for me!"

Technically, they call this cinderblock building an animal shelter, but I'll bet the dogs inside call it *the pound* or *the joint or the big house* or something worse. They don't want to be here. They miss their people—even the lousy bums who abandoned them

That's what we figure happened to Barkley.

Ceepak and I found him without a collar, hiding underneath the boardwalk. When we crawled in to fetch him, he immediately started sniffing Ceepak's cargo pants, because my partner always carries dog treats in one of the pockets. My dad did the same thing. He was a USPS letter carrier. Treats in one pocket, mace in the other.

Barkley's sort of shaggy. Got the white whiskers, droopy tail, and hind-leg shuffle you see on old dogs. But he also has this twinkle in his eyes, especially when he smells Pupperonis or Snausages.

Ceepak gives Rita a quick kiss and then, holding hands, they head in to visit the dog nobody else has any use for today. I wave goodbye, but they don't see it. The fact that I'm kind of a lonely stray myself these days doesn't occur to them. But that's cool. Sure, my apartment is filthy, but at least it's not a cage.

Dogs are kept here for two weeks, in hopes that their owners will come claim them. After that, they go up for adoption. If no one wants an old, shedding bed-hog who probably farts, well, I don't know what happens.

I'm pretty sure they don't set the dogs free.

Man—this is turning into one of the most depressing Sundays ever.

I head toward the causeway—the long bridge that's the only way on or off the barrier island we call Sea Haven Township.

I wonder how many hours it'll take to drive the final five miles home.

I catch a break.

Traffic's not that bad. Of course, it's almost four o'clock, so anybody who wanted to soak up some sun has already squeezed their way across the bridge.

My cell phone chirps.

Since I'm only doing about twenty miles per hour and Ceepak is no longer sitting next to me, I go ahead and answer it, even though I know it's against the law in New Jersey to drive and talk. On the phone, I mean. You can talk to other people in the car.

"Hello?"

"Hey, Danny! Where are you?"

It's my buddy Jess.

"Crawling toward the causeway."

"Cool. Head over to The Sand Bar."

"Why?"

"Olivia's here."

Jess and Olivia have been together for about two years. They're getting married next Christmas.

"And?" I know there's got to be more.

"Aubrey's here, too. By herself. Looking totally hot."

Aubrey is a long-limbed beauty who waitresses at a greasy pit of a restaurant called The Rusty Scupper. Ever since Katie left, Jess and Olivia have been trying to fix me up with somebody. Anybody.

"She's out of my league, bro," I say and maneuver into the right-hand lane.

"Dude? She asked us about you."

"Seriously?"

"Totally. She said, 'Where's Danny?'"

"No way."

"Way. Come on, man. You gotta climb back on that bicycle."

He means horse. I think the bicycle is the thing you never forget how to do. The horse is the thing that throws you for a loop but you have to climb back on anyway. I think Katie is more of a horse than a bicycle.

"You out on the deck?" I ask.

"Of course."

"I'll swing by."

"Excellent. We'll alert Aubrey."

I snap the cell shut and toss it onto the passenger seat.

For some reason, traffic slows down right before the causeway and then it speeds back up again. Probably some sort of rubbernecking delay. I hope nobody's had an accident. Could be an overheated radiator. Maybe a flat tire. I'll check it out, see if I can help. Hey, a cop is never really off duty. Ceepak tells me that, all the time.

I move closer to the bridge. I see this curvy girl standing on the shoulder of the road. She's wearing rolled-up military shorts, cowboy boots, and a bikini top. Actually, the top looks more like a bra than a bathing suit. She's sticking out her thumb and every car with a still-breathing male behind the wheel is slowing down to sneak a peek.

I pull over and roll down the passenger-side window.

The girl heads over to my Jeep and sticks her head inside. She leans over far enough to give me a pretty good idea of what's holding up the bikini top.

"Hey," she says, all breathy and husky, like she thinks a sexy woman is supposed to sound. Her hair is red. Actually, it's more an orange rinse over black roots.

There's a small stone sparkling near her left nostril, and she's stuck an earring through her right eyebrow—for balance, I guess. I'm figuring she's sixteen, maybe seventeen, tops. She has a Hello Kitty backpack.

"Got room for one more?" She swipes her tongue slowly across her top teeth. It might actually be sexy if her teeth weren't so grungy.

I reach over to the passenger window for her backpack, toss it into the back.

"Hop in," I say.

She does.

SIX

W.W.C.D?

What would Ceepak do?

I should get a hat made like the W.W.J.D. ones the born-again Christian kids wear at the Life Under the Son booth up on the boardwalk. They're always asking, "What Would Jesus Do?" But Jesus never owned a Jeep, so he probably never picked up a semi-naked teenage hitchhiker who sits with her cowboy-booted legs tucked up under her butt in a way that shows off a ton of thigh.

We're on the island now, approaching the traffic circle right next to King Putt Golf, this miniature golf course where I once scored a hole-in-one on Cleopatra's Loop-D-Loop. You have to shoot your ball up an alligator's snout and wait for it to twirl out the tail.

Finally, I come up with something to say.

"So, where you headed?"

"The beach."

"Cool. Which beach?"

She giggles. "Um, the one near the ocean?"

I laugh. She laughs. I laugh some more.

"I mean what street? See, down here, we sort of name the beaches after the streets that dead-end into them. Like Oak Beach is near the east end of Oak Street. Tangerine Beach, Tangerine Street. Maple. . . ."

"Maple."

Maple Beach is pretty close to where I used to hang out when I was her age. Like a decade ago.

"Where do you live?" I decide to ask.

"Jersey," she says.

Oh.

"What exit?"

In the great state of New Jersey, it's standard practice to pinpoint someone's hometown by either their Turnpike or Garden State Parkway exit number. Some lucky people even have both. Me? I'm Exit 62 on the GSP. The Turnpike doesn't come down the shore—it goes to Delaware, instead. Guess it's a much more serious roadway.

My passenger doesn't answer.

We're at the red light at the traffic circle.

"Come on—what exit?"

"Sorry," she says. "Not on the first date."

"Oh? Is this a date?"

She leans forward. Her lip gloss smells like test-tube strawberries or some other kind of chemical fruit.

"If you want it to be. . . ."

Fortunately, the stoplight changes to green and the New Yorker behind me wastes no time blaring his horn up my bumper.

"Fuck you!" the girl screams, and flips the guy the finger. "Asshole!"

I concentrate on making the right turn. Applying pressure to the gas pedal. Letting the New Yorker pass me. Grinning foolishly when he shakes his fist and shouts something you'd never hear in a Disney movie.

"I'll drive you to where you're going."

"Thanks," she says.

"So, you hitched all the way down?" I ask.

"Cheaper than taking the bus."

"True. . . ."

"I don't have my own wheels."

"I see. What about your parents?"

She doesn't answer that one.

"It's totally easy to hitch."

"Totally dangerous, too."

She gives me a "whatever" rise and fall of the shoulders. "I'm careful. I never climb in with any, you know, raggedy-ass skeezers or anything."

She says this like I should be flattered.

"Of course," she adds, "I'm always willing to pay my way."

"Unh-hunh."

"Always."

"Unh-hunh."

"There's a couple totally happy truck drivers on the Turnpike right now."

"Hunh."

I'm focusing on the road but I can feel the heat radiating off her skin as she leans in closer. I smell strawberries again. It reminds me of that weird, day-glow-red stuff they pour on top of ice cream at Skipper Dipper for the folks who don't do hot fudge. Suddenly, a wet tongue is swirling around inside my ear.

We swerve into the left lane.

"Sorry," I say, regaining control of my vehicle—if of nothing else.

"You want to pull over and mess around some?"

"No, thanks."

"We could party."

"I'm kind of late."

"For what?"

"I'm meeting some friends."

"Really? Where?"

"The Sand Bar. Burgers, beer, that kind of thing."

She moves back into her seat. Thinks for a minute.

"I'm hungry," she says. "I forgot to eat lunch."

I see my out.

"Well, if you're planning on hitting the beach, you really need to wait until after you go swimming to eat."

Yes! This is what Saint Ceepak would do: he'd lecture this Nympho of the Highways about stomach cramps. He'd do his duty and obey the Scout Law: to help other people at all times; to keep himself physically strong, mentally awake, and morally straight.

Morally straight.

That's the part I need to concentrate on right now.

"What's your name, anyway?" she asks.

"Danny. Danny Boyle. How about you?"

"Stacey."

"Stacey what?"

"Just Stacey for now, okay?"

"Sure. Stacey."

"A nice, cold brew would be totally awesome."

"Yes, it would. But are you anywhere even close to twenty-one?"

She leans forward in her seat. I glance over just to make sure there's no tongue aiming at my ear.

"Do I look twenty-one?"

She looks like trouble, is what she looks like. I'm starting to wonder if I should take this girl back to the mainland. Maybe Avondale. Trenton. Edison. Sea Haven, after all, is the only Jersey township I'm sworn to protect.

Instead, I make a right turn and we head to The Sand Bar.

SEVEN

The Sand Bar is a vinyl-sided three-story building on the bay side of the island, with three levels of party decks under blue canopies out back.

I figure I'll take Stacey inside and feed her—buy her a burger, maybe some curly fries—but no beer. Then I'll call Ceepak. Ask him what to do.

After we're parked, Stacey reaches into the back to unzip her backpack and pull out "something a little nicer" to wear for dinner. Good thing, since she's dangerously close to violating the eatery's longstanding "NO SHIRT, NO SHOES, NO SERVICE" edict in her bra-and-combat-shorts ensemble.

"Where's my top?"

Finding it seems to require wiggling her bottom a lot. I decide it's time for me to step away from the vehicle, as we say on the job.

I check out the restaurant's upper deck, where my buds usually hang.

Jess sees me, waves down.

"Hey!" he hollers. "Where you been?"

"Traffic."

"Too bad. Aubrey had to split. What took you so long?"

As if on cue, Stacey climbs out of the car. She's wrapping on this prairie skirt and adjusting a turquoise tube top. It fits her like a sausage skin.

Jess leans back and shoots me a double thumbs up.

It's not what you think, I gesture.

He gives me a *sure, sure* nod 'n' wink.

As Stacey walks toward me, the tube top is straining to keep everything in place. I try not to pay attention to the struggle.

"Where's the little girls' room?" she asks, giving me a bored look. Now that we're here maybe she's thinking it's not her kind of scene.

"Go to the bar and make a left."

She puts her hands on her hips, leans back, checks out the upper deck. "Those your friends?"

I see that Olivia has joined Jess at the railing. They're both cradling longneck Buds. Watching us.

"Yeah."

"Cool. I'll meet you guys upstairs."

"Where'd you find her?" Olivia asks.

There's no bullshitting Olivia. She's way too smart. She's goes to med school up in New Brunswick and comes home in the summer to earn money for the stuff all her scholarships don't cover. And Olivia's pretty intense. I guess that's why she and Jess are such a good combo. He's totally mellow—works as a house painter when he's not too busy goofing off or surfing.

"She was hitchhiking," I say. "Causing a traffic jam near the causeway."

Jess nods. "So you took prudent police action, right?"

"I figured I needed to take her someplace safe. Yes."

"Sure," says Jess. "Someplace safe. Like a seaside bar. Good call. It's like a convent in here."

"This is only temporary," I say. "I'm calling Ceepak. We'll try and find her a bed. . . ."

Jess raises an eyebrow.

I fling an onion ring, nail him on the nose.

Olivia shakes her head, takes a pull on her beer. Jess and I reach for the onion rings. We're all sharing a basket before we decide what we actually want to eat.

"So," she asks, "you think your friend got lost trying to find the bathroom?"

I check my watch. She's right. Stacey should have joined us half a bottle ago.

"I'll be back." I head downstairs.

The place is packed. Lots of guys and girls making a mosh pit around the bar. Lots of noise. Music. The bleeps and bloops of electronic pinball machines.

I don't see Stacey.

I check the hallway outside the restrooms.

"Excuse me," I shout to the girl at the head of the line. There's bass-thumping music blasting out of the concert-sized speakers suspended from the ceiling. "Are you waiting for a redhead to come out?"

She looks puzzled.

"What?"

"The girl who's in there—is she a redhead?"

"No. Blonde." Now she grins. "You like redheads?" She steps into a dusty beam of light.

She's a redhead. She's also extremely drunk.

"I'm looking for my sister," I lie.

"Too bad."

The music breaks into a fuzz-box guitar solo that growls enough to cover my exit. I head back into the bar. No Stacey. Frustrated, I decide to head through the crowd and make my way outside.

I see more people clustered just beyond the door, smoking cigarettes and laughing.

Then I see my Jeep.

Both doors are wide open.

I hustle over. The Hello Kitty backpack is gone. The papers and crap I stow up under my sun visor are scattered all over the driver's seat. Looks like everything is still there except, of course, the twenty-dollar bill I keep hidden for emergencies.

Next, I check the cup holder. My coins have been cleaned out, too. At least she left me my Dunkin' Donuts coffee mug. At least I no longer have to search the yellow pages for the local Runaway Teen Shelter .

My cell phone—which, thank God, I had tucked into my shorts before heading into The Sand Bar—chirps. I wonder if it's Stacey, Little Orange Robbing Hood. I wonder if she found my number somehow, and is calling to laugh at me.

I snap it open.

"Hello?"

"Danny?"

It's Ceepak. I dial down my rage.

"Hey. What's up?"

"Are you busy?"

"Not really. Why?"

All of a sudden I hear this big "woof."

"What's that?" I ask.

"Barkley," says Ceepak.

"You're still at the shelter?"

"No. We're home."

Another woof. I guess it was inevitable. Ceepak adopted the prisoner.

"It's all good, boy." I hear Ceepak say, and suddenly Barkley is quiet. I think somebody just got another Pupperoni. Ceepak comes back on line. "Sorry about that."

"What's up?"

"Danny, if it's convenient, can you meet me at Captain Pete's?"

"When?"

"Tonight. Now. Say five, make that ten minutes?"

"Sure. What's up?"

"The captain went treasure hunting this afternoon."

"Oh. Did he find another old shoe?"

"No. A charm bracelet."

I roll my eyes. I can't believe this. Ceepak wants me to spend my night off gawking at a charm bracelet?

"Danny?" he says, as if he can read my mind over the telephone.

"Yeah?"

"It should prove extremely interesting. Pete found something else."

"What?"

"A picture of the girl who lost it."

EIGHT

I say my goodbyes to Jess and Olivia, snag one last onion ring, and walk the two blocks up Bayside Boulevard to Gardenia Street and Cap'n Pete's Pier House, where he keeps his boat and runs his charter business.

It's not really a house. Looks more like a motel office straddling a dock. There's an ice machine out front, a picnic table, and a little sign detailing the daily tide table and Pete's hourly rates. There's also a wide breezeway along the side of the building that takes you out to the dock and the *Reel Fun*, Cap'n Pete's trusty sport-fishing vessel.

The building's decorated with funny coconut pirate heads and party lights—brightly colored ones shaped like flamingos, tropical fish, and chili peppers—strung all over the place. Hanging near the front door he has one of those battery-powered parrot-in-a-cage things that flaps its wings and repeats whatever you say. Inside, there's a rubber Billy The Bigmouth Bass that sings "Take Me to the River."

You go fishing with Cap'n Pete, even if you don't come back with anything but a sunburn, you're guaranteed to have a good time.

Looking around, I don't see Pete anywhere, so I go to the office and knock on the screen door.

"Cap'n Pete?"

No answer. I shield my eyes, peer inside.

The singing fish plaque is hanging on the wall behind the little desk where you hand Pete your credit card or sign the clipboard with the liability waiver papers. Next to it is a framed photo of Pete's wife and kids and, next to that, one of his mother. When we were kids, we used to call his mom, Mrs. Molly Mullen, "Cap'n Hag." Not to her face, of course. She used to run the office and hated kids. Thought we made everything we touched sticky. Yelled at us to wait outside while our parents went into the office to fork over their cash.

We didn't mind. This meant we got to hang out on the dock with Pete, pick out our fishing rods, laugh at his goofy jokes and riddles. Guess the Cap'n got his funny genes from his father, because his mom sure didn't have any. Maybe that's why she left Pete's dad and moved to Sea Haven.

Anyway, old Molly Mullen died about fifteen years ago, and Pete took over the whole operation. That's when all the decorations went up and children of all ages rejoiced.

I knock again.

"Yo! Cap'n Pete?"

I move around the office, walk under the breezeway, and hit the dock. There's a plastic table out here where Pete cleans and guts fish for the folks who want to cook what they caught but prefer to see it looking like it does at the grocery store. But instead of Styrofoam and shrink-wrap, he tidies up their catch and presents it to them in newspaper. A pile of the *Sea Haven Sandpaper*, our local weekly, is stacked inside a milk crate.

"Danny?"

It's Cap'n Pete, behind me.

"Hey!"

"Johnny here?"

"Not yet. But he called me, so I know he's on the way."

"You want a pop while we wait?"

"Sure."

"Come on, laddie."

He unlocks the door. Inside his office, he keeps one of those old-fashioned Coke coolers, the kind with the thick aluminum sides where you lift open a lid and sink your arm into icy water to fish out your favorite kind of soda. Pete calls it "pop" because he and his mom moved down here from Chicago. Must be why he keeps the Mike Ditka mustache, too. I think when they first came to town, Mrs. Mullen hired a different captain every summer. When Pete hit eighteen, he took over the full-time skipper duties, even got the official yacht cap with the gold cord and life-preserver-plus-anchors patch.

"Who wants a pop?" he says—and all of a sudden the parrot flaps its wings and shrieks, "Who wants a pop?" Pete must've flicked the plastic bird's switch before he came out back to find me.

"Polly wants a pop!" he cracks, and the bird, of course, parrots it right back. Pete is chuckling so hard I think his baggy-butt jeans are going to slide down another inch.

Ceepak pulls up to the pier on his sixteen-speed trail bike.

"Evening, Captain."

"Evening, Johnny," says Pete. Then the parrot flaps and says it: "Evening, Johnny." It's getting pretty annoying. Danny wants Polly to stick a cracker in it.

Fortunately, Pete decides it's time to flip the switch off.

He unlocks the office door. "Come in and look at my pirate booty!"

I fish a Stewart's Orange Cream soda out of the cooler. Ceepak passes.

"You sure?"

"No, thank you. I had a root beer earlier."

"With Rita?"

"Roger that."

Pete is in the back room retrieving his find.

"Give me a second, guys," he calls out from behind the thick curtains, which look like old army blankets. "I put my little treasure in a

shoebox. Now, I just have to remember where I put the shoebox!"
More laughs. He cracks himself up sometimes.

"Take your time," says Ceepak.

"So, where's Barkley?" I ask.

"Sleeping on the sofa."

Suddenly, I want to tease him. I don't know why. Maybe it's an orange-pop-induced sugar rush. Maybe it's because my last female companion stole my emergency twenty. Whatever the reason, I'm in the mood to bust my partner's chops again, to give him a little grief about his girlfriend. Maybe it's because I don't have one myself.

"So," I say, knowing, of course, that John Ceepak cannot tell a lie, "is Rita up there with Barkley?"

"10-4."

"Is she gonna spend the night with you guys?"

Pete steps into the office with his shoebox.

"Affirmative," says Ceepak.

Poor guy. He's blushing—but The Code won't let him fib, fudge, or weasel.

"She's sleeping over two nights in a row? Awesome." I flash a manly wink at Cap'n Pete.

Pete doesn't wink back.

He's grinning but I can tell it's a strain. In fact, he looks the way the old nun from elementary school used to look whenever she caught us upside down on the monkey bars practicing our swear words.

"So," I say, quickly changing the subject, "you found a charm bracelet, hunh?"

"Yep," says Pete. "I got lucky for a change. All it took was following in the footsteps of our able friend here. I went back to where you found that ring, Johnny."

"Oak Beach?"

"Right. Figured it might not be a bad idea. Might be something else buried there. It was just a hunch—but it paid off!"

He puts the box on the desk and angles down a gooseneck lamp so we can better see his find.

"I tried not to touch anything. Just like you said at the meeting. Pulled it out with hot dog tongs."

"Let's see," says Ceepak. He snaps open the cargo pants pocket where he packs his tweezers.

He snags the bracelet and holds it up under the light. The gold still sparkles in spots. Now he pulls out his photographer's bulb-brush. He keeps that one in his knee pocket. He gently dusts the charms.

"A charm bracelet is like a piece of frozen—or, in this case, buried—history."

"We're all ears," I tell him. Pete nods agreement.

Ceepak pulls a magnifying glass out of yet another pocket. Clearing his throat, he begins. "The wearer went to the 1984 World Expo in New Orleans, Louisiana. Or else someone brought her back a souvenir."

"What else?" I ask. Come on—that one was pretty easy.

Ceepak fingers another of the charms.

"I also suspect this young lady was an Italian-American. She liked rock music and cats. And she either enjoyed going to church or someone encouraged her to do so." Go, Sherlock.

He shows us the little Fortuna, the curved goat-horn that Italians say wards off the evil eye. Next comes a tiny electric guitar, then two kittens in pounce poses, and a silver church with a steeple.

"Mary," says Cap'n Pete. "Her name was Mary!" He sounds like a gypsy reading Tarot cards.

I point to the last charm, the one cut in the silhouetted shape of a girl's head. "Because that's what's engraved on the back side of that one, right?"

Pete looks properly mysterious. For an instant.

"That . . . and this."

He holds up the shoebox with both hands like he's the high priest in *Raiders of the Lost Ark* right before all hell breaks loose and the Nazis melt.

"I told you I had her picture."

He turns over a plastic bag sitting in the bottom of the box to reveal a cutout panel from a wax-paper milk carton. It's one of those missing children mug shots. A teenage girl, seventeen or eighteen. I read her name: Mary Guarneri.

"This was buried in the same spot as the bracelet," he explains. "Look!" He points to the top edge of the cardboard.

Embossed letters read AUG 12 85.

I say what we all know: "The milk's expiration date."

NINE

I head back to The Sand Bar.

It's only about nine P.M. but Jess and Olivia are long gone. Four sorority sisters sipping Aqua Velva-blue cocktails now occupy our table on the upper deck. They wear neon-green wristbands to prove they're old enough to get smashed. They shimmer in Lycra sundresses and muscle-cut T-shirts to show off gym-sculpted muscles and their honey-colored skin.

I love the sentiment stretched across the chest of the blondest blonde: NEW JERSEY. ONLY THE STRONG SURVIVE.

I head back down the steps.

It's still the weekend for another three hours. I figure I'll spend it flirting with Debbi, the bartender whose work outfit usually involves tattered logo wear and torn-off short shorts with frayed threads trickling down her thighs. On Debbi, it works. Trust me.

When I reach the bottom of the staircase, I feel like Jacques Cousteau fighting his way through a school of scantily clad tropical fish. All the girls flash ultra-bright smiles because teeth look even whiter when faces go cocoa brown. All of them are twentysomething. They're loose and giddy, made merrier by mango margaritas and pineapple martinis and raspberry mojitos—all served in frosty plastic cups instead of glasses so nobody will be seriously injured once they're totally tanked and start dropping their drinks.

Strings of Coors Light and Bud Light and Corona Light pennants flutter overhead. It looks like the grand opening of an indoor gas station that only pumps low-cal beer.

Lots of T-shirts call out to me as I sidle through the crowd. They're like personal ads these beach bunnies can post on their chests. I see JERSEY FRESH on one. MEN SHOULD BE LIKE DESSERT: SWEET AND RICH on another. One babe seems particularly pleased with hers: on the front it instructs passersby to REMEMBER MY NAME, while on the back it says, YOU'LL BE SCREAMING IT ALL NIGHT.

Oh, the poor neighbors.

But I'll spend *my* night wondering about Mary Guarneri and who buried her charm bracelet on Oak Beach along with her picture from a milk carton stuffed inside an old-fashioned sandwich bag.

It was Ceepak, of course, who had pointed out that the plastic bag was a relic of School Lunches Past.

"See how the flap tucks in?" he said. "No Ziploc top. No yellow-and-blue-makes-green sealing strip. Those were all technological advances yet to come."

Yes, thanks to my partner, I now know the sandwich bag development timeline.

Ceepak is big on the forensic stuff. In fact, he started the whole metal-detecting, treasure-hunting deal as a way to further hone his investigative skills in the downtime between cases. He finds stuff buried in the sand, takes it home, and tries to decipher its secrets.

You or I might find a coat button on the beach and fling it at an overly annoying sea gull. Ceepak picks up the same button and does enough homework to tell you it most likely came off a very expensive fur coat purchased at Bergdorf's in 1959 and that, coincidentally, the mayor's wife had worn just such a fur coat to the beach one December day back in the early 1960s when Santa Claus used to kick off the

Christmas shopping season by coming ashore in a lifeguard's row boat. Then, he'd whip out a Xeroxed article from the December 5, 1962, issue of the *Sea Haven Sandpaper* and hover his magnifying glass over the accompanying photo to show you where Mrs. Ellen Bullard, the mayor's wife at the time, was missing a button on her coat.

"Why do you think the bracelet was buried?" Cap'n Pete had wondered.

"It's unclear," Ceepak had replied. "We don't have enough information, just two pieces of a larger puzzle."

However, he did have more factoids to share with us.

For example, the use of milk carton panels to spread information about missing children wasn't initiated until the mid-1970s. A missing New Yorker named Etan Patz was one of the first so-called "milk carton kids." The use of this breakfast table search technique hit its peak in the 1980s.

Of course, the World Expo charm had already placed our time capsule in the '80s. So had Mary's hairdo. Very *Charlie's Angels*.

Ceepak also brought up Lisa DeFranco—she of the jerk-for-an-ex-boyfriend and the miserable-excuse-for-a-mom. After all, the same stretch of sand had yielded the 1983 class ring she'd been given.

"Unlike Ms. DeFranco, Mary Guarneri had concerned people actively searching for her. We should be able to learn what happened to her. Perhaps she eventually came home. Or a body was found." He uttered this last possibility with appropriate gravity.

Cap'n Pete closed up the shoebox. He handed it over to Ceepak, entrusting him with its hidden truths. "I hope you find us an answer. I surely do. . . ."

Ceepak said he would try his best.

Me, I was going back to The Sand Bar.

Tonight is not my night.

I finally find a stool at the bar but Debbi, my tattered T-shirt temptress, is not the bartender. I guess she doesn't work Sundays anymore. Instead, I get Ralph.

"Hey, Danny."

"Hey, Ralph."

We're both kind of bar-shouting—speaking loud enough to be heard over the din of drunks.

"Where's Katie?" Ralph asks.

"California."

He nods. Small talk is officially over. "What are you drinking?"

"Beer."

"Bud?"

"Yeah."

"Glass?"

"Nah."

He marches over to the cooler to fish me out a longneck.

Ralph has been doing this bartending gig way too long. He's about forty-five and hates his job. I know this because I worked here one summer as what they call a "bar-back." I was the guy who went downstairs to the ice machine and scooped up the five-gallon buckets of cubes to dump into the ice bin. Mostly, I stood around and cleaned glasses and listened to Ralph gripe about the "skanks" and "sluts" he had to serve.

Ralph *looks* angry, too. Shaves his beard and head every third day—wears stubble in both departments on the days in between. And when he slices up limes and lemons into wedges, I believe he gives them names first.

"Here's your beer."

"Thanks, man."

I put a five on the counter.

Ralph waves it off. "Keep it. You're family." He strokes his chin. "Not like these other motherfuckers. . . ."

Then he flashes a big fake grin.

"Hey, whataya need, pal?" he says to some guy in a pink polo shirt standing behind me.

"Coors Light and a piña colada."

"Comin' right up."

I sip my Bud.

"Asshole," Ralph mutters.

I notice that Pinkie has moved away from the bar to wait for his drink order alongside his lady friend.

"Blender crap." This is Ralph at his best. "All night long it's fucking blender crap." He only disses his customers to their backs — the tips work out better that way.

He attacks the ice with the blender jug, using it like a snow shovel.

"I'm getting too old for this shit, Danny Boy."

"Yeah."

Ralph has lived in Sea Haven all his life. Maybe he stays in town because he has just about the coolest house in the world: it's a boat. A houseboat — pretty much the same great set-up as that private investigator from Florida in those old paperback mysteries my dad loves.

Ralph tips juice bottles, booze bottles — sloshes all sorts of syrupy stuff into the ice. He jams the jug onto its base, slaps on the lid, punches the grind button. I think this is his favorite part of the job — listening to sharp steel gnashing against hard ice.

While I'm watching him, a guy moves behind the empty stool immediately to my left. He's in my peripheral vision zone, so I turn. Our eyes meet. Now I need to nod.

"Hey," I say.

"Hey." He says the same thing. Nods. Doesn't sit. We've both firmly established that neither one of us is gay.

Ralph pours the finished concoction into a frou-frou glass. It comes out slow and thick — like cold applesauce.

Pinkie returns for his order, slaps a soggy ten on the bar, and says, "Keep the change."

"It's twelve bucks," says Ralph.

Pinkie puts another five on the counter and wiggles away in time to the rap number rocking the rafters. I check out his girl. She, of course, is wearing a T-shirt: JERSEY GIRL. I NEVER PUMP MYSELF. Some gag writer hit pay dirt when he realized how the New Jersey state ordinance prohibiting self-serve gas stations could actually sound fashionably sleazy.

"What do you need?" Ralph now asks the guy who came up to the bar after Pinkie.

"What was that he had?"

"A royal pain-in-the-ass piña colada."

"I see. How about a beer?"

Ralph stalks back to the cooler.

"Is he always in such a good mood?"

"Nah. I think he took his meds tonight. Usually he's real crabby."

The newcomer nods. He doesn't really belong here. Sure, he has on a T-shirt, but all it says is PRINCETON. And, I'm sorry, his blue jeans are creased. He obviously sends them out to the cleaners, probably has them starched, too. The same with the tee. It's too crisp. Plus, the guy is about fifty. Hard to tell exactly how old he is because he's fit and trim and has his white hair all crimped and spiky and gelled like he's still twenty-two. He also smells. Like a muskrat frolicking in a very expensive pine forest.

"You know, I believe that fellow worked here back in the good old days," he says.

"Really? Ralph?"

"Uhm-hmm. Of course, he was a lot younger. Had hair. I was in college. Med school. Came down the shore to unwind."

While he yaks away, I realize: I've seen him before.

Didn't like him then, either.

TEN

"Not much has changed," says Mr. Princeton. "No indeed."

He turns around to admire the sea of healthy young girls swirling all around us.

"Sea Haven has always been my private island paradise."

Who he is, is the tourist in the Docksiders-without-socks from the bagel shop this morning. The one whose wife stomped out the front door.

"Here you go," says Ralph, putting a cold beer on the bar.

"Thanks." Mr. Princeton creases a twenty into a horizontal fold and slips it under a coaster. He sips his beer like it's wine. Sniffs the foam. "Ah. Excellent. Very refreshing."

"Beer's five bucks," says Ralph, like the guy is purposely trying to kill him by making him hike all the way back to the cash register. "You got anything smaller?"

"Keep the change." The guy tips his frothy glass toward Ralph.

Since Ralph knows the guy expects him to smile over a fifteen-dollar tip, he doesn't. He just swabs at the bar with a tattered rag and glowers.

"Excuse me." Mr. Princeton taps me on the shoulder. "Sorry to be a bother but where might one purchase beer to go at this hour?"

"Your best bet is Fritzie's. It's a package store."

"Fritzie's? They're still here?"

"Yeah. They're open till ten."

"Fantastic." He checks his watch. "I'm meeting a young lady friend out front at nine-thirty."

He winks. I nod. Why do I suspect the "lady friend" is not his wife?

"Fritzie's is still the spot, then, eh?"

"Yeah. It's a couple blocks down Jacaranda Street. . . ."

He holds up his hand. Nods. "I know: where it hits Ocean Avenue. The corner there. Correct?"

"Yeah."

"Fantastic. Good to know some things never change. Thank you."

"No problem. But do me a favor," I say. "Don't even think about drinking and driving."

Mr. Princeton drains about half of his mug.

"And who, pray tell, are you? My mother?"

"No. I'm a cop. Sea Haven Police Department."

"Really? You seem awfully young."

I shrug. "Me being young only means I can run fast and catch the bad guys. Especially the older, slower ones."

"I see. Well, not to worry. My friend and I simply intend to grab a cold six-pack and head over to an establishment three or four blocks up the street. We'll walk. Smuggler's Cove. Another oldie but goodie." He chuckles.

He checks his watch again.

"Well then. . . ." He polishes off his beer. "Early day tomorrow. Taking a charter out. Maybe catch a few bluefish."

"Have fun," I say, since it's our civic duty to say that kind of stuff to tourists.

He heads toward the door, checking out every midriff-baring babe he passes along the way. A few of the girls check out Mr. Princeton, too—the ones in the naughtier T-shirts.

As I said, I don't like this guy.

I don't like his spiky hair or creased jeans. I don't like him trying to buy Ralph's love for fifteen bucks. And I absolutely hate the fact that his plans for the evening include grabbing a six-pack and heading over to Smuggler's Cove, our local Hotel No Tell, for his own private version of *Girls Gone Wild*.

"He was in here last night, too," Ralph now says to me.

"Yeah?"

"Yeah. That bit with the twenty? He pulled the same shit. Then he waltzed out with this totally tanked chick young enough to be his daughter, you know what I'm saying?"

"Yeah."

I think it's pretty clear why Mrs. Princeton was so pissed this morning. Hubby probably crawled home ten minutes before I saw them. And maybe when she'd last seen him, he was wearing his socks.

I put my five-dollar bill back on the bar.

"Thanks."

"Hey, I told you—it's on the house."

"If he can tip you, so can I."

Ralph cracks a grin and slides my money into his tip jar. "It's really not a club you want to join."

Yeah. And I probably couldn't afford the membership fees.

Both doors of my Jeep are closed and locked. The top is zipped into place. No one has broken in to steal my loose change again, but it doesn't really matter since I was totally hoovered out the first time.

At the far end of the lot, underneath a streetlamp, I see Mr. Princeton. He's looking at his watch again. Guess his lady friend stood him up.

Good. Serves him right. Maybe he'll have better luck tomorrow, hooking up with some striped bass.

Time to head home. Roll call comes early: seven-thirty A.M.

"Hey, Teddy!" I hear this female voice from the darkness. It sounds familiar. Husky. "Am I like totally late?"

"Well, my dear, we did say nine-thirty."

"Sorry. . . ."

Okay. I'm at least thirty feet away but now I can hear all sorts of slurpy lip-smacking.

When the streetlamp catches the orange glints in her hair, I realize: Stacey has returned to the scene of the crime. She's not currently robbing her new guy—unless, of course, she's simultaneously picking Mr. Princeton's pockets while kneading his butt cheeks with both hands.

Finally, they break out of their lip-lock.

"Come on!" he says.

They race up the sidewalk.

She's wearing the Hello Kitty backpack.

Somehow, I don't think my twenty's still in it.

ELEVEN

You have a good weekend, Danny?"

"Not bad," I lie. "How about you?"

"Excellent, my friend. Absolutely excellent."

"Awesome."

"Oh, yeah."

It's 7:25 on a Monday morning but behind the front desk, Sergeant Reginald Pender is already feeling frisky, despite the fact that the big man never drinks coffee—says it only serves to dehydrate an individual. He's our new desk sergeant, having taken over from grumpy Gus Davis who retired last winter after almost thirty years on the job.

Reggie couldn't look more different than his predecessor, who was old and white and hipbone scrawny; Reggie is young and black and carries a small paunch above his belt buckle. He looks like a football player who doesn't run his wind sprints anymore but still eats everything on the training table. A lineman.

"You better hustle, Officer Boyle," he says with a jerk of his head toward the wall clock.

I check it out: 7:27.

I head for the duty room.

Ceepak, of course, is already seated in the back row. He likes to say, "If you're not five minutes early, you're ten minutes late." I still don't really understand what that means—guess that's why I'm always the last cop in the room.

Ceepak has his notebook open on his desk. His pencil looks freshly sharpened. Every hair on his head is neatly combed and plastered into its pre-assigned position.

Ceepak likes to be prepared.

I know thinking ahead helped save his ass a couple times over in Iraq. Once, he saw a dead dog lying by the side of the road and, since he'd done his homework, he knew that canine carcasses were often used by the insurgents to hide their improvised explosive devices. He saved everybody in his Humvee that day because he saw the wires sticking out of the animal's jaws before its belly blew.

All the other cops in the room are busy finishing their coffee and doughnuts, scanning the *Sandpaper* to see if they made the Crime Blotter, waiting for Chief Baines to make his 7:30-sharp entrance. Old Buzz likes to do the early Monday roll call himself. The rest of the week, he lets Pender handle it.

"Find a seat, Boyle," snarls Dominic Santucci. He has his sunglasses on—indoors. He likes the way they make him look menacing and mysterious. He also doesn't like me so much.

"Danny?" Ceepak motions to the chair next to him, which he has saved for me like kids used to do for their friends on the school bus.

"Thanks."

When I sit down, my holster squeaks. The leather is that new. Last summer, I was a part-timer without a gun. This summer, I wish I didn't have to carry one. Unfortunately, last summer, I also saw what bullets could do.

Now Ceepak checks off an item on a list he has inside his spiral notebook.

"I ran the milk carton data by Officer Diego," he says. "She's going to run some searches on Mary Guarneri."

"Cool."

"She'll also do a data sweep on Lisa DeFranco. See what she comes up with."

Special Operations Officer Denise Diego works in the computer room here at Police Headquaters, what we all the station house. She's a self-proclaimed techno-geek. I think that's how come she can recite every line from *The Lord of the Rings*. All three movies.

"Of course," Ceepak continues, "Officer Diego will only work on this project during downtime and lunch hours."

"Of course."

"We don't want our private investigation interfering with the normal flow of official police business, no matter how fascinating."

"Right."

Truth be told, Ceepak's a lot more charmed by the Case of the Buried Charm Bracelet than I am. But I don't let on.

He flips through his notebook and stops when he reaches a page near the middle. I lean over to see what he's looking at.

There, in the center, surrounded by a spiral of circles, is one word:

DOVER

I have no idea what it means. Maybe he wants to visit the white cliffs in England. Maybe he's thinking about fish for dinner tonight. With Ceepak, sometimes you just never know.

Chief Baines strides into the room. You could set your watch by this guy, which I go ahead and do since mine thinks it's eight P.M. on a Tuesday. I got it free from *Sports Illustrated*.

Buzz Baines has a chiseled, movie-star face and thick, fluffy hair. He's good at his job and even better at posing for pictures in the newspaper.

"Gentlemen. Ladies. According to the calendar, we're halfway through the summer and, so far, things have been dull, quiet, and boring." He looks smugly around the room. "Let's try to keep it that way, shall we?"

We all answer dutifully, "Yes, sir."

"Fine. Now. Not much to report from the night shift. At one A.M., Pete Turner noticed a car running without its lights. When he pulled the young man over it became readily apparent that the driver was unable to locate the headlights switch on his dashboard, or the nose on his face."

Dutiful once again, we give a collective chuckle.

"All right, guys. Today starts a new week and a lot of well-earned vacations for our visitors. Ceepak and Boyle?"

"Yes, sir?" Ceepak answers for us.

"You're working the sand castle set-up over on Oak Beach?"

"Roger that."

"Let folks enjoy the show but try to keep the kids a safe distance away from the heavy machinery." Chief Baines checks his notes like he can't believe what he's reading. "They actually use backhoes? To make sand castles?"

"And bulldozers," says Ceepak. He's done his homework again.

"Whatever happened to the old-fashioned sand bucket and plastic shovel?"

"They use those as well, sir. However, many of the master sand sculptors prefer nursery plant containers. The holes pre-cut into the bottom help drain away excess water while maintaining even pressure against the sand grains."

Roger that. By now, everyone in the room is used to this sort of stuff from Ceepak.

"Oh-kay," says Baines. "Thank you, Officer Ceepak. Now everyone get out there and keep Sea Haven a safe haven!"

I can't complain.

We've pulled a pretty cushy assignment today, basically sitting on the beach working on our tans. We've set up two folding chairs near the entrance to what will eventually become the Sand Castle Kingdom. It's a fifty-foot by two-hundred-foot plot of white sand situated between the high tide mark on Oak Beach and the sea grass up on the dunes. The Chamber of Commerce has roped off the area with white plastic chains strung between portable PVC posts sunk into the sand every eight feet or so. It's an outdoor, summer version of Santa Land at the mall.

Today, the heavy equipment is being off-loaded. Tomorrow, the sand sculptors show up and start to work. Wednesday, they finish up. Thursday, the public will come gawk at a gigantic sea dragon, a chess set with life-size kings and queens, and a '57 Chevy convertible—all made out of sand.

It's now almost three P.M. The most exciting part of the day so far was when Ceepak told me to take five about an hour ago. I wound up helping this kid from Indiana learn how to ride his skim board. That's a flat wood disc you stand on, then slip and slide up and down the wet sand ahead of the waves. It should be an Olympic sport by 2012.

I'm glad Ceepak has settled into a groove here on the island. Over in Iraq, he saw even worse stuff than dead dogs blowing up by the side of the road. Somehow, my partner came out of it all with his soul intact. I think it was The Code that pulled him through. As long as he could hold on to that, he could hold on to who he is.

Anyway, it's good to see my man sitting in a folding chair, guarding the entrance to Sea Haven's First Annual Sand Sculpture Competition, smiling up at the sun warming his face. He's earned it.

I finish a quick stroll around the perimeter and plop down in my beach chair.

"Tough duty."

Ceepak smiles. "It's all good."

I reach into the small cooler we brought along and grab a bottled water.

"Officers!"

I squint. A hairy guy is huffing and puffing up the sand toward us. He's bare-chested but wearing a gold neck chain and several gleaming gold bracelets on both wrists.

"Officers!"

A chubby kid who has to be the man's son is following behind him.

"Is there some problem?" Ceepak is up and focusing fast.

"Yeah." The dad catches his breath, props his hands on his hips. His heaving chest looks like a curly shag carpet. So do his arms. He could comb the tops of his shoulders. "Thief," he pants. "Robber. Girl."

"She tried to steal my wallet!" his son squeaks.

"Tell us what happened," says Ceepak.

"Tell them, Max."

"Okay. I was like on my boogie board and all, and when I came out of the water I saw this girl in a bikini and she was like looking inside our beach bags and so I like yelled at her and my dad, that's him, he came running up as fast as he could from the ocean and we both kind of like scared her away and stuff."

"I almost nabbed her," says the father. "Had my hand wrapped around her wrist but she slipped away. I'd been down in the surf, putting sunblock on my wife's back . . . "

Ceepak nods.

" . . . so my hand was kind of greasy."

"Did she take anything?"

"No," says the boy. "She almost got my new wallet but Dad stopped her."

"Can you describe this girl?"

"She had orange hair," says the boy. "And. . . ." He stops. Looks at his dad.

Ceepak sinks down on his haunches so he can look the boy in the eye.

"And what?" he asks gently.

The boy's eyes cut up to his father.

"Go ahead, Max. Tell him."

Max still hesitates. "She had big boobs," he finally says.

Ceepak nods. I try not to smile.

"I saw something else," says the father.

Wow. Wonder how he managed that?

"What was it, sir?" asks Ceepak.

"She had this thing stamped on her hand. You know, like they do at Six Flags so you can get back in after you exit?"

"Yes, sir. What did this stamp look like?"

"It was a sun. An orange, smiling sun."

TWELVE

Ceepak reaches for our radio, which had been enjoying the shade underneath my folding chair.

"The Life Under the Son Ministry," he says.

"The guys who run that booth on the boardwalk?"

"Roger that. They also operate a soup kitchen of sorts in the motel nearby."

"The motel lets them do that?"

"The ministry owns the building. Has its offices inside. Rita volunteers there some mornings when she isn't busy at the bank. They serve a hot breakfast to anybody who walks in hungry, no questions asked. However, to gain access to the chow line, you need to have your hand stamped."

"With a bright orange sun."

Ceepak nods. "I'm going to radio in a request for the chief to relieve us, assign another team to this location."

"So we can head over to the boardwalk and check it out."

"10-4."

• • •

Billy Trumble, the evangelist guy who does the early morning preach-a-thon Sundays on WAVY radio, also runs the Life Under the Son Ministry.

Their booth up on the boardwalk is staffed by born-again Christian kids who sit inside and reach out to all the young sinners happily strutting through life in string bikinis and Speedos. They'll tell you about the hell that awaits those who fornicate outside the sanctity of marriage — and they don't just mean the hell of having to wake up with each other after the beer goggles wear off. They'll even try to convince you not to gamble at the boardwalk arcades, to avoid the Wheel of Chance, which, if we're honest, is just another spin on roulette, and even the humble Whack-A-Mole, this game where you bop furry little critters on the head with a mallet while more moles pop up in the holes you're not whacking.

It's very hard to win at Whack-A-Mole. Even attempting to do so, the Life Under the Son Ministry will advise you, is the first step down a slippery slope that leads directly to losing your shirt and pants and the family farm at Trump's Taj Mahal in Atlantic City. Next stop after that? Hellfire and damnation.

It's a tough sell.

But they do, apparently, serve a hot breakfast to anybody who walks in hungry.

The chief approves Ceepak's plan, freeing us to head up the island to The Sonny Days Inn, the motel that doubles as worldwide headquarters for Reverend Trumble's ministry and outreach programs. I think it used to be a Days Inn. They only had to paint two extra words on all the signs to make the switch.

A young girl comes out of the office to greet us. She's probably seventeen, with a bright open smile and a gray T-shirt that says CHASTITY IS REAL LOVE. The "o" in Love is a heart.

I see other girls up on the second-floor balcony, leaning against the railing, wondering why a police car just pulled into their seaside sanctuary. Some of them stand next to vacuum cleaners. Others hold armloads of linen. They must be the Lord's handmaidens doing double duty as chambermaids.

"Good afternoon, Officers," says the official greeter. "How can I help you?"

"We're investigating a minor incident on the beach," says Ceepak.

"Oh, dear. An incident?"

"Minor, ma'am. We'd like to talk to Reverend Trumble."

Her face blossoms into a beautiful ball of tranquility. "Of course." She leads us toward the motel office. "Would you gentlemen care for some lemonade while you wait?"

"Lemonade would be wonderful," says Ceepak.

"I'll tell Reverend Billy you're here," she says.

"Thank you, ma'am."

As she walks away, I check out the sky. It's gone greenish gray. The thunderheads bubbling up over the ocean all day long look like they're finally ready to unload a torrent of rain—or hailstones.

In a few moments, our personal handmaiden comes back. We follow her through the small lobby, past the front desk, and into the Reverend's office. After she leaves, a different girl soon appears with two frosty glasses of lemonade and a plate of sugar cookies. She's a blonde. Maybe seventeen, too. Looks wholesome, like she grew up in Nebraska.

Ceepak takes his lemonade. "Thank you . . . I'm sorry, I don't know your name."

"I'm Rachel."

"I'm John. This is Daniel."

I can't believe Ceepak just called me that. Daniel's what my mother used to call me—but only when she was real mad.

"Thank you for the refreshments, Rachel."

She leaves. Ceepak puts down his glass and drifts behind the small desk to study the framed photographs hanging on the paneled walls.

"Interesting," he says.

The pictures all have that hazy, washed-out look of snapshots that have been sitting in the sun too long.

"These photographs were taken during a baptism on the beach," says Ceepak. "Out in the ocean."

"These, too." I point to a frame holding six pictures: 5-by-7s laid out comic-strip style, telling a story from left to right.

"Look," says Ceepak. "This man in the clerical collar is leading a fully clothed girl out into the surf." He's now in full analytical mode. "The man with the Bible is most likely a young Reverend Trumble."

He continues narrating the story as it unfolds across the panels. "Reverend Trumble holds up his arms in prayer. He dunks the girl under an incoming wave. She emerges from the water, jubilant. Everyone on the shoreline applauds. . . ."

"Verily, they rejoice," someone croons smoothly behind us. "'For what was lost, now is found.'"

It's the Reverend Billy Trumble. I recognize the buttery voice from his radio show.

"Of course," he continues, "those photographs were taken many years ago. Before my hair turned white."

Ceepak extends his hand.

"Reverend Trumble?"

Trumble clasps Ceepak's hand with both of his.

"That's right, brother. And you are?"

"Officer John Ceepak. Sea Haven Police. This is my partner, Daniel Boyle."

"Danny," I say and hold out my hand.

Trumble gives me the double pump, too, and locks his eyes on mine. They're crystal blue and set off by a rich tan—the kind you can only get from a spray can.

As we shake hands, the sky explodes with a roar of thunder that makes the windows rattle. I think Reverend Billy just read my mind and called in a retaliatory lightning strike. I look out the window. Fortunately, it's just raining buckets of water, not frogs or anything biblical. Droplets the size of quarters ping and splatter off car roofs.

"Guess we better build an ark," I joke.

"No need, son. The next time God destroys the earth it shall be with fire, not water!"

When he says "God," it sounds like a three-syllable word: "Ga-uh-uhd." Why is it even New Jersey radio preachers sound like they grew up in North Carolina?

"Second Peter. Chapter Three." Trumble continues. "'But the day of the Lord will come like a thief, and then the heavens will pass away with a mighty roar and the elements will be dissolved by fire, and the earth and everything done on it will be found out.'"

I nod because I can't change the channel like I do when this guy invades my radio.

"Now then, Officers—how may I be of assistance?"

"We're looking for a girl," says Ceepak.

"Is she a lost soul?"

"Perhaps. We have reason to believe she came here for breakfast this morning."

"Very likely. Many do. They come to seek sustenance. Physical *and* spiritual."

It's beginning to sound like Reverend Billy has some endless loop of sermon tapes spooling through his brain.

"She had an orange sun stamped on her hand," says Ceepak, unmoved by our host's holiness.

Trumble lifts his hand to show us the sun mark on his own. "As do I. For we are all sinners, marked so with Adam's stain."

"She has orange hair, too," says Ceepak.

Trumble sits in the swivel chair behind his desk and smiles knowingly. He puts his hands together to form a steeple in front of his lips.

"In Scripture, evildoers are often identified by red or orangish hair. Judas had red hair. Eve, as well." He pauses. "Was this red-haired girl a runaway?" he suddenly asks.

"We have no way of knowing at this juncture. We can assume, however, that it is a distinct possibility."

"I'm not surprised. So many of the children who flock to my table are runaways." He shakes his head sadly. "Why do they choose to leave their homes? To flee loving parents?"

I figure maybe they just listened to Springsteen's "Born to Run."

You know: *"We gotta get out while we're young, 'cause tramps like us, baby, we were born to run."*

"There are several reasons," says Ceepak, who knows a thing or two about loving parents. His own father was a drunk who smacked his mother around and picked on his little brother. I'm guessing that, in his teens, young John Ceepak considered running away from home but decided to stick around to do his duty and protect his mom and kid brother. "Often times the teenage runaway. . . ."

Reverend Trumble holds up his hand to silence Ceepak.

"You gentlemen are sworn to uphold the laws of man. I, however, answer to a higher authority. A God who commands that all children honor their fathers and mothers—*no matter what.* Exodus 20:12."

Ceepak's back goes ramrod stiff. "'And, ye fathers,'" he says, "'provoke not your children to wrath.' Ephesians 6:1–4."

I'm impressed. Something that happens on a daily basis when you work with John Ceepak.

Trumble's hands reform the steeple below his nose, only this time the rafters are bent and wobbly because he's squeezing hard. I think he's used to having the last word.

"Is there a number where I might call you gentlemen should a girl answering this description return to our table?"

Ceepak pulls one of our cards out of his shirt pocket.

Reverend Trumble takes it, studies it.

"John Ceepak. Unusual name. Tell me, son—are you a Christian?"

"Call us if anyone matching her description shows up."

"I certainly will."

"We'd appreciate it. We suspect she may be stealing money and credit cards from vacationers."

The Reverend sighs. Shakes his head. "Placing her soul in mortal jeopardy by defying the *Eighth* Commandment as well: 'Thou shalt not steal.'"

Ceepak nods.

That one's part of his Code, too.

THIRTEEN

The clouds have parted and sunbeams pour down as Ceepak and I march out of the missionary's motel office.

"Now where?" I ask.

"We'll hit the house. Make a report. Advise all units to be on the lookout. . . ."

A beat-up old Toyota crunches into the parking lot. It's Rita. I recognize her clunker.

"Hi, guys," she says as she climbs out.

Ceepak, always the gentleman, holds the door for her. It's a good thing, too—it looks ready to fall off its hinges.

"What're you boys doing over here?" Rita asks. "I thought you were supposed to sit on the beach all day."

"Duty called," says Ceepak. It's good to see him smile again. I think the silver-haired and -tongued preacher man hit too close to home with that pious little lecture about obeying your father and mother. Depends on the father and mother, if you ask me. I can tell Ceepak wants to kiss Rita but he won't—not while he's in uniform, not while he's on the job.

"What happened?" Rita asks. "Nothing serious I hope."

"Routine run. Possible 10-92."

"That's a robbery, right?"

"Roger that."

My god: Ceepak has his girlfriend memorizing police 10-codes. They are definitely getting serious.

"Male or female?" she asks.

"Female," he answers. "We suspect she had breakfast here."

"Poor kid," says Rita.

That's Ceepak's lady in a nutshell. She's more worried about what drove a young girl to steal than what was stolen from somebody's beach bag. Rita hauls a pile of clothes out of the back seat of her car, clutches the bundle against her chest.

Ceepak springs into action. "Need a hand?"

"No, thanks. It's not heavy. I'm just dropping off some of T. J.'s old T-shirts and jeans. Stuff he's grown out of."

Clever move. Clean out the kid's closet while he's on vacation up in the city. I think that's how I lost my baseball card collection.

"I thought maybe some of the boys here could use them."

"They have boys?" I wonder aloud. Thus far, all I've seen here are upright and courteous young girls. From the look of things, Reverend Billy could be running a mission for reformed cheerleaders.

"Of course," Rita laughs. "The food's free."

"How long have you known Reverend Trumble?" Ceepak now asks.

Rita hesitates. "A long time."

Ceepak doesn't push it—not in public.

"Yes, ma'am."

"Don't call me *ma'am*, John. Makes me sound old."

"Roger."

Her face warms. "Do you even know how to say 'yes' or 'no'?"

"Negative."

She shakes her head. Laughs again. "I'll see you later."

We watch her carry her bundle up to the second floor.

"She's a good lady," says Ceepak as we head off. "An inspiration."

"Yeah."

With Ceepak and Rita, it's a case of likes, not opposites, attracting. If he's a goody-goody, she's a better-better. Last spring, she rescued this sea gull she found lying in the middle of Ocean Avenue. First, she had to dodge traffic to reach it. Then, she took it home, mended its broken wing, fed it with an eyedropper, and nursed it back to health. She even gave the gull a name: Jonathan Livingston—I forget why. In June, she set the bird free. She and T. J. and Ceepak went down to the beach and made sure the gimpy gull was able to swoop with its own kind. They took pictures.

"Rita does enough good for both of us," Ceepak once told me.

The thing is, his own choices haven't always been easy ones. I've never asked him if he's killed anybody, but I've seen how he looks when other idiots do.

"Did you kill anybody over there in Iraq?"

They always whisper when they ask it.

"What's it feel like?"

Ceepak never answers. He usually just walks away.

We're in the car, driving toward headquarters, when the radio squawks.

"Unit Twelve, this is base."

Ceepak snatches up the microphone.

"This is Twelve."

"That you, Ceepak?"

"Yes, Sergeant Pender. Over."

"Chief Baines said to bounce this one out to you, seeing how you're in the neighborhood."

There's this long pause.

"Go ahead," says Ceepak.

"Yeah. Sorry. Don't know what to call this one. Tempted to say it's a 10-37."

That's a mental case.

"What's the situation?"

"You know that tiny museum up on Oyster Street?"

"The Howland House?"

"10-4. Woman just called, said she's the curator, sounded hysterical. Says some children found something 'horrible' but she wouldn't tell me what it was."

"We are 10-17. Out."

10-17 means we're en route.

Ceepak hangs up and does a three-finger hand chop toward the horizon. "Oyster and Bayside. The Howland House Whaling Museum."

"Roger. Should I 10-39 it?"

Ceepak looks at me. Hey, I memorized all these 10-codes for the final exam at the academy. I figure I need to use them or I might lose them like I've lost everything I memorized back in high school: atomic weights, the metric system, who did what to whom in 1066. It's all gone.

"No need for lights or siren, Danny. Let's keep it 10-40."

"10-4."

He means *keep it quiet*.

I mean *okay*.

FOURTEEN

The Howland House is this two-story brick building that used to belong to a whaling ship captain named Jebediah Howland.

About fifty years ago, a bunch of ladies, the "Daughters of the Sea," got together and raised enough cash to buy the place before it was torn down to make room for another miniature golf course. Now it's a museum nobody goes to.

I guess few vacationers want to walk around a dank house looking at dusty furniture during their week off from work. Sure, there are a couple of ship models in glass cases mounted on the walls. There are even three or four model ships in glass bottles. But mostly, it's moldy furniture and velvet drapes.

The museum doesn't give tours or anything. In fact, nobody is ever there. Somebody comes by in the morning and unlocks the front door. They come back in the afternoon to lock up. There's a plexiglass box on a desk in the front hall with a hand-written sign: SUGGESTED DONATION $2.

"Is that Norma?" Ceepak asks as we pull up to the curb on Oyster Street and see a figure on the porch.

"Yeah, I think so."

Norma Risley, a dignified Daughter of the Sea, is seventy-five years old and works part-time as a hostess at Morgan's Surf and Turf, the restaurant where Rita waitresses. When Norma leads you to your table, you have plenty of time to contemplate the daily specials. In fact, you have time to do your laundry.

"Officer Ceepak!" She is waving hysterically. "Hurry! Please!"

Ceepak speeds up the brick pathway. I'm right behind him.

"Norma? Are you injured?"

"No. No." Her hand flutters near her chest.

Ceepak reaches her in time to catch her when she faints.

"Danny?"

I grab an arm. We haul Norma inside, find a velvety chair in the foyer, and sit her down.

About fifteen seconds later, she comes to.

"Oh, my."

"Norma, do you need an ambulance?" Ceepak asks.

She shakes her head. Lifts up an arm. Points down the hall.

"What is it? Was something stolen?"

Another head shake.

"Take it slow. Tell us what happened."

She swallows. Nods. "I came by during the thunderstorm. Figured I might as well lock up early today. When I got here, I found a family inside, waiting for the rain to let up. The mother started screaming at me. 'How dare you!' she said. 'How dare you put something like that on display in a museum?' Her youngest, a little girl—oh, she was bawling her eyes out. Something had scared her, that's for sure."

"What was it?"

She shakes her head. It's so atrocious, she can't even tell us. So, once again, she points up the hall. Her arm trembles.

"The Scrimshaw Room." She chokes out the words."Bookcase. Top shelf. Two jars."

"Jars?"

Norma nods. Breathes in deep.

"Plastic jars with screw-on lids. Small." She curls her knotted fingers to make a tiny fist.

"Okay, Norma. You stay here. My partner and I will investigate. . . ."

Her hands fly up to her chest again. If she doesn't have a heart attack, she might give me one.

"Danny?" Ceepak says. "Secure the front door. Use your evidence gloves."

I put on these lint-free gloves Ceepak insists I always carry so I won't contaminate potential evidence, such as fingerprints on a doorknob. Ceepak pulls on a pair, too.

I close the front door.

"We'll be right back, Norma," says Ceepak.

We head up the carpeted hallway.

We reach the door to the Scrimshaw Room and Ceepak does this series of hand signals to indicate how we will enter.

He'll lead. I'll follow.

The room looks like it always looks. Dark bookcases. Overstuffed furniture. Framed oil painting of men in a boat harpooning a gigantic whale on one wall, carved figurehead of an Indian lady in a red headdress on another.

We see them at the same time.

On the top shelf of the bookcase on the far side of the room

Two small jars filled with clear liquid and something else — something pinkish and blobby with stringy bits floating in the fluid. It could be somebody's jellyfish collection or one of those pig fetuses in formaldehyde they give you to dissect in junior high biology class. There's writing on both jars. Labels. We move closer.

Ceepak sucks in a deep chestful of oxygen.

"They're ears," he says. "Severed human ears."

I feel the sausage-and-pepper sandwich I had for lunch move an inch up my esophagus. I choke it back down and lean in for a closer look.

The label on one jar reads: RUTH. SUMMER. 1985.

The other jar doesn't have a name, just a date: SUMMER. 1983.

No name because it doesn't need one.

The ear lobe suspended in the specimen jar has an earring stuck through its pale flesh. It spells out a girl's name in sparkly letters.

"Lisa," Ceepak whispers.

I guess he's thinking what I'm thinking: Lisa DeFranco might've lost more than a class ring that summer she visited Sea Haven.

FIFTEEN

Ceepak called Rita on her cell phone.

She swung by the museum and gave Norma a ride to the restaurant. Norma isn't supposed to be working the door there tonight, but she agreed with Ceepak and Rita: after all she'd seen today, better not to be home alone. Besides, Morgan's has a fully stocked bar and Norma could use a hot toddy or two, heavy on the rum.

"Be sure you lock up, Officer Ceepak," Norma called out as she and Rita drove away.

"Will do," Ceepak said. I think one day he may find himself an honorary Daughter of the Sea.

"Danny? We need to investigate this crime scene."

"Right."

I knew that's what we'd be doing as soon as Norma was safe, secure, and gone. Ceepak loves a good Crime Scene Investigation — on the job or off. When he isn't working, he's usually at home watching all twenty different versions of *CSI* on CBS. Sometimes, he's told me, he watches with the sound switched off so the actors' banter doesn't distract him from the clues.

We've already radioed in and alerted the house as to what we found. Chief Baines agreed with Ceepak: we should gather what evidence we can and bring it in for further analysis. I suspect Chief Baines is most interested in removing the specimen jars from public view. Floating body parts are not the kind of attractions you want on display when you're running a resort town big on family fun in the sun. Pickled ears belong in a sideshow up in Seaside Heights, in the freak show tent with the bearded lady and the fire-eater—who, I think, are married to each other.

Ceepak uses his forceps to remove the jars from the bookcase and place them in the evidence bag.

"Doubtful that we'll find any fingerprints on either jar," he says while placing them gingerly into the sack. "But it remains a remote possibility, and therefore, we must treat the evidence accordingly."

"Right," I say, and experience another acid reflux episode as I watch the ears slosh around in slow motion.

"Unfortunately," he grouses, "this museum's too small to utilize security cameras or guards. If someone broke in when no one was here, we'd see it on the tape."

I could point out that no one is *ever* here, but I don't.

"Be that as it may," Ceepak says, "we can still check the guest registry up front."

"You think whoever did this signed in?"

"Doubtful. Unless they did so as a prank. But even that could prove fruitful. If they wrote down a false name we can still use it to work up a handwriting analysis."

"Yeah," I say. "Maybe they signed in as Vincent van Gogh. I think he lopped off his own ear. . . ."

"Indeed so," says Ceepak. "And, legend has it, he then delivered it to a prostitute he knew at a nearby brothel."

I remind myself never to play *Trivial Pursuit* with John Ceepak— unless, of course, we're on the same team.

He drops to his knees and examines the worn-down Oriental rug in front of the bookcase. He reaches into his right hip pocket and pulls out his magnifying glass.

"Hmmm."

The glass goes back in and out comes a small roll of Scotch tape. Ceepak snaps off a piece, presses it down into the carpet, pulls it up, and stores the tape strip in a small envelope retrieved from his knee pocket.

"What was that?" I ask. "What'd you find?"

"Sand particles."

"Cool! That should help. Right?"

"Unlikely. As you know, Danny, sand is quite common here in Sea Haven. Most people carry it around on their shoes, their socks, inside their pant cuffs. Difficult to distinguish one grain from another or to determine where it came from. There is, however, always the remote chance that it might offer us a clue, and so we collect it. Remind me to ask the museum staff when this rug was last vacuumed."

I jot down a memo to myself. Ever since I put on the badge, I've been carrying my own small spiral notepad around. Usually, I use it to remind me of stuff. You know—pick up bologna, buy a new toothbrush, question career choice. Stuff like that.

"So, what've we got?" I ask. "Diddly or squat?"

"We've got the ears, Danny. I suspect they have been preserved in formaldehyde or a similar embalming fluid. Their DNA signatures, therefore, remain intact and could help us identify the two girls."

"Do you think the 'Lisa' is our Lisa? Lisa DeFranco?"

"It's certainly one possibility. We should contact the girl's mother."

I can just imagine how delighted the wicked witch of the A&P is going to be to hear from us again.

"Even if she can't provide us with a sample of her daughter's DNA, we could test hers. There would be a definite familial pattern."

"Are those ears even real? Maybe they're just, you know, made out of rubber like the ones you can buy for Halloween. George W. Bush ears or Spock ears. . . ."

"I'm quite certain they're real. I also fear they may point to picquerism."

I'm afraid to ask but I do: "What's that?"

"The act of mutilating a victim beyond what is necessary to kill her. It is a common trait among serial killers."

Jesus. Serial killers?

"So all of a sudden there's a serial killer on the loose in Sea Haven?" I ask.

"We cannot yet call our perpetrator a serial killer, Danny."

"Good."

"The FBI defines a serial killer as someone who has killed at least three victims."

Oh. I see. Two down, one to go.

"And whether he is on the loose, as you say, is questionable. We can surmise from the dates on the jars that these mutilations took place in the 1980s."

"Wait a minute," I say. "We don't even know if these two girls are dead. What if, I don't know, what if both Ruth and Lisa were caught up in some kind of big kidnapping scheme where the kidnapper sends an ear with his ransom demands to prove he means business."

"Then the cars wouldn't be here, would they? They'd be wherever the kidnapper sent them. And, again, remember the dates written so meticulously on the jar labels: Summer 1983. Summer 1985. Two kidnappings, two years apart? Both involving severed ears as proof of life? Again, highly unlikely."

He's right. I'm clutching at straws. Rehashing plots from DVDs I've rented.

Ceepak frowns. "I suspect that what we've discovered here is evidence of the sixth phase of the typical serial killer cycle. The totem or trophy stage: the taking and keeping of souvenirs. It's an essential act for the serial killer because the souvenirs create the link between his fantasies and the reality of what he has actually accomplished."

"So," I say, "the ears in the jar are his version of the snow globe you bring home to remind you of all the good times you had on vacation?"

"Exactly."

"Then why's he getting rid of his souvenirs? I mean he's had them for, what? Over twenty years? Why's he all of a sudden donating his stuff to a whaling museum?"

"That, Danny, is the question we must strive to answer. The sooner the better."

The way he says it, I know he thinks something bad is about to happen.

"Maybe we should check that visitors book in the now," I suggest. "Maybe we can find the family that was in here during the thunderstorm. They might have seen somebody or something. . . ."

Ceepak nods. "Good idea."

Feeling like I'm on a roll, I come up with what I think is another good one. "But first—we should check that glass for prints." I point to the bookcase, which is one of those old-fashioned oak jobs where every shelf has its own window to keep out the dust.

"No need," says Ceepak. "Whoever dropped off the jars wore gloves. See here? And here?"

He points to two smudged sections. The only two clean spots on the otherwise grimy glass. Even though it's the middle of July, I don't think the Daughters of the Sea have gotten around to their spring cleaning. The two areas, about eighteen inches apart, were wiped clean when our guy pressed his gloved hands against the glass.

Ceepak re-pockets his gear. "Let's go check out that guest book."

SIXTEEN

We catch our first break.

Well, we actually catch two. First: the family that discovered the jars while they waited out the thunderstorm did, indeed, sign the guest book. Second: they were admirably thorough and filled in every detail requested: NAME(S), AGE(S), HOME ADDRESS, ADDRESS WHILE VISITING THE ISLAND.

Ceepak suggests we take the book with us.

"Not many visitors," he remarks. "About two or three a day. However, given the apparent lack of basic housekeeping and the low level of museum security, there is no telling when those two jars were placed in the bookcase. We may eventually need to talk to every person listed in this register."

So we pack up the green book, secure The Scrimshaw Room, lock up the museum, and head off to the Seahorse Motel to visit the Pepper Family of Okemos, Michigan. Warren, Brenda, and the kids: Heather (13), Warren Jr. (10), and Maddie (6). I figure Maddie was the one howling like a miniature banshee when she saw the ears bobbing up and down inside their little glass bottles. I don't blame her: I would have done the same thing.

• • •

The Seahorse is an L-shaped brick building with a neon-green sign jutting out from the wall facing Nutmeg Street. At night, the neon flashes through a series of poses turning the tubular seahorse into an underwater bucking bronco.

We walk past the rattling ice machine and head into the office. The nice girl watching TV behind the front desk tells us we're in luck: she just saw the Peppers heading for the pool, which is located around the back of the building.

We say thanks and head that way. The day is cooling off after the thunderstorm, but not the steamy air around the motel. As we walk around to the pool, we're blasted by hot exhaust from the ice machine, the Gatorade vending machine, the coin-operated dryer vent, and every dripping air conditioner we pass.

We round a corner and smell chlorine. I see three kids splashing in a cool blue rectangle about the size of a postage stamp. The parents are sitting in white plastic chairs on the pebbled concrete path lining the pool. The chairs are the kind they always have on sale at Wal-Mart and in the seasonal aisle at the grocery store.

The kids are playing Marco Polo, thrashing and splashing in their blind frenzy to find each other. The pool is, as I mentioned, tiny. Maybe ten feet wide by twelve feet long. It's an in-ground pool but the motel didn't have much ground left to put it in.

Mrs. Pepper sees our uniforms and nudges her husband.

"Warren? It's the police!"

Warren wakes up.

"Hmmm?"

He reaches for his sunglasses and knocks over a beer can snuggled in a foam Koozie.

One of the kids just did a cannonball into the pool. I know this because the seat of my shorts just got soaked.

"Mr. and Mrs. Pepper? I'm Officer John Ceepak of the Sea Haven Police Department. This is my partner, Danny Boyle."

Ceepak pulls out his pad. "We'd like to ask you a few questions about what you saw at the Howland House Whaling Museum."

"You mean those . . . *things?* In the jars?" whispers Mrs. Pepper.

"You mean the ears?" a boy blurts out from the pool.

"They were gross!" screams the teenaged girl.

"No, they weren't! They were awesome!" I'm figuring the boy is Warren, Jr. "Maybe some sailor lost them to scurvy! We read about scurvy in school. He didn't eat his limes so his ears fell off and then they pickled them!"

Now I hear bawling. A little girl in water wings who wants her big brother to shut up.

"Mommy, make him stop!" Must be Maddie.

"It was disgusting," says her mother. "I told that woman—she should be ashamed."

"How long will that ear exhibit be in there?" her husband now asks Ceepak. He sounds genuinely interested.

"Warren?"

"Well, the boy wants to go back . . . maybe take the cousins . . . it's kind of educational. . . ."

"The museum will remain closed for the foreseeable future," says Ceepak.

"Really?" Mr. Pepper sounds disappointed. "I was just telling the guy in 109 about it. He's been coming down here for fifteen years and never even knew they had a museum, let alone one with, you know, mummy ears."

"Were those King Putt's ears?" Warren Jr. has climbed up the ladder and hauled himself out of the pool. Currently, he is standing beside me, shivering and dripping on my shoes. "Dad says they were probably from like a caveman. . . ."

Ceepak ignores the boy. "Did you see anyone else at the museum, ma'am?"

"No," says Mrs. Pepper. "We were the only ones inside. It's not a very popular spot. I can see why."

"Did you see anybody coming out when you were going in?"

"No."

"You're certain?"

"Positive. We ran in when the thunderstorm started. I told the kids they could look around. Nobody else was in the building until the old lady showed up."

Ceepak nods. "Thank you, ma'am. Sir. Danny?"

He puts away his notebook and we head back to the parking lot.

"That was certainly helpful," I say as we drive away. "They can go into the Witless Protection Program."

"Now, Danny, you know that police work involves a lot of walking down trails that turn into dead ends. However, walk down them we must."

Ceepak checks the time. It's nearly six P.M.

"Where to now?" I ask. "Any more dead ends we can get out of the way today?"

The radio on the drivetrain hump between us bursts with static.

"Unit Twelve?" It's a female voice. "This is Special Officer Diego. Over."

Ceepak picks up the microphone. "This is Twelve. Go ahead, Officer Diego."

"Where are you guys?"

"Seahorse Motel."

Or more correctly, traveling down a dead-end street to Nowheresville.

"Can you swing by the house?" she asks. "Like right away?"

Ceepak snaps down the microphone button with renewed vigor. "Did you find something on Mary Guarneri?"

"Oh, not much. Just Miss Milk Carton's mother."

SEVENTEEN

C hief Baines recognizes the significance of our recent finds," says Ceepak, "and agrees that they warrant further investigation."

We're huddled around Denise Diego's computer workstation: just the three of us.

"However," Ceepak says, lowering his voice, "Chief Baines also requests that we keep this matter under the tightest operational security. We three are the only individuals he wants in the know on this. I will personally update the chief regarding our progress on a periodic basis."

"Should we have like a secret handshake or something?" asks Diego. "I could work up a code. . . ."

Ceepak smiles. "No need, Denise. Just don't discuss this matter with your fellow officers, friends, or family."

She shrugs and buries her arm in a bag of Cheese Supreme Doritos. I think she's disappointed that the Sea Haven Police Department doesn't afford more opportunity for Dungeons & Dragons–type tricks.

"Whatever," she says.

Diego is a little older than me. And a lot smarter. Her family is

Cuban—the ones who said *adios* to Havana back in the '60s when Castro came to town. She's got a sweet face and a cute figure. When she tries to talk tough, her big brown eyes usually give her away. She also likes to eat Doritos. Breakfast, lunch, and dinner. She told me once that Doritos are the perfect food. I called them "chemical chips" and she said, "Exactly! That's what makes them such an efficient fuel."

"Tell us what you found," says Ceepak.

Diego licks her fingertips and starts clacking on the keyboard.

"This one was pretty simple," she says. "I did a quick history on those milk-carton pictures. They started putting missing children on the side panels in the late '70s and early '80s—after Etan Patz in New York and all those kids in Atlanta disappeared."

Ceepak nods. Like I said—he's more of a forensics history buff than I am.

"Anyhow, I went to missing-kids-dot-com. It's run by the National Center for Missing & Exploited Children. They even have an 800 number: 1-800-THE-LOST. Creepy, hunh? Sounds like a vampire movie. But, then I realize—all the information about missing kids is centralized over at the FBI. So I tap into the NCIC. . . ."

Even I know this one: she's talking about the National Crime Information Center, a computerized database filled with all sorts of info about fugitives, stolen property, and missing persons. The data is available to all federal, state, and local law enforcement agencies 24 hours a day, 365 days a year.

"Anyway," Diego continues, "I put in the name Mary Guarneri, and the computer spits out the next of kin who posted the original missing child alert: Martha W. Guarneri, 24 West Grove Street, Fresno, CA, 93706."

"Fresno?" says Ceepak. "That's a long way from New Jersey. . . ."

"Yeah. So, I checked her background. She used to live in West Pennsylvania. Erie. Up near the lake. No husband. Never married. You guys tell me her daughter left home and came to Sea Haven in the summer of 1985. Well, mom left Erie, PA, in 1992."

"I wonder why," Ceepak muses.

"You can ask her." Diego hands him a purple Post-It note. "That's her phone number. She's sixty years old, and she should be home right now. She lives in a one-bedroom rental close to the Fresno Airport. That's why her rent's so cheap."

Diego winks at me.

"You got all that off the Internet?" I ask.

"Yep. Took me almost an hour." Another wink. "Be careful, Danny. Big Sister's watching you."

I nod. I will.

"How do you know she's currently at home?" asks Ceepak.

"Well," she says as her fingers play across the keyboard, "it's partially supposition on my part. We know she works the early morning shift at Country Waffles on Blackstone Avenue. She gets off at three P.M. and, according to her credit card bills, takes the FAX bus, that's the Fresno Area Express." She glances at her wristwatch. "It's six fifty here, means it's ten to four out in Fresno. The bus ride takes ten to fifteen minutes."

I give her a wrinkled brow of disbelief. How could our new Nancy Drew know that?

"Danny," she says, "FAX posts its schedule online. I simply plotted the shortest route from her job to her home and factored in. . . ."

Ceepak picks up a phone. "Awesome work, Officer Diego." He glances at the number. "Let's give her a call." He nods to a vacant desk. "Danny, pick up when I give you the signal."

"10-4."

"Denise?" he asks. "If you'd like to. . . ."

"No, thanks." She gives her Doritos bag a good shake. Crumbs sprinkle down to mingle with the crusty triangles already scattered on her mouse pad. "I need a refill. Can I get you guys anything?"

Ceepak cups his hand over the telephone's mouthpiece, shakes his head. Then he gives me the single-finger hand-chop point. I figure that's my "go" signal to pick up the phone, so I do.

"Hello?" says a tired voice.

"Hello, is this Ms. Martha Guarneri?"

"Yes. . . ." Now she sounds suspicious. "Who's this?"

"Ms. Guarneri, my name is John Ceepak. I am a police officer in Sea Haven, New Jersey."

There's this tense pause.

"Have you found her body?"

EIGHTEEN

I hear Ms. Guarneri taking in a deep breath to steel herself.

Her voice trembles anyway. "I always knew this day would come. You'd find her body. I'd get a call. . . ."

"Ms. Guarneri? We have not recovered your daughter's body. We do not even know if she is alive or dead."

"I see. I see." She heaves a deep sigh. Relief, I guess.

"We did, however, come upon what we suspect is her charm bracelet."

"Her. . . ."

"Ma'am, did your daughter wear a charm bracelet?"

"Yes, sir. All the time."

"Do you remember any of the charms she had on it?"

"Sure. Some of 'em. Not all. They were pretty, I remember that. I bought her a couple whenever my tips were good enough. I worked at the Perkins Family Restaurant back then. In Erie."

"Yes, ma'am."

"Did she still have that one from New Orleans? I bought her that one. We went down to the World's Fair together in July 1984. I remember the trip. It was a good one. We drove all the way down to

Louisiana in my beat-up Buick." I hear a smile creeping into her voice. "It was real hot and muggy because it was right along the Mississippi river, near that French Quarter they have down there. I guess it was the last summer vacation we ever took together."

"How old was your daughter when she left home?"

"Seventeen. We'd just had a huge fight."

"May I ask what about?"

"What else? Boys. She was fooling around like teenagers do, spending too much time with this boy and that. I warned her what could happen. Told her she could get in big trouble if she weren't careful. Told her that's what happened to me."

"You became pregnant as a teenager?"

"Yes, sir. I ain't proud about it, but I won't lie to you, neither. At the time, I thought I was giving Mary good advice, trying to stop her from doing what I done wrong. She, of course, turned it all around, took it the wrong way. Thought I was saying I wished I'd never had her, which weren't true at all. I loved my baby girl. But she was always Mary, Mary, Quite Contrary. Ran away the day after we had that argument. June 14th, 1985. You think it's strange I still remember the date after all these years?"

"No, ma'am."

"I went crazy looking for her. Couldn't afford to hire no private detective or nothing like that but I did what I could. Put her picture up everywhere I could think. Even slipped it into the menu binders there at Perkins. The police in Erie put me in touch with the milk carton people and they put her face in front of the whole country for about a month. . . ."

Her voice drifts off.

"Ms. Guarneri?"

"Yes?"

"Why did you think we had found your daughter's body?"

"You said you was from Sea Haven. Sea Haven, New Jersey?"

"That's right."

"Mary sent me a postcard from there one time. Only one I ever did get after she took off. Only time I ever even heard from her. I still have it hanging on my refrigerator. 'Greetings From Sea Haven, New Jersey,' it says. Looks like a nice beach."

"Did Mary tell you anything about the time she spent here? Did she write any kind of message on the back?"

"Not much. Just . . . hold on . . . I'm here in the kitchen. Just a second. . . ."

We wait while she walks from the phone to the fridge and back again. I wonder how many times she has stared at that particular postcard, how many times she's read the words scribbled on the back.

"Here we go," she says when she returns to the phone. She's sniffing back tears. "I'll read it to you. 'Dear Mom. How are you? I am fine. I am here with some new friends. They are my new brothers and sisters. Do not worry. I am fine. Please forgive me. He already has.' That's all she wrote."

"Who is *he*?" asks Ceepak. "The one she says forgave her?"

"I don't rightly know. I figure it must be the boy—the one who got her pregnant. I figure she had an abortion."

"Was your daughter pregnant?"

"I don't know. If she was, she never did tell me. But I always figured that might be what made her run away like that—'specially after I scared her off with my little lecture. Soon as I got that card, I called the police down there in Sea Haven. Spoke to a man . . . I believe his name was Gus. Yes. Gus. I remember because I had me an uncle named Gus and he sounded a lot like this fellow did. Kind of put-out, you know what I'm saying? Like a customer who hollers at you to hurry up and bring him his coffee because he ain't had any yet."

Sounds like our retired desk sergeant: Gus Davis. Or, as we used to call him, "Gus The Grouch."

"Was this police officer able to help you in any way?"

"No. Not really. I called him three or four times that summer and into the fall. Called him near Christmas time, too. He said he'd get back to me if there were any new developments. Guess there never were none. He never did call back."

"I'm sorry."

"Well, sir, I don't blame him. Guess it's hard for you folks to find someone if they don't want to be found—'specially when they go and change their name."

"Your daughter changed her name?"

"Yes, sir. 'Ruth.' That's how she signed the card. Of course, I recognized her handwriting and all. Mary never were no Ruth. That weren't even her middle name. I have no idea why she signed herself that way."

Ceepak and I look at each other.

Ruth.

It's the name somebody wrote on that specimen jar we found at the Whaling Museum.

NINETEEN

We drive toward the setting sun, over to the bay side of the island.

Retired desk sergeant Gus Davis spends most of his time on his fishing boat, especially in the summer. He says it helps his marriage: he and his wife get along better if they only see each three times a day—coffee, dinner, and the ten o'clock news.

Gus's boat, a thirty-eight-footer, is usually docked at the public pier near Cherry Street. Ceepak and I park in a crumbling patch of asphalt close to the pier pilings.

"Here he comes," says Ceepak, pointing to a puttering fishing boat followed up the inlet by a flock of hungry gulls.

Then I hear Gus, yelling at the birds swooping down to check out his catch.

"Get outta here, you freaking mooch birds! Find your own freaking fish. . . ."

It's a wonder the birds don't snag their wings on all the poles and antennae and outriggers jutting out above the boat. Gus pulls back on the throttle, churns up some water, and reverses engines to wharf in his berth.

"Throw me the line, Danny," he hollers. "Freaking mooch birds!"

I pick up a coil of rope and toss it down to Gus. He wraps it around a cleat. The birds keep circling and squawking.

"Here you go, you greedy bastards!"

Gus scoops his hand into a five-gallon bucket and tosses a tangled chunk of chopped squid as far out as he can. The birds dive bomb and attack it.

"They can have the freaking bait," Gus says with a raspy laugh. "But the fluke is all mine." He hoists a Styrofoam chest up and over the side. I grab it.

"Good day?" Ceepak asks as Gus moves around the cockpit closing things down.

"Not bad. You ever eat fluke?"

"Roger that. However, I believe the restaurant called it 'summer flounder.'"

"Same difference. I'll be eating good tonight, boys. I cleaned and gutted on the way in. That's why the birdbrains were giving me the winged escort. I told Fran to drag out the corn meal and pickle relish."

Fran is Gus's wife. It's why his boat is called the *Lady Fran*.

"You boys be sure to think of me when you're grabbing a cup of bad coffee and a shrink-wrapped sandwich over at the Qwick Pick."

Gus just described the typical cop's dinner, purchased at any friendly neighborhood convenience store. Of course, this cop usually adds in a bag of chips, some Ring Dings, and a can of Mountain Dew. Ceepak goes with the bag of baby carrots.

Gus climbs over the gunwale and up onto the dock. "So, what's up? Fran called on the cell, said you boys were looking for me."

"Roger that," says Ceepak. "We need to ask you a couple questions. About an old case."

Gus grimaces. His face is brown with leathery seams. His wispy hair has been bleached white by the sun. I can tell he doesn't much want to talk shop, doesn't want to play cops and robbers anymore. He's retired. Put in his time, picked up his pension. Now all he wants to do is fish and breathe in the salty sea air until the day his lungs conk out.

"Can we make this quick? I'd like to eat my fish while it's still fresh."

"Of course," says Ceepak. "Do you remember a case involving a teenage runaway named Mary Guarneri?"

"No. Should I?"

"Perhaps. The girl's mother spoke with you several times. She had reason to believe Mary was in Sea Haven."

"What kind of reason?"

"She received a postcard from her daughter."

"Is that so? Hunh. Well, I got to be honest—I don't remember any Mary Guarneri. When was this? Couple years ago or something?"

"1985."

"1985? Jesus, Ceepak. That's freaking ancient history."

"Agreed. However, the mother spoke with you several times over the course of that summer. Again right before Christmas. I thought perhaps. . . ."

"Listen, Ceepak—I realize you're relatively new down here, but let me give it to you straight: we have moms and dads calling about their kids all summer, every summer. Sea Haven is a very popular destination for your juvie types. They figure they can head down here, hang out on the beach, sleep under the boardwalk—live the dream, you know what I'm saying? Nothing but sun, sand, and sex."

"We have reason to suspect that this girl could have become the victim of foul play."

"What reason?"

"Recently uncovered evidence." Ceepak doesn't go into the grisly details.

"Hey," Gus says with a shrug, "if her mom called, I'm sure we put her name up on the board with the rest of 'em. But I guarantee you we didn't bust our hump searching for this Mary Guarneri kid. Summers, we're crazy busy. You know that. Forty-some officers. Twelve men a shift. We never had the time or manpower to provide station house adjustments for every kid that comes down the shore looking for a good time without telling her parents about it first."

"Did you write up an incident report when Ms. Guarneri called? Maybe if we re-examined your records. . . ."

Gus shakes his head.

"You're not listening. There aren't any records, no paper at all. These runaway kids were never what you might call a 'high priority.' Most of them were druggies or worse. Now if this kid got into some kind of trouble, say she was ripping people off or, you know, dabbling in drug dealing or prostitution or what have you, then we might have something on her."

"Do you have reason to suspect she might have been engaged in criminal activity?"

"Most of these runaways are troublemakers. I wouldn't be surprised if her parents kicked her out of the house, told her to take a hike."

"This particular girl's mother was actively searching for her."

"Then she's the freaking exception to the rule. Most of these kids, they're like the garbage you fling out your car window, you know what I'm saying? You're happy to be rid of it. Maybe somebody comes along and cleans up your mess, maybe they don't, but you don't really give two shits either way."

Ceepak nods but gives Gus the sad eyes that say he could have and should have done better.

"I gotta go home." Gus picks up his cooler. "Fran's waiting."

Ceepak puts away his notebook, clicks his pen shut.

"Say 'hello' for me."

"Yeah." Gus shambles toward his car. Stops. Turns to face Ceepak. "You might ought to check with that Jesus freak on the boardwalk."

"Are you referring to Reverend Trumble?"

"Yeah. Most of these runaways, sooner or later they get hungry or stink so bad they end up at his place for a hot meal and shower." Gus shrugs. "Sorry I can't, you know, give you guys anything more."

Ceepak smiles. "Don't worry, Gus. It's all good."

Gus opens his car door. His lips twitch down into a frown. I get a feeling his fried fluke won't taste so good tonight, no matter how well Fran breads and spices it.

As his car crunches out of the lot, Ceepak turns to stare at the sun setting behind the skyline of boat antennae. The view kind of reminds me of this fake oil painting that's bolted to the wall in my apartment. My apartment used to be a motel room. Motels use bolts on all their works of art.

I hear Ceepak sigh.

"What's up?" I ask, because when he heaves a sigh like that, I always know something is.

Ceepak turns. Squints. It's not the sun that's causing his eyes to tighten. He's seeing something he'd rather not, something that happened in the past. Something bad.

"Antwoine James," he says.

"Who's he?"

Ceepak stays quiet. Nods. Finally he says one word: "Exactly." Then he repeats my question. Slowly. "Who is he?"

Okay. I think we're entering one of those Ceepak Zen Zones where the complexities of a cruel universe get boiled down to a single simple question that somehow answers everything. At least for him. Me? I've got nothing.

"Antwoine James was a good man," he says. "A good soldier. Sixty-seventh Armor Regiment out of Fort Hood, Texas. He was riding in the deuce-and-a-half behind our Hummer . . . we were on point. . . ."

He's back in the sandbox. Iraq. The day his topside gunner on the SAW, the Squad Automatic Weapon, took out a taxicab full of innocent civilians. The day the truck behind him was blown to bits by an IED, a roadside bomb.

"This was early in the conflict. Before we started doing hillbilly armor improvements. Sheet metal sides and firing ports. Of course, the brunt of this particular blast came up through the undercarriage. Side panels wouldn't have helped all that much."

Ceepak stops. Water laps against the pilings. Happy gulls chirp in the sky. Soothing seashore sounds surround us, like the mood music you hear on New Age CDs in gift shops. I don't think Ceepak hears any of it. I think he hears exploding bombs and screeching metal and the screams of men who just lost both their arms or legs or worse.

"Private James did not make it. He died before the choppers arrived. Died with his head in my lap. They shipped his body home in a steel casket with a flag draped over the top. They shipped him home to Dover Air Force base. Delaware."

Dover.

The circled word I saw in Ceepak's notebook.

"Unfortunately," he continues, "Antwoine James had no family except the Army. No home except Fort Hood. He was a tough kid from the streets of Houston who joined the Army because he wanted to become something better. When his body arrived in Dover, no one claimed it. No one was allowed to see his coffin in the newspaper or on TV. There was no one to take his folded flag, the flag given on behalf of a grateful nation."

Ceepak says the last two words with as much sarcasm as he ever musters. Then he turns to look me in the eye.

"I'm afraid the nation was too busy to show its gratitude for a young black soldier who grew up in the wrong part of town. He was considered 'less dead.'"

Less dead.

And so, once again, Ceepak helps me understand the significance of solving the Mary Guarneri puzzle.

Dover. Private Antwoine James.

Sea Haven. Runaway Mary Guarneri.

In Ceepak's world, every life is worthy of honor and respect, no matter how shady the circumstances surrounding it. No man is less dead than any other. No child less missed.

"You hungry?" I say.

Ceepak blinks. I think I just shocked him out of his dark musings, which was exactly what I was hoping to do.

"I'm starving," I chirp like one of those gulls tracking Gus's boat.

"Maybe we should head over to Morgan's. We don't have to do the whole surf and turf deal but maybe we could grab some crab cakes or a bowl of chowder. . . ."

I'm rambling.

I'm also not really hungry.

I just think my partner needs to be reminded of what's still good and decent in this world.

I think he needs a little Rita time.

TWENTY

Morgan's Surf and Turf is one of the few restaurants on the island that actually covers its tables with a tablecloth made out of cloth instead of paper.

And they don't give you a glass full of crayons to scribble on it, either.

When we got there, around eight P.M., Rita was working five tables. She looked pleased to see us, even if she was busy. Now we're sitting in a big booth at the back, right near the swinging kitchen doors where we can hear dishes clatter and bells ding and the cook yell in Spanish while we wait for our steaming bowls of Morgan's World Famous Clam Chowder to cool down. Only they spell it "Chowda." All the restaurants down here do. Guess it makes New Jersey sound more like New England. Maybe Cape Cod.

I'm also eating crackers. They have good ones at Morgan's, not just your basic Saltines. Morgan's gives you variety: Waverly Wafers, Ritz, Melba Toast—even those Sociables with the baked-in black specks that I think are pepper, maybe poppy seeds. Each cracker couple comes sealed inside its own individually labeled cellophane wrapper and they all sit in a tidy row inside a black-and-gold wire basket.

Classy.

I have a pile of tooth-torn cellophane wrappers heaped up next to my fork. I also have a light dusting of crumbs in my lap.

Not so classy.

I slurp some soup. It's good. Thick and creamy.

Ceepak has nibbled maybe the corner off one Saltine. For him, chowda is something you stir with a spoon while you ruminate.

"Hey, Danny!" It's my friend, Olivia Chibbs, the med student. She works summers at Morgan's, which is why she is currently balancing a mammoth tray loaded down with crab-stuffed lobster tails and something that smells like overcooked broccoli. "Hey, Ceepak."

"Good evening, Ms. Chibbs."

"Where've you been, Danny?" Olivia asks.

I point to my cop uniform. "Working."

"I thought you were on days."

"I am."

"It's night."

"We needed to put in a little overtime," says Ceepak. I notice he doesn't offer any additional information as to *why* we're working later than usual. I think it's his hint for me to do likewise, to keep our current mission under wraps as the chief requested.

"Do you guys get time-and-a-half when you pull OT?" Olivia asks

Ceepak nods. "Yes, ma'am. We surely do." He nibbles another corner off the same Saltine. For a tower of power, the guy eats like a sparrow on a low-carb diet.

"Awesome," says Olivia. "So Danny, Becca's been trying to text you for like two hours."

Becca Adkinson is another one of our mutual friends. She and her family run the Mussel Beach Motel over, as the name suggests, near the beach.

"What's up?"

"You and Aubrey Hamilton. She's willing to give you a second chance."

Aubrey is the girl Olivia and my buddy Jess tried to fix me up with last night.

"Becca set it all up. Tonight. Nine-thirty. The Sand Bar. Be there. On time, this time!"

Olivia shoots me a wink and bustles away with her clattering tray.

"Have I met this girl Aubrey?" Ceepak asks.

"Maybe. Waitress. Rusty Scupper." When I'm nervous, I tend to speak in quick, incoherent bursts.

"Nice girl?"

"Oh, yeah. Very, you know, nice. Real nice."

"You know, Danny, I suspect your friends think it's time you moved on. Tested the romantic waters."

"Yeah. I guess."

"When one door closes, another door opens."

"Yeah," I crack, "but it's hell in the hallway."

"You still miss Katie?"

I'm about to say, "Nah," when I remember Ceepak's Code. Not only won't he lie, cheat, or steal, he also won't tolerate anybody who does. I am, therefore, once again compelled to tell him the truth.

"Yeah. Sort of."

He nods his head like the big brother I never had.

"Understandable. Katie is a wonderful woman."

"Yeah. Must be why she moved all the way across the country to get away from me."

Now Ceepak shakes his head. "Not you, Danny. The memories. Her secret sadness. I believe Springsteen says it best. . . ."

Of course he does.

"'Some day they just cut it loose, cut it loose or let it drag 'em down.'"

He's quoting "Darkness on the Edge of Town" again.

"Danny, Katie had to cut herself free from Sea Haven and what happened here or it would have dragged her down for the rest of her life."

As usual, The Boss and Ceepak are correct, but it doesn't really make me feel any better. So, I tear open another cracker wrapper.

Ceepak tilts his wrist, checks his watch.

"You should definitely meet up with this young lady. Aubrey. It's only twenty-fifteen. Finish your soup and we'll swing by the house so you can pick up your Jeep."

"Don't you want to go talk to Trumble like Gus suggested? He's right, you know. A lot of the teenage runaways eventually end up there."

"10-4. However, I feel it might be best if we pay the Reverend a visit first thing tomorrow morning while he's serving breakfast. I find people are often most forthcoming when they're too busy to play games or plot deceptions. Who knows—maybe our redheaded friend will be there as well."

The thief from the beach. I had forgotten all about her.

Ceepak leans back in the booth and stares off into space, his face softening. I swivel in my seat to see what he sees, what he's smiling at.

Of course. It's Rita. She's over by the bar with her soft blonde hair backlit by the golden glow of a neon Corona Beer sign. She beams back at him and waves something in our general direction.

"Wonder what that might be. . . ." As if she heard him, Rita does a quick scan of her crowded tables to make sure everybody has everything they need for the next two seconds, and then darts across the dining room to join us.

"Look you guys—T. J. went to the top of the Empire State Building!"

She puts a postcard down on our table.

"That's wonderful," says Ceepak.

"John, he's having such a great time. . . ."

Ceepak sort of blushes. He doesn't want the whole world knowing he paid for Rita's sixteen-year-old kid to go see King Kong's perch. Not that he's embarrassed about doing it. It's praise that usually makes Ceepak feel all squirmy. I think it's why he never talks about the ton of medals he earned in the Army.

"Neither one of us can ever thank you enough," says Rita. "He went to Greenwich Village and this free rock concert in Central Park. . . ."

Ceepak allows a slight smile to cross his lips.

"I never could have afforded to send him up to my sister's . . . not on my own . . . I mean not with everything else . . . you know, back-to-school clothes and school supplies and. . . ."

"Rita, I'm very glad to hear that T. J.'s having fun," Ceepak says softly. "He's a good kid."

Rita leans down because she can't resist giving him a quick peck on the cheek.

Ceepak's grin grows so wide his wiggling dimples look like parentheses quivering on either side of his nose.

Rita giggles when she finds a tear in her eye.

"Look at me. I'm a mess." She dabs it away with her thumb. "Thanks again, honey."

"You are very welcome."

Romance fills the air. Almost enough to cover up the smell of over-cooked broccoli and lobster brine. Who knows, maybe I'll get lucky. If not tonight, sometime soon. If not Aubrey, someone else.

"He'll be home on Friday," says Rita, composing herself, brushing invisible wrinkles out of her crisp white blouse. "They need him on the boardwalk. Apparently, they're expecting big crowds on account of the Sand Castle Competition."

T. J. works part-time at this game booth on the boardwalk, helping people lose their money by flinging rubber rings at two-liter Coke bottles in a frantic attempt to win their girlfriend some kind of cuddly stuffed monkey.

"Miss?"

A man three tables away, a huge man with a napkin tucked under his three chins and a glob of sour cream dotting the tip of his nose, is waving his arm like a little boy who needs permission to use the bathroom.

"We need more butter, miss."

"Right away!" Rita says.

She scoots into the kitchen. Ceepak watches her fly through the swinging double doors. I look down and check out T. J.'s postcard. Naturally it reminds me of the one Mary Guarneri sent *her* mother all those years back. The one she signed "Ruth," for whatever reason.

When I look up, I can tell Ceepak is thinking the exact same thing. He pushes his chowder bowl aside and reaches into a cargo pants pocket to pull out a stack of Polaroids.

"Let's recap. What do we have thus far?" he asks rhetorically as he flips his evidence photographs down on the table like Uno cards. "The two jars left at the museum. The name Ruth written on the one label—the same name Mary Guarneri used on her postcard home to her mother. The Lisa earring." He flips down another Polaroid. "We also have the museum guest book."

"We should check all those names—the people who came in before the Pepper family."

"Roger that." He flips down two more pictures. "We have Cap'n Pete's treasure: the milk carton and Mary's charm bracelet."

"Yeah. Guess she lost it before she changed her name."

Ceepak agrees. Taps the "Mary" charm.

"What's that?"

Rita has come out of the kitchen with a big bowl of melted butter for the heart-attack-waiting-to-happen over at table fifteen. She's staring at the charm bracelet picture.

Ceepak deftly flips over the more gruesome photos.

"A charm bracelet Captain Pete found buried in the sand."

Rita looks surprised. "He actually found something?"

Ceepak nods. "On Oak Beach. Close to where I found the high-school ring."

Rita leans down for a closer look.

"Cool," she says. She focuses on the tiny doodads strung along the chain. "I had a kitten charm like that. . . ."

"Miss?" Tubby at table fifteen must smell his butter.

Rita taps the picture.

"I had that one, too," she says.

"Which one?" asks Ceepak.

"The church," she says. "Reverend Billy gave it to me."

TWENTY-ONE

We wait while Rita serves the big man his butter.

"Anything else?"

The guy's mouth is a mush pit of half-chewed broccoli and bread. "I need more sour cream." He says this while stuffing the crusty heel of a dinner roll into his face.

"No problem." Rita dashes back toward the kitchen.

Now Ceepak's the one holding up his hand, trying to catch the waitress's attention by waggling his fingers.

Rita sees him. Stops before she hits the doors.

"You guys need more chowder? More crackers, Danny?"

"Negative," says Ceepak. He taps the charm bracelet photograph. "However, I would like to discuss. . . ."

"Sure. I'll be right back."

Boom. She hustles into the kitchen.

"Actually, I could use a couple more crackers," I say. Waverly Wafers. You can never have enough.

Boom. Rita cannonballs out the double doors with a quart-sized mountain of sour cream scooped into a salad bowl.

"Here you go, sir," she says to Tubby, who has too much bread and meat in his mouth to even mumble anymore.

"Miss?"

A woman with a helmet of hard hair is tapping her lipstick-rimmed coffee cup with an index finger—the universal symbol for *fill-'er-up*.

"Regular, right?" Rita's still smiling.

"Right."

While she's on her way to the coffee pots, a woman at another table—with what looks like all her sisters and their husbands—holds up a half-full breadbasket.

"Excuse me? Miss? We need more of the rolls with the salty tops . . . not the brown ones . . . no one likes the brown ones. . . ."

Rita, that smile permanently planted in place, grabs the basket.

"No problem."

When she gets to the Bunn coffee warmer, this old guy nearby tugs on her skirt with one hand, slurps his coffee with the other.

"I could use a little more decaf."

"Of course."

The guy holds out his cup like a beggar under the boardwalk.

Suddenly, Ceepak slides out of our booth and marches toward the center of the dining room. As he walks, he unpins the badge on his shirt, holds the shiny shield in the palm of his right hand, raises it high above his head.

This is so cool: Ceepak's going to tin the entire dining room.

"Ladies? Gentlemen? May I have your attention please? I am Officer John Ceepak of the Sea Haven Police Department."

People turn. Forks lower. Chewing ceases. Even Tubby shuts his trap.

"Because of an ongoing police investigation, your waitress will be temporarily unavailable to serve you. If you require anything, kindly wait until Ms. Lapczynski returns to the floor in approximately five minutes. Thank you and enjoy the rest of your dinners. Ms. Lapczynski?"

Ceepak tilts his head, indicating that Rita should follow us outside. Immediately. She is trying very hard not to laugh. With a big grin on her face, she accompanies us out the front door and into the parking lot.

• • •

"He gave one to all the girls who came to the Life Under the Son Ministry. The church roof tilts back. And inside are these teeny little pews. I think I still have it somewhere. . . ."

Ceepak watches her closely.

"When exactly did you go there first?"

Rita drops her head. "1991. Sixteen years ago." She waits a second. Then looks up. "When I was pregnant with T. J."

Ceepak nods. I see no judgment in his eyes. Neither does Rita, so she continues.

"I was just a kid. I made a mistake."

"We all make mistakes." Ceepak's voice is steady but soft. "That's . . ."

"You're not going to tell me 'that's why your pencil has an eraser' again, are you?"

In fact, Ceepak probably was going to tell her exactly that, because that's what he always says whenever somebody else goofs up.

"No, ma'am."

"Good. Because T. J. isn't a mistake."

"Of course not."

"His father was long gone. I'd only known him for a few weeks. We were kids, John. Teenagers hanging out on the beach. He was just this cute boy, a summertime fling. He lived outside Philly, I think."

She pauses. Ceepak nods again, encouragingly.

"Anyway, I stayed there at the Inn for a couple months. My parents wanted nothing to do with me. I'd come down here with a bunch of friends from high school, all of us looking for summer jobs. We rented a cheap apartment. Slept three to a room. My bed was an air mattress on the floor."

Been there. Done that.

"When I told my mother I was pregnant, she said if I was grown up enough to get knocked up, I remember that's what she called it, knocked up. . . ."

Her lips curl into a sad, remembering smile.

"She said if I thought I was mature enough to become a mother, then fine—I could fend for myself. She wouldn't help. Neither would my father."

"But Reverend Billy would?"

Rita nods. *"Hate the sin, love the sinner.* That's his motto. He fed us. Gave us motel beds to sleep in. Even put us in touch with doctors and counselors and social workers. Of course he wanted me to confess my sins, accept Christ, and be born again."

"How so?"

"He used to do these surf baptisms. Not as much as he did back in the '80s, but every now and then. You'd walk out into the ocean at low tide, all the way out to where the waves were breaking. He'd say a few prayers, you'd ask Jesus for forgiveness, accept him as your personal savior, and then Reverend Billy would, you know, dunk you backward under the water three times."

"So, you were you baptized by Reverend Billy?"

"No. I kept putting him off. Told him I wasn't ready. He told me to keep praying on it. And I did. But then I met this very nice woman who stopped by the motel one day to donate some food. She was a little older than me—not much, maybe five years. We started talking. She told me she had been in my 'situation' herself a few years back. Even spent time with Reverend Billy at the motel. Her own pregnancy ended badly."

"Abortion?"

"Miscarriage. Anyway, I guess she took pity on me. The next thing I know, she's offering me a job in this store she just opened—plus free room and board in the small apartment above the shop. She even gave me paid maternity leave when T. J. was born, though I'd only been working for her a couple months."

"Does she have a name?"

"Yes. A very good one. In fact, she's currently one of this town's most prominent and respected merchants. Nobody knows about her past and how she almost became an unwed mother at the age of eighteen. No one knows that she put in time at The Sonny Days Inn. She'd like to keep it that way. So would I."

I don't think that was the answer Ceepak was looking for when he asked, "Does she have a name." I think a simple "Michele" or "Judy" would've sufficed.

Ceepak stares at Rita.

"She sounds like a wonderful woman," he says.

"She is."

"I'd like to meet her."

"And you will. If and when you really need to."

Ceepak considers his options. Makes his decision.

"Thank you," he says. "I appreciate that."

Rita looks down.

"I'm sorry I never. . . ."

"It's all good. If we absolutely need to talk to this woman, I'm certain you will provide us with her name."

"I promise," says Rita.

"You don't have to. You already said you would do it. Your word is good enough for me."

Rita turns to face me.

"Are you okay with this, Officer Boyle?"

"Oh, yeah," I say. "Me, too. Your word's good to go."

"Thank you, Danny."

"No problem. Hey, like Ceepak says: *'Everybody's got a secret, Sonny.'*"

Rita laughs. "That's not Ceepak. That's Springsteen."

I wink at her. "Same difference."

One of the cell phones clipped to Ceepak's belt chirps. He wears two of them. I'm not exactly sure why.

"Excuse me," he says and flips open the silver clamshell. "This is Ceepak. Yes, Chief. Right. Roger that. Will do."

This can't be good. The chief doesn't work nights. He clocks out at five or five thirty. Then again, the poor guy has to wear a suit and tie every day. I'll stick with late nights, bad coffee, and hitting the streets. We get to wear shorts in the summer.

Ceepak snaps his phone shut.

"Danny? You may want to contact Ms. Aubrey Hamilton and postpone your date at The Sand Bar. We need to be at The Treasure Chest. ASAP."

"Everything okay?" asks Rita. "My tables must be going crazy."

"Something's come up."

"Something serious?"

Ceepak nods.

"Going to be a long night?"

"Definite possibility."

"Okay. Uhm, do you need me to take the dog out for a walk later? After I'm done here?"

"I'd appreciate it. So would Barkley."

"What's going on, John?"

"I'd rather not say at this juncture."

When Ceepak starts using words like "juncture," you know he's shifting back into supercop mode. Typically, you also stop asking him questions.

"Okay." Rita reaches out, squeezes Ceepak's left hand. "You be safe, you hear?"

"Will do."

"Promise?"

"I give you my word."

"Rita?" Olivia has found us. "They need us inside. Time to sing 'Happy Birthday' at the four-top up front."

"I really gotta run."

"Us, too."

"Okay." Rita finally lets go of Ceepak's hand. As soon as she and Olivia are through the door, he turns to me.

"An employee at The Treasure Chest souvenir shop at 105 Ocean Avenue just discovered a severed human nose floating in a jar of formaldehyde."

"A nose?"

"Affirmative."

It's like we're playing Whack-A-Mole. Body parts keep popping up all over town.

"Was there a label on the jar?"

Ceepak nods.

"Miriam. 1980."

TWENTY-TWO

Kitsch.

That's what my mom would call the souvenirs and stuff they sell at The Treasure Chest. Crappy kitsch.

Spoon rests, jumping dolphin paper weights, rubber sharks, salt and pepper shakers shaped like lighthouses, ceramic coffee mugs where the coffee comes out of a fish mouth so you're basically kissing a fish first thing every morning.

I think people's brains must go on vacation when their bodies do. It's the only answer. Vacationers buy things they wouldn't normally buy. If they'll pay thirty dollars for a sand-dollar wall clock to hang in the rumpus room, it must be because their mental faculties have taken the week off.

I think the main purpose of the Sea Haven souvenir shops is to keep New Jersey's Goodwill and Salvation Army thrift stores stocked for the remainder of the year. And garage sales. Jersey is the capital of Garage Sale Nation.

The Treasure Chest is right across the street from The Bagel Lagoon and Ceepak's apartment on Ocean Avenue. It's a squat, block-long building with pirate flags fluttering every ten feet along the mansard roof. With curb-to-ceiling plate-glass windows painted with slogans like DOCK HERE FOR BIG $AVING$, it kind of looks like a giant furniture showroom, only the floors are cluttered with T-shirt racks and beach ball bins instead of Barcaloungers.

We arrive without lights or siren, since Officers Adam Kiger and Dylan Murray had radioed in to say they'd already secured the scene. The parking lot is empty except for their cruiser and a small Honda.

Our headlights sweep across the two cops as we pull in. I notice they're with a young woman in a purple polo shirt. I look closer and see that it's my old friend from high school, Amy Decosimo. She used to work over at Pudgy's Fudgery, where she was in charge of slicing quarter-pound slabs off the big bricks and making up the assorted-flavor two-pound boxes for people to take home to cat-sitters.

I now recall hearing that Amy has moved up to a management position here at The Treasure Chest. I have a hunch she's the one who found the item that wasn't listed in the store's inventory: one souvenir nose. She looks terrified.

"What've we got?" Ceepak asks Kiger.

"You talk to the chief?"

"Roger that."

"This is Ms. Decosimo," says Kiger. "She's the one who found the object in question."

Amy looks at me. "Hey, Danny."

I remember the last time I saw her—at the start of the whole Tilt-A-Whirl thing. She helped me clean up the bloody little girl I hauled inside the fudge shop.

Don't get me started. It's a long story.

"How you doin', Amy?" I ask.

"I . . . I'm. . . ."

I forgot: Amy Decosimo doesn't deal with crisis situations all that well. Her first instinct is to panic and say, "Ohmygod"—a lot.

"Ohmygod, Danny! It's horrible. . . ."

There she goes.

"Ohmygod!"

"Are you okay?" I ask.

Her frozen doe eyes become gigantic.

"Have you locked down the area?" Ceepak asks Kiger.

"We left everything just the way Ms. Decosimo found it."

"I . . . I . . . " Amy sputters a little more.

"Ms. Decosimo?" says Ceepak.

"Hmmm?"

"Were you alone in the store when you made your discovery?"

"Hmmm?"

"Were you alone?"

"When?"

"When you found the jar."

"Oh. Yes. Ohmygod. I was all alone!"

"Was the front door locked?"

"Yes. I always lock it at eight. Maybe five past, if we have a straggler . . . none tonight . . . no stragglers."

"Did you notice any unusual customers?"

"No."

"Do you have security cameras in the store?"

"Uhm-hmmm. Yeah."

"Good. That might help us find whoever. . . ."

"They don't work."

"Come again?"

"The video cameras don't work. Mr. Mazzilli just put up these fake ones to scare off shoplifters. The actual cameras and recorders and stuff cost way too much money. . . ."

Mr. Mazzilli is Bruno "The Boardwalk King" Mazzilli. He owns The Treasure Chest and half the junk shops and lemonade stands up and down the boardwalk. He is also notoriously cheap, even though he charges six bucks for a twenty-cent corked glass bottle filled with free seashells and equally free sand.

Now Ceepak turns to me.

"Danny?"

"Yes, sir?"

"Do you have the digital camera?"

"Yeah."

"We're going in."

We make our way up the center aisle of the store. Usually, the place is packed with families in flip-flops and shorts milling about, mesmerized by brightly colored plastic bathed in fluorescent light. Usually, this place gives me a splitting headache.

We pass the cardboard displays for Party Poppers and Pinwheels.

We squeeze through a maze of circular clothes racks jammed with Sea Haven sweatshirts, most of which have the same SH logo silk-screened on the front. It's like we're telling the rest of the world to be quiet.

"There it is." Ceepak uses his Maglite flashlight like a laser pointer. "Next to the snow globes."

I see it, too.

Another small jar. Glass with a metal screw-on lid.

It's on the top shelf. On either side of it are dozens of "snow" globes all depicting the same diorama: an open pirate chest, a skull, and two palm trees stranded on a plastic desert island. If you grab one and give it a good shake, the water becomes filled with a swirling flurry of gold sparkle flakes and the skull's jawbone yaps up and down. I know this because The Treasure Chest has been selling their signature Pirate Globe to boys like me for nearly twenty years.

"Danny? Focus."

Ceepak can usually tell when my mind is drifting off to someplace other than where it should be.

"Take a picture before I spray the jar."

"Right."

I power up the Canon and press off a few images. The one with the flash is a mistake: the jar's glass reflects back and my picture looks like a big white blob. I trash that one. Check the others.

"We're good."

"Zoom in tight. Use the macro lens."

"Okay."

I do. I also make the mistake of checking out the viewfinder as the lens pushes in.

First I see a pinkish triangle suspended in somewhat murky fluid. As the image becomes sharper, I know it's a nose. I can see the two smooth nostrils devoid of any nasal hair. A strand of flesh flops out of one naked hole and just hangs there. Poor girl. I know for certain it belonged to a girl because it's one of those cute buttons of a nose—the kind that would look ridiculously out of place on any guy unless he was a pixie.

"Note the cut marks. Along the edges," says Ceepak.

I do. I also take another picture—close along the sides of the nose. I sidle around to frame up a reverse angle. I've never been behind the inside of a nose before. I hope I never am again.

"Very clean incisions," says Ceepak. "Whoever did this was quite skillful, their blade quite sharp."

"You think they did this with a knife?"

"Or a scalpel," says Ceepak. "Perhaps a razor—although that would present a problem once they reached the cartilage—the tough elastic tissue connecting the flesh of the nose to the nasal bone of the skull. One would need a saw of some sort to cut through that."

I feel all those free crackers from the Morgan's basket creeping up my windpipe to protest.

"Photograph the label," he says.

"Right."

I move a step to the left and zoom in again.

Miriam. 1980.

"Odd name," says Ceepak.

"Even for 1980?" I ask—making the '80s sound like prehistoric times, which, to me, they are. That's when Springsteen used to wear a sweatband on his head and people drank Crystal Light while they did aerobics with the blonde from *Dynasty* named Krystle, who also wore a sweatband. Lot of sweatbands back then. Sweatbands and break dancing. I've seen history books.

"I don't believe Miriam has ever been one of the most popular names for girls in America, except, of course, in Jewish families." Ceepak now produces a spray can. "This is ninhydrin," he says. "A chemical substance that reveals latent fingerprints in porous surfaces such as paper."

He aims the spray nozzle toward the paper label affixed to the jar and spritzes it.

I snap my head back. "Oh, man." It stinks.

Ceepak starts fanning his hand near the jar. "It's best to do this in a well-ventilated area. . . ."

Now he tells me. I think they shut down the A/C inside The Treasure Chest when they lock the front door. The air in aisle four isn't ventilating at all except for Ceepak fanning it in my face. It smells like the Turnpike up near Rahway.

"We need to wait for the ninhydrin to dry," he says. "I wish I had my steam iron. . . ."

I cough. "Maybe they sell them here."

"Doubtful."

"I could go look. . . ."

Ceepak stops fanning the fumes. "No need. Whoever placed the jar on this shelf was most likely wearing gloves."

"We need those security cameras," I say. "If they were real . . . if they were working. . . ."

"Indeed. An individual wearing gloves, if only for a moment, would certainly stand out in a sea of summertime shoppers."

"Yeah."

The smell of the stink-spray is still strong. I'm thinking about heading over to the next aisle where I see scented candles sculpted in the shape of pink flamingoes.

"Two ears. One nose," says Ceepak. "Why? Why isn't this another ear?"

"Maybe he got bored with ears. Maybe we're dealing with two different killers."

"Who both store their trophies in labeled jars of formaldehyde? Doubtful, my friend. Doubtful."

"Okay, so what's next?"

"I'll examine this evidence more closely this evening. Put it under my microscope. Discuss this new development with the chief. He'll undoubtedly initiate calls to the press. Ask them to sit on the story. He'll likewise ask the Pepper family to do the same thing. . . ."

"Well, what do you want me to do?"

"Get a good night's rest. First thing tomorrow morning, we need to go talk to the Reverend Billy Trumble."

TWENTY-THREE

I drop Ceepak off at headquarters.

He has a little high-school chemistry lab set up on the second floor. The chief arranged for it after Ceepak saved his butt on the Mad Mouse case. It's not a huge deal, but he's got a microscope plus a computer that can do automated fingerprint searches or match tire tracks to a database of known tread patterns. He even has this program called SLIP for "Shoewear Linking and Identification Program." He's all geared up for the first season of *CSI: Sea Haven* if, you know, CBS decides to do that instead of, say, *CSI: Des Moines*.

I head back over to Ocean Avenue. When I cruise past The Treasure Chest and The Bagel Lagoon, I check my rearview mirror and see Rita coming down the staircase from Ceepak's apartment with Barkley the dog. It's a slow go. Barkley needs to contemplate each step before taking it.

By my watch, it's nine forty-five P.M. I figure Aubrey Hamilton might still be waiting for me over at The Sand Bar. I figure this because I forgot to let her know I wasn't coming at nine-thirty as planned.

Oops.

I hang a right and head back to the bay side of the island. I know I'm supposed to head home and get a good night's sleep, but I need a beer. Something to wash the stink of Ceepak's fingerprint spray out of my nostrils. Something to wipe the image of Miriam's severed nose out of my memory bank.

She's gone.

Long gone, according to Ralph the bartender.

"She's the blonde with the long legs, right?"

"Yeah."

"Always dresses in white, to show off her tan?"

"Yeah. That's Aubrey."

"She's a tramp, my man." He stares at an empty stool two down from mine at the bar. "Had most of the buttons undone on her blouse . . . everything all hanging out."

"Unh-hunh. . . ."

"Keep away from that one. Skanks like her are nothin' but trouble. Trust me. You want a beer?"

No, I want somebody to put me out of my misery. But a beer will have to do.

"Yeah. A Bud would be great. Thanks."

Ralph plops a cold longneck down in front of me.

"Oh, shit," he says. "Dorkface."

He sees somebody I don't.

"Why does this fucking asshole have to come into my bar every night?"

I turn around. It's Princeton. The fiftysomething tourist who was heading off to Smuggler's Cove last night with my sweet little hitchhiker.

He sees me. Waves like we're old pals, fraternity brothers. Acts like I have a tiger tattooed on my butt, which, I'm told, is what all the guys who go to Princeton do—even the ones who eventually grow up to become Secretary of State and whatnot.

"Good evening, gents," he says as he straddles the stool next to mine, even though there are about a dozen empty seats up and down the long bar. This is Monday night. The bar scene in Sea Haven doesn't really start cooking until Wednesday or Thursday. Sometimes Tuesday. Tuesday is Ladies' Night. Mondays, however, are nothing. Mondays are for drinking Busch at home.

Ralph swabs at the bar with his damp cloth. "What're you drinking?"

Princeton rubs his palms together like he's warming 'em up. "What's good tonight?"

"Beer."

"Ah-ha. Do you have Stella?"

"Yeah."

"On tap?"

"Yeah."

Stella Artois is this Belgian beer all the college kids go nuts about.

Princeton holds up two fingers. "One Stella. Two fingers of foam if you please."

"Oh, shit," says Ralph. "I forgot. Tap just broke. You want a bottle? That way you can pour as many fucking fingers of foam as you want."

Princeton blinks and smiles, and Ralph stomps off to fetch his beer. "Excellent suggestion." His stool squeaks as he swivels in my direction.

"What a foul-tempered cretin," he confides.

I shrug. Sip my Bud.

"You're with the police, if I remember correctly."

"Yes, sir."

"I'm not driving this evening."

"Then I'm not having a problem."

"Excellent. I'm Teddy Winston."

"Danny Boyle."

"Here's your beer." Ralph delivers Teddy's bottle with a hard thump that sends some of his precious foam sloshing up the top and down the sides.

Teddy whips out a hanky and dabs at the puddle.

"Do you happen to have a coaster?"

Ralph plops a paper one down.

"And a glass?"

Ralph reaches for a mug.

"The classic chalice?" Teddy asks.

"Nope. Just mugs."

Princeton blinks again. "Sorry. I don't mean to be intractable. I'm just something of a perfectionist. I suppose most surgeons are. . . ."

Ralph wipes his way up the bar away from us. He wants nothing more to do with Dr. Teddy Winston.

I, however, need to ask a few questions.

A perfectionist and a surgeon? Welcome to my suspect list.

Most surgeons know how to use a scalpel, and Ceepak says serial killers are usually perfectionists. All of a sudden, I'm wondering whether Teddy Winston, MD, is an Ear, Nose, and Throat specialist.

"You're a surgeon?"

"Indeed I am."

"And you used to come down here, back in the '80s?" I ask.

"That's right. When I was in college and med school. Sea Haven offered a welcome respite. I'd put down the books, pick up my fishing pole. . . ."

"Right. Cool. You ever hang with a girl named Miriam?"

"Miriam?"

"Yeah. She could've been a Jewish girl."

He thinks. Pouts out his lower lip.

"No. Not that I recall. I don't remember any chicks named Miriam. . . ."

Chicks? This guy is totally stuck in the '80s. Maybe the '70s.

"How about a Ruth?" I ask.

"Another Jewish chick?"

"I don't know. I think she was from Pennsylvania. Up near Erie."

Teddy tilts his mug and pours a perfect foamy head. He takes a sip, smacks his lips obnoxiously to show his appreciation for the Belgian brewmeister's skill.

"Ah. There's nothing quite as refreshing as a crisp, hoppy, pilsner, is there?"

"Yeah. So—did you know a Ruth back then?"

"Maybe. There were so many scrumptious young things roaming the beaches back in the day. But tell me, since we're discussing fine female flesh—do you know a young redhead who calls herself Stacey?" He looks wistful. "Enormous breasts. Quite fetching."

"No," I say. "I don't know any Stacey."

Except, of course, the one I picked up hitchhiking. The same one I saw in the parking lot with this doofus last night. Sure I'm lying, but frankly, I don't care if Princeton has a Code.

He sighs. Way too dramatic. "Too bad. Amazing young woman. I need to find her."

"How come?"

"She slipped away before I could jot down her phone number."

"I see."

"She also pilfered about a hundred dollars."

"She robbed you?"

"So it would seem."

"You want to fill out a complaint? Press charges?"

"No. No need. She earned it. Every penny. In fact, I was hoping we might hook up again later this week."

"Is she a prostitute?"

"Heavens, no. The money she took was a gift. An honorarium, if you will."

"Sure," I say, because I want him to keep talking.

"However, that motel, Smuggler's Cove, it's even worse than I remembered. You're lucky you have your own pad."

I think a pad is where you take chicks. I should watch *That '70s Show* more often.

I gesture toward Ralph, who's down at the far end of the bar reading a wrinkled copy of *Salt Water Sportsman*.

"Ralph's even luckier," I say. "He lives on a boat. A houseboat."

"I am envious," says Teddy. "Fortunately, I was able to get out on the ocean this afternoon. Usually, I rent my own vessel. Captain it myself. Today, however, I took a quick charter with my wife."

I cock an eyebrow.

He gets it.

"Now before you condemn me as an adulterous scoundrel, hear me out: my wife takes certain antidepressant medications that serve to suppress her libido, forcing me to seek 'relief,' if you will, elsewhere."

Some people take Rolaids, he takes redheads.

"We're staying at a *bed-and-breakfast*," he says, making it sound like a sewage treatment plant. "Place called Chesterfield's. God, how I hate B&Bs."

"How come?"

"Nothing but middle-aged couples hoping to rekindle some semblance of their fading romances. Housewives desperate to get laid at least once a year so they drag their husbands into tarted-up Victorian houses filled with dishes of potpourri. There, one is encouraged to eat breakfast in a communal dining room with these . . . people. Fat people, mostly. Obese. You should see them scarfing down the homemade cranberry-pineapple muffins. As they ooh and aah over the scones, you are compelled to imagine them naked—aahing and oohing while they do what you know they did the night before."

Now he's grossing me out worse than Miriam's nose. I change the subject.

"So you went fishing?"

"Indeed. I thought a quick fishing expedition might cheer my wife. Revive her sagging spirits. She, however, quickly became seasick. Vomited over the starboard railing. We had to turn about and come back to dock early. The charter captain, by the way, was a very decent fellow. Only charged me for the hour we were out, not the three we booked. Quite gregarious, too. On the way back, he told the most amusing stories."

"Was it Cap'n Pete?"

"Yes. Do you know him?"

"Sure. Everybody knows Cap'n Pete. He's a local institution."

"As he should be. Anyway, if you see this redhead, let me know."
He hands me a business card. "Call my cell."

I tuck the card into my shirt pocket—not because I want to pimp
for Theodore "Teddy" Winston but because I'd like Ceepak to meet
this guy. Call me crazy but I have a hunch he'll want to ask this
scalpel-wielding perfectionist a few more questions about "chicks"
named Ruth and Miriam.

Maybe even Lisa.

TWENTY-FOUR

Tuesday morning starts like Monday: at seven-thirty A.M. in the roll call room.

Only today Sergeant Pender is manning the podium instead of Chief Baines. I think the chief's in his office. Blow-drying his hair.

"Ceepak," says Pender, "you and Boyle can continue your 'special investigation' until oh-nine hundred. After that, we need you guys working crowd control at the Sand Castle site. The heavy machinery starts rolling at ten A.M."

Ceepak isn't happy. "Will do. However, that gives us insufficient time to follow up some very significant leads."

Pender shrugs.

"Sorry. The chief gives me the marching orders; I pass 'em on to you."

Ceepak nods. "Roger that. Understood."

Pender looks down to the podium, checks his notes.

"We almost done here?" says Dom Santucci, yawning and leaning back in his chair. "Me and Malloy are working a special investigation, too."

Sergeant Pender looks confused.

"I don't see anything in the book. . . ."

"That's because it's *super*-secret. The chief doesn't even know about it." Santucci pauses. Looks around the room. Acts like he's about to say something he shouldn't, which is what he does all day.

"You see. . . ."

We wait.

He whispers: "We're trying to locate and apprehend a decent cup of coffee."

Santucci's partner, Malloy, smirks and crosses his thick arms across his washing-machine-size chest. The two of them like to act bored every morning because they think they're better than all the other cops in the room. They also like to roll their short-sleeve shirts up into a cuff so everybody can see just how big and impressive their bulging arm muscles look this early in the day.

Reggie Pender frowns.

"Funny, Dom. Real funny. Maybe you guys will be able to track down that coffee up on the North End. You're working it today."

Malloy moans. "The North End? Jesus, crap. . . ."

"We have seniority," says Santucci. "We've been on the job longer than anybody in this room. Longer than you *or* the chief. We want the beach and boardwalk."

"Sorry. Ceepak and Boyle have that assignment."

"How come?"

"That's what the chief wants."

"We used to have some rules around here, you know? Rules regarding seniority and who works where. . . ."

"Look, Dom—you have a complaint, take it up with the chief. Right now, do your job. Hit the streets. Hit the North End. Go find that damn coffee. Dismissed."

Pender gathers up his notes.

Santucci's seething. His face is so purple he looks like the Fruit of the Loom grape. "We're not done here, Sergeant Pender."

"Yes we are. Like I said—you have a complaint, take it to the chief."

Pender marches out the door.

The second he's gone, Santucci gets in Ceepak's face.

"You bucking for detective?"

"Excuse me?"

"You heard me. I've been hocking the chief for months to bump me up to detective grade. This department needs one. Full-time. We need a good one."

"I have never once discussed job titles with the chief."

"Bullshit."

No. If Ceepak says it, it's true, because Ceepak cannot tell a lie. If he ever chops down a cherry tree, he'll hand you the axe and arrest himself.

Santucci won't let it drop. "So how come the chief gave you that Mickey Mouse microscope upstairs?"

"I have an interest in forensics that Chief Baines finds useful to our ongoing mission to keep Sea Haven safe."

"Bullshit. You want to fight me for the detective job? Fine. Bring it on. I know my shit. Backwards and forwards. So when you and junior here screw up whatever it is you're investigating, don't worry—me and Malloy will bail your ass out." He turns to his partner. "Come on, Mark. Let's go investigate us that cup of coffee."

"Roger that," says Malloy, mocking Ceepak. "Roger-dodger that!"

The two cops march out of the room, hiking up their gun belts so they can swagger even better.

"Danny?"

"Yes, sir?"

"You ready to roll?"

"Roger that," I say with a smile

Ceepak smiles back. "Then it's all good."

Since we don't have much time before we're back on Sand Castle duty, Ceepak picks Reverend Trumble as our most pressing lead. We hop in the Ford Explorer and set out for his headquarters. Ceepak takes the wheel.

"What's eating Santucci?" I ask. "Whataya think crawled up his butt?"

"Can't say for certain," says Ceepak. "Furthermore, I've never been inclined to investigate."

I think he just cracked a joke. He does that sometimes. More since he met Rita.

"I suspect, however, he finds himself in an uncomfortable position. I am, indeed, still somewhat new on the Sea Haven Police Force. Perhaps I have violated some unwritten code and inadvertently disrupted Sergeant Santucci's perceived career path."

I change the subject.

"Hey, how about that doctor I was telling you about? The vacationing surgeon who was coming here all the time in the '80s?"

Ceepak nods.

"He definitely makes our list, Danny."

We pull into a parking slot out front of The Sonny Days Inn. It's eight A.M. Very early morning or—judging from the bleary-eyed looks on the kids standing in the straggly chow line—very, very late at night.

Ceepak tells me the plan. "We spend fifteen minutes questioning Reverend Trumble about Mary Guarneri and the church charm. See if he remembers her. Immediately afterward, we survey the scene." He nods toward the line of hungry young beach bums. "Try to spot the pickpocket. See if she showed up for breakfast again this morning."

"Right."

"Then, time permitting, we can follow up on this Dr. Theodore Winston you encountered last evening."

"Who maybe started practicing his surgical skills before he had his medical license?"

"Let's not jump to any conclusions, Danny."

"Yeah, I know . . . innocent until proven otherwise. But, trust me— he's definitely guilty of being an asshole."

"Let's roll," is all Ceepak says.

We take our place at the end of the breakfast line.

One of the blondes we saw yesterday is automatically inking her rubber stamp as each person approaches. When we reach the head of the line, she's all set to brand a shining sun on our hands to prove we're good to go for grub.

"We're not here to eat," says Ceepak. "We're here to see Reverend Trumble."

"He's busy. In the kitchen."

Exactly how Ceepak wanted him.

"This is important," he says.

"So is breakfast—for the weary and the lost."

"Yes, ma'am. However, this is a pressing police matter."

She looks at us. The morning sun glints off Ceepak's badge. I should probably polish mine more often.

"I see. Catherine?" She calls to a nearby girl whose smile is way too sunny for 8:05 A.M. It looks pasted on. "Please take over here."

"Of course, sister."

Sister? I'm starting to wonder if the Reverend Billy's acolytes are all nuns. Maybe Moonies.

"This is not the best time," says their leader.

"The Sea Haven Police Department appreciates your cooperation."

I love how Ceepak can kick butt and sound polite doing it.

We're with Reverend Trumble in his office. He didn't want to talk to us in the kitchen; too many devoted followers eavesdropping while they juggled their cast iron skillets. Scraping up scrambled eggs instead of loaves and fishes. French toast for the faithful. Saving souls with Entenmann's Danish rings.

"Tell us about the church charms," says Ceepak.

Trumble, though impatient, answers carefully. Whatever he had been expecting, it wasn't this. "For several years, I gave one to every girl who sought solace here. Charm bracelets, however, are no longer fashionable. So I stopped doing it."

"But when you were handing them out . . . ?"

"I gave away dozens. I ordered them from a catalog . . . a jewelry company in Pennsylvania. . . ."

"New Bethlehem Creations?"

"Yes, I believe that's correct."

I take it Ceepak put the sterling silver charm under his microscope last night, identified the company mark stamped into its bottom.

"The tiny church had an open roof," says Trumble. "A beautifully symbolic representation of our Lord's open and loving spirit. Jesus longs to take His wayward children back into His loving embrace."

"Tell me, Reverend," says Ceepak, "do you remember a young girl named Mary Guarneri?"

Trumble shakes his head. "I'm sorry. I do not ever reveal the names of those in my flock."

"You might have known her as Ruth."

"Again, Officer, I must insist on protecting the privacy of those who seek shelter here."

"What about a Miriam?"

Trumble is silent. Then, we get another, "I am sorry."

But Ceepak doesn't give up. "How about Lisa? Lisa DeFranco?"

"I cannot help you."

"Did you *know* Lisa DeFranco?"

Reverend Billy sighs. "If this Lisa DeFranco was here," he says, "she was obviously a short-term resident."

"Do you remember her?"

"No. But I can tell you: this girl did not elect to repent her sins."

"How so?"

"Any young woman who chose to follow our path for any significant length of time would have taken a new name to celebrate her rebirth in Jesus Christ. A biblical name. Anyone named 'Lisa' would not be counted among the saved."

"Why do their names have to be changed?"

"In the sacrament of Baptism, they are asked to choose a new name. One from Holy Scripture to help them remember the day they became a new person, the day they were born again."

"And so a Mary could become Ruth?"

"I have talked with you enough." He looks at us steadily.

Ceepak makes some notes in his spiral notebook.

"What happens to these girls once they leave your ministry?"

Trumble shakes his head sadly. "Hard to say. I suppose most return home to their parents or find gainful employment here in town. Others simply drift away. I only hope I am able to make some lasting impression on their young souls."

I, of course, am thinking about the impressions someone made with a sharp blade on their young faces.

Ceepak closes his notebook, giving up. For now. I can tell he has a grudging admiration for Trumble's desire to put young people on the right path. But I know he'd admire the guy more if the Reverend answered his questions.

"Now, if you gentlemen will excuse me, I still have hungry souls in need of their daily bread."

Ceepak nods. Trumble heads for the door.

I think about these young girls who, years ago, came through the doors of the Sonny Days Inn. How they picked up church charms and biblical names. How maybe some of them suffered fates that hardly resembled "salvation."

You have to wonder. Was the French toast worth it?

TWENTY-FIVE

We follow after Trumble into a room set up with six cafeteria tables and three dozen folding chairs—all currently occupied by hungry young folk scarfing down breakfast off thin paper plates.

The Reverend moves behind a chafing dish to scoop up portions of what looks like scrambled eggs but could be yellow cottage cheese. He has given us all the information he plans on serving up today. Ceepak doesn't push it. Not this morning. But I have a hunch we'll be back.

"What about redheads," Ceepak asks, his eyes scanning the chow line. "I don't see any girls. . . ."

"Me neither."

Suddenly, I spot Stacey. She's standing by the door.

I know I should point her out to Ceepak. But I don't. I'm not exactly sure why. Maybe I don't want him knowing that, on my days off, I spend my time picking up jailbait I find hitchhiking by the side of the road. I know she's a thief, stole my twenty and Dr. Teddy's hundred, but there's really no evidence to suggest that she's the beach bandit, too. Except, of course, the eyewitness description. And the fact that she's here with a rubber-stamped hand.

Okay, I'm embarrassed.

If I finger her, she'll just ID me right back. Tell Ceepak and Reverend Billy's assembled multitudes what kind of skeeve I truly am.

I decide not to say anything.

I'll just have to take full responsibility for any twenties she swipes down the line from upstanding Sea Haven residents and unsuspecting tourists.

It's not what Ceepak would do.

But I am not Ceepak.

I take a second look. She still hasn't seen me. Luckily for me, Stacey has a new hair color. She's spray-dyed it green.

"No redheads," I mutter in Ceepak's general direction.

Technically, I'm off the hook.

"Roger that." He checks his watch. "We better hit the beach. We'll check up on your Dr. Winston lead later."

On his belt, one of the cell phones beeps. He answers it.

"This is Ceepak. Slow down. Take it easy, Pete. Okay. Breathe in. Try to calm down. Tell me what you found."

Now we have another reason to hurry back to Oak Beach, besides our official bulldozer-watching duties.

Apparently, Cap'n Pete returned there first thing this morning, hoping to find more buried treasure. He brought along a friend's metal detector.

"She started humming right away," Pete says. "Lights blinking. Noise in the headphones. Knew I found something. Yes, indeedy. Didn't know it'd be this. No, sir. Not this. . . ."

We're west of the roped-off area where the sand castle sculptors will soon start erecting their colossal creations. I can see their backhoes covered with tarps.

The beach, itself, is practically deserted. Some surfers are happily catching the waves before the lifeguards show up to tell them to knock it off. A few joggers are doing the *Chariots of Fire* thing down where the sand is wet. Two middle-aged romantics in matching sweat-suits stroll up the beach holding hands.

All is as it should be.

Except, of course, for what Cap'n Pete and his borrowed metal detector found buried three feet deep in the sand.

Ceepak crouches next to the hole.

"Did you touch it?"

"No, sir, Johnny. I called you right away. I wouldn't touch it. Still not sure what made this thing start beeping." He motions toward the metal detector lying on its side in the sand. "It's Bill's. Bill Baiocchi's. You know him, Johnny. From the Treasure Hunter club. He let me borrow it. It's a CZ-20."

Ceepak nods.

"The CZ-20 is an all-weather detector," he says. "It's leak-proof to a depth of two hundred and fifty feet, with electronics able to ignore the destabilizing effects of saltwater, making it ideal for working a wet, sandy beach."

"That's just what Bill said. But what made it start beeping?"

Ceepak grimaces.

"Uncertain."

The thing in the hole looks like a salad bowl. An old-fashioned Tupperware container like my mother used to have.

Ceepak carefully pries off the lid.

Now we see what might be a soccer ball wrapped in newspaper. Ceepak reaches into one of his many pockets and draws out his forceps. He uses it to work open the sheet of newsprint, which is still dry, thanks to Mr. Tupper's famous watertight seal. He peels back the paper like you'd work open a head of lettuce.

"The *Sandpaper*," he says, identifying the newspaper as our local weekly. He studies the top edge. "The Friday, August 4, 1979, edition."

He splays open the paper. Unwraps the top of the package.

It's not a soccer ball.

It's a human skull.

TWENTY-SIX

I still don't understand," says Cap'n Pete. "If it's a skull, nothing but bone, what set off the detector?"

Ceepak points to the jawbone. "I suspect that several of these teeth have fillings. Metal fillings."

"This is horrible," says Cap'n Pete.

A human skull wrapped in the Sports section from a twenty-eight-year-old newspaper, then packed into a re-sealable salad bowl and buried three feet deep on the beach? You ask me, that's *worse* than horrible.

Ceepak looks solemn.

We're about thirty feet up from the high tide line, close to the sea grass and rolled-out fencing. Fortunately, we're so far up from the ocean, no kid ever thought about building his castle on this patch of sand.

"Danny? Hold open the bag."

He clamps onto the skull with his forceps, gripping it snugly.

I hold open one of the brown paper grocery sacks we always keep stowed in the back of the Explorer. Ceepak says paper bags are better for evidence storage; they don't sweat like plastic. The bag boys at Acme let me take as many as I want. They even gave me a stack of those double-insulated ice cream bags you don't see too much anymore.

"Danny? Focus."

Ceepak is tonging the cranium like I've seen Homer Simpson do with a rod of radioactive uranium. Only Ceepak is much more careful. When he lowers the skull into my bag, I wince to feel its weight.

Next he uses the forceps to lift out the sheet of newsprint. It's stained. I figure dried blood. Maybe worse.

I hold open another bag to take it from him. I'm sure it's loaded with clues. Maybe DNA.

"What's that?" says Cap'n Pete.

Taking out the newspaper revealed something shiny on the bottom of the Tupperware bowl.

"Plastic baggie. Fold-down top." Ceepak's speech patterns get clipped when things get serious. "Note card inside. Typed message. Folded paper behind note card."

Ceepak sinks back on his haunches. He's thinking.

Cap'n Pete crouches down for a closer look.

"Captain Pete?"

"Yes, Johnny?"

"This area is about to become a very major crime scene." This is what he's thinking about.

"Yes. I imagine it might . . . what with the skull and now what looks like a secret message sealed inside a plastic bag. . . ."

"I anticipate an influx of forensic personnel from the County and State Police. Possibly the FBI."

"Oh, yes. Of course. They'll be interested in this, that's for sure. The FBI."

"We might be better able to perform our tasks if you were to vacate this area and return to your fishing vessel."

"I see. Yes. Of course. You're right. Besides, I have my morning charter. Mustn't keep them waiting. They paid in advance, you know. Cash. Let me grab Bill's metal detector. . . ."

Ceepak holds up his hand.

"Let's leave it here. We might have further use for a CZ-20."

"Oh. Okay. But what'll I tell Bill?"

"That I will bring him his metal detector. Possibly this evening. I'm sure he'll understand. We'll also want to talk to you again."

"Me?"

"We'll need to take a more formal statement."

"Yes. I see. Very good, Johnny. Of course. I'll be back at the dock by noon and I don't think I head out again until two . . . unless of course there's walk-in traffic . . . sometimes I get walk-ins . . . no reservations. . . ."

"We might not get to you today, Pete."

"No. Doesn't have to be. Not today. No, sir. Whatever's good for you, Johnny. I'm flexible. Schedule's wide open. . . ."

"Thank you. We appreciate your assistance and cooperation."

"See you later, Pete," I say.

"Yes. Of course. See you later, Danny."

The guy won't leave. He leans over, takes another peek into the hole.

"Pete?" Ceepak is losing his patience, but not his courtesy. Not yet.

"Right. See you later. When you come to take my statement. We'll talk then. Should I jot down some notes? Just to make certain I remember everything? While it's still fresh. Are notes allowed?"

"Good idea. Write everything down. Do it now. And please—for the time being, do not tell anyone else what you discovered. Not even your wife or sons."

"Of course not. Won't breathe a word. Sorry to have . . . you know . . . ruined your day."

"We'll be fine, Pete."

Pete does a quick sign-of-the-cross. Head, heart, chest, chest. Turns. Walks away.

Ceepak waits until he is absolutely certain Pete has crested the dune and is on his way down to the street.

"Danny? Camera."

I hand him the digital.

Ceepak snaps a half-dozen shots of the plastic bag resting at the bottom of the bowl.

"I am now going to remove the bag from the bowl."

I just nod. Ceepak sounds like he's narrating brain surgery for the first-year students up in the cheap seats of one of those operating rooms they always have on doctor shows.

He pulls out tweezers from another pants pocket.

"Inspecting first item. Typewritten note on 3-by-5 ruled index card."

He holds the note card with his tweezers in one hand, fishes out his magnifying glass.

"Message appears to have been typed on an IBM Selectric. Pica 10 Pitch font."

"What's it say?"

"We start with a name. Centered and underlined: 'Delilah.'"

Delilah. Samson's girlfriend. The hairstylist.

"Another name from the Bible," I say.

"10-4. Beneath the name is recorded a date: 'Tuesday. 8-1-79.'"

The creep marked down the harvest date—just like some people do on freezer bags full of summer corn.

"Under the date there is a typed quote. It too appears biblical in nature: 'Thus will I make thy lewdness to cease.'"

I figure it's the "thus" and "thy" that peg it as coming from Scripture.

He offers no interpretations. Not yet. Not about the mention of lewdness. Not about the date, 1979—which sort of puts the skull back in the disco days with the ears and nose we already found. Ceepak never conjectures right away. First he examines all the evidence. That means tweezering and unfolding the other piece of paper tucked into the baggie because it's only halfway visible behind the index card.

"Map," he says. "Hand-drawn. Permanent black marker on foolscap paper."

It looks like a treasure map drawn on that old-fashioned parchment stuff you always see in souvenir shops with the Declaration of Independence printed on it .

I see there is a big X on the map.

And a dotted line—like footprints.

And, in the corner, one of those orientating compass deals: N, E, S, W.

"Ten paces due north," says Ceepak as he studies the map.

Then he turns to me.

"Danny, I believe we're going to need the field shovel."

TWENTY-SEVEN

We keep an Army-issue field shovel stowed in the back of our cop car with the flares and rolls of POLICE LINE DO NOT CROSS tape.

The sun glints off the tinted glass and I can already tell: this day's going to be a scorcher. Probably hit 90, maybe 95 degrees. And the wind has shifted. It's blowing across the island from the bay to the ocean. West to east. That means the greenhead flies will be blowing this way, too.

The greenheads are vicious little devils, our local locusts, the shore's summertime plague. Their heads aren't really green. They take their name from their big buggy eyes. Huge green peepers popping out of humongous black bodies. These suckers fly slow—maybe because their eyeballs are so huge. They sort of lumber through the air like one of those C-130 military cargo planes that shouldn't even be able to fly. You swat at a greenhead, it'll stare at you, ask if you've got some kind of problem, then loop back to take a snap at your ankles.

Ouch. All this, and greenheads, too.

• • •

Ceepak is waiting for me — standing on a clump of sea grass ten feet north of the first hole.

I hand him the shovel. He looks like he's ready to play some serious Whack-A-Mole. Like he's there to bop anything that dares pop up out of a hole in the sand.

"I radioed the chief," he says.

"And? Is he calling the FBI?"

"Not yet."

"I think we should."

"As do I. However, the chief reminded me that we retain primary jurisdiction in the case for investigative purposes unless and until we determine that these individuals were killed elsewhere and transported across state lines."

Chief Baines never does like the FBI dropping by Sea Haven. They scare away more cash-carrying tourists than all the sharks in *Jaws I, II,* and *III* combined.

"Record my location," says Ceepak, ready to shoulder the grim responsibility of moving forward.

I pull out the digital camera and snap a frame. I check the viewfinder. The shot looks like one of those groundbreaking ceremonies for a new bank.

"Got it."

Ceepak nods.

Digs.

Shovels up several buckets of sand, making a tidy pile to the left of his hole.

"Approximate depth: one foot."

He keeps digging. The sand is soft.

"Two feet."

The pile of powder next to his hole grows taller. Sugary sand slides off the peak, trickles down along the sides.

"Three feet."

I hear steel tap plastic. Ceepak stops. Steps away from the hole. Lays down his shovel and drops to his knees.

"Danny? Will you please bring me a paintbrush?"

"On it."

I slap one into his open palm and say, "Paintbrush."

"Thank you."

I crouch down and watch Ceepak start to dust off what we both know is going to be the lid to another Tupperware bowl. Ceepak whisks away the sand with his brush, an umpire cleaning off home plate for the next batter up.

I see a translucent top with the raised ridge of a lip. The famous, vacuum-sealed lid designed to keep the bowl's contents fresh and crisp. Even if you store your head of lettuce—make that a *human* head—in the hot sand.

Of course, it's another skull.

A small oblong ball, really. Maybe five inches wide, eight inches tall, six inches deep. Wrapped in another newspaper.

"Again, a Friday edition of the *Sandpaper*. July 12, 1980."

There's another baggie in the bottom of the bowl. Inside the baggie, another note card and another little folded map.

"'Miriam,'" Ceepak says, reading the index card. "'Monday. 7-8-80.'"

"Oh, man," I whisper, even though I feel like screaming. "Miriam."

Ceepak just nods.

We have to assume it's the same Miriam whose nose we found with the local souvenirs back at The Treasure Chest.

Ceepak holds up the card and reads what's typed along the bottom: "'Thus will I make thy lewdness to cease.'"

"He's repeating himself."

"They usually do."

Ceepak puts the index card into an evidence bag, and then uses his tweezers to unfold the little map. I study it over his shoulder: it's dotted with dashes of footprints leading to another X. Ten feet due west this time.

"Of course!" says Ceepak. He's having one of his eureka moments. "It was near the pirate chests."

"Pirate chests?" I'm a little behind him, somewhere south of *Eureka!* "What pirate chests?"

"At the souvenir shop. Remember? The jar was on a shelf surrounded by snow globes depicting pirate chests filled with gold doubloons. The killer was being cute. Alluding to his private necropolis filled with treasure chests."

"So you think this Miriam is the same Miriam who, you know. . . ."

"I do."

Usually, he says, "It's a possibility." Not today. Today, he's definite.

"The nose, most likely, was the souvenir the killer kept for himself during the totem stage of his cyclical spree. During or after the murder, the killer performs a ritualistic taking of trophies, often involving mutilation of his dead victim's corpse. He needs a souvenir, something to help him perpetuate the erotic pleasure sparked during the actual killing."

"Jesus."

"It's no wonder he placed his formaldehyde jars in a museum and, later, The Treasure Chest. One building storehouses trophies, the other contains nothing but souvenirs. This man is taunting us."

"Why?"

"He wants us to know he's back in town. Perhaps to complete another killing cycle. A serial killer is very similar to a drug addict, Danny. Sooner or later he will give in to his cravings and return to the one thing in the world that gives him pleasure."

Ceepak pulls a pair of latex gloves out of his hip pocket, snaps them onto his hands. Next, he finds his magnifying lens. Finally, he uses his free hand to hold the skull. He looks like Hamlet crossed with Sherlock Holmes. I make sure no one's watching.

It's amazing. The beach is still empty.

"Can you see it, Danny?"

I lean over his shoulder, try to look through the lens, but all I'm getting is a rubbery, funhouse-mirror close-up of white.

"See what?"

"Between the eye sockets. Where the nasal bone is joined to the frontal bone."

I see an upside-down Valentine-heart-shaped hole between the skull's two eye sockets. Not much else.

"Definitely nicked," says Ceepak. "Slightly notched. There are noticeable groove marks where a blade sawed too close to the bone when severing the cartilage forming the support structure for the nose."

He flips the skull around in his hand and zooms in for a look at the ear canal.

"Here, too. I note chipping near the exterior auditory meatus. A cut line crossing into the adjoining temporal bone."

"He cut off Miriam's ears?"

"Yes, Danny."

"But we didn't find her ears."

"Not yet. Most likely, those were the souvenirs he chose to keep for himself, in his personal museum."

Ceepak slips the skull back into its paper sack.

"I believe we may have just isolated the killer's signature."

Ceepak hikes back across the sand to Hole Number One and the ring of evidence bags circling it—everything we found with "Delilah's" skull.

Ceepak reaches into the bag, pulls out the skull, and examines it with his magnifying glass. First the front, then both sides.

"Again. The nose and both ears were chopped off. The cuts in this instance were much cruder, less skilled. I note a false start with a serrated blade high up on the nasal bone, along an imaginary line running between the girl's pupils."

I don't want to imagine that line. I don't want to imagine some lunatic drawing it in with a stubby carpenter's pencil or snapping a blue chalk line across the girl's face so he could saw off her nose with a serrated steak knife.

"He kills his victims, decapitates them, then cuts off their nose and their ears. This is his signature."

"Why?"

"Unclear."

He puts away Skull Number One and marches over to Hole Number Two.

"We need to call Officer Diego. Have her run down the Bible quote."

"Diego doesn't come in until nine."

"Let's radio the house. Have Dispatch call her at home and instruct her to report for duty ASAP."

"It's only like a half hour until. . . ."

"Danny? Time is of the essence."

"Yes, sir."

"We should also request uniformed backup to help us secure this crime scene and work crowd control. The beach will be filling up soon. We should contact the municipal garage. See if we can procure some privacy screens. You know, the type of tarps the Highway Patrol puts up around serious accident scenes on the Interstate."

"Right."

"I will once again urge the chief to request county, state, and/or federal assistance. He should also contact the Chamber of Commerce. Postponement of the Sand Castle Competition would seem the most prudent course of action."

"Yeah."

"Danny, if you had any plans for this evening, please cancel them."

"Yes, sir."

"We need to move fast. This killer may not wait for Chief Baines to call the FBI before striking again."

And I was worried about the greenheads.

TWENTY-EIGHT

One hour later, we have two more holes, two more plastic containers, two more skulls pulled up from the sand.

Hole Number Three. Rebecca. Tuesday, August 13, 1980.

Hole Number Four: Deborah. Tuesday, July 29, 1981.

Each skull was wrapped in the local newspaper from the following Friday. Each was stored in Tupperware-type bins slightly different from each other and the ones we found earlier, but big enough to handle the job. All four plastic containers held sandwich bags with neatly typed index cards identifying the victim and proclaiming, "Thus will I make thy lewdness to cease."

Each find also contained a map leading us gruesomely onward.

One hour later, we have company. Lots of it. First came the lifeguards. Now the beach is almost full, fed by a steady parade of sun worshippers. They march across the sand and claim their territory, planting the family umbrella. They haul lawn chairs, ice chests, boogie boards, and rolling laundry carts stuffed with towels, paddleball paddles, and brightly-colored sponge toys. They wear bathing suits, sarongs, sun visors, and the occasional unfortunate Speedo. Children squeal and splash at the foamy edge of the shallow water, down where the sand sucks at your toes. Parents lounge in low-slung chairs. Every now and then, the lifeguard up on his platform blows a whistle, calling foul on some hotshot boldly venturing beyond the safety flags staked fifty feet out from his chair. The flags tell you where it's safe to swim.

Today I wonder if any place on this particular beach is safe. There are dangerous, hidden spots nobody can see. Deep black holes where young girls disappear. Young girls nobody was watching out for. The invisible dead. What Ceepak, only yesterday, called the "less dead."

You dig up four skulls in under an hour, you start thinking creepy stuff like that.

Ceepak decides we should stop digging even though we are in possession of Map Number Four, which indicates that if we venture seven paces to the east we will unearth Skull Number Five.

The four female skulls already excavated sit in grocery bags over near Hole Number One. From a distance, it looks like Ceepak, me, and two extremely hungry lumberjacks brought huge sack lunches with us to work today.

About ten feet down from the brown bags, I see the recently erected FIRST ANNUAL SEA HAVEN SAND CASTLE KINGDOM banner snapping in the breeze near the entrance to a rolled-out rectangle of bright orange construction fencing. The banner's got half-moon wind vents cut into it, so it won't roll up on itself. Behind the fence, I see guys climbing aboard backhoes, finishing their coffee and rolls and Little Debbie Honey Buns.

"We need to wait for backup," says Ceepak. "Lock down this primary area of interest. Set up a secure perimeter. We may need to seal off the Sand Castle site as well."

I nod because I know we can't have tourists and backhoes traipsing all over what might be the east wing of Sea Haven's beachfront boneyard.

When I was a kid, my mother used to tell me it was a sin to walk across somebody's grave. Sacrilegious. You don't want to step on their souls, she'd say. Made me wonder how cemetery groundskeepers mowed their lawns if it's against the rules to walk on top of anybody's coffin.

Who knew that the unintentionally irreverent have been playing hacky-sack for years on top of our secret cemetery: Oak Beach.

"So far," Ceepak says, "it seems the killer only struck in the summer."

"Yeah."

He rattles off the facts. "One victim in the summer of 1979. Two in the summer of 1980. . . ."

"And one in 1981."

"So far."

"Yeah. So far."

"He also seems to kill early in the week. Monday. Tuesday."

I nod. "And he always uses the Friday newspaper."

"Indeed. However, the *Sandpaper* is a weekly. I believe it is only published on Fridays."

"Yeah."

"Still, you make a cogent observation, Danny. In all instances, the killer waits three or more days before wrapping up the skull, sealing it inside the plastic storage container."

"Yeah," I say. "The kill date always comes before the paper date. . . ."

"Precisely. The perpetrator also premeditates his next kill—at least where he plans on burying the next skull. Otherwise, he wouldn't be able to put the maps in the bag with the note card. Each kill is a prequel to the next."

I nod again, then restate the most obvious fact we've uncovered thus far: "He also cuts off their ears and noses."

We examined all four skulls. There were cut marks.

Ceepak checks his watch.

"What's keeping Diego?"

He's eager to pinpoint the lewdness quote, hoping it might give us a clue as to the perp's twisted motivation.

Unfortunately, Denise wasn't home when Dispatch called. They finally tagged her on her cell. She was at the 7-Eleven picking up breakfast. Cool Ranch Doritos and a Diet Pepsi would be my guess.

"Hey, Danny Boy!"

I squint. Some guy smoking a cigarette is waving at me from the wooden plank walkway cutting through the dunes.

"Friend of yours?" asks Ceepak.

"I'm not sure," I say, because I don't recognize him. He saunters over toward us, takes one last drag, flicks his butt in the sand.

"Sir?" Ceepak calls out. "Kindly retrieve your refuse."

The guy stops. Seems surprised.

Ceepak points to where the man tossed his cigarette.

"Please deposit your trash in a proper receptacle."

Now the guy shrugs, bends down, searches in the sand. He finds his cigarette butt and picks it up.

"Sorry, man." He coughs, rolls the stubbed-out filter between his finger and thumb. Tucks it in his shorts. He shambles over toward us.

It's Ralph. The angry bartender. I didn't recognize him at first because I've never seen the guy in direct sunlight—just under dim neons in the dark bar. He's also wearing a Phillies baseball cap pulled down tight to shade his bleary eyes.

"Hey, Ralph," I say. "You're up early."

"Yeah." He hacks to clear out his lungs a little. "Excuse me. Think I'm catching a summer cold." He catches sight of our grocery sacks. "What's in the bags?"

I answer because I don't want Ceepak blurting out the truth.

"Stuff."

"Police stuff?"

"Roger that," I say, sounding *way* official.

Ralph sticks a fresh smoke between his lips. But he doesn't light up. Something distracts him.

"Jesus, look at them, would ya," he says, the cigarette bobbing up and down in the corner of his mouth. He motions toward a group of young girls giggling up the beach in their bikinis. I figure it's the first of many such trios that will strut their stuff on this particular stretch of sand today.

"Would you let your daughter dress that way in public?"

He shoots this one to Ceepak.

"I'm not married," says Ceepak. "I have no children."

"Yeah, well me neither, but fucking-a. Look at that. What are they? Fourteen? Fifteen? Why don't they just walk around naked?"

I have often asked myself the same question—but not in the same hypercritical tone Ralph's using. With me, it's more of a dream-come-true type thing.

"What're you doing out of bed so early?" I ask Ralph, hoping to nudge him off his rant.

"It's Tuesday morning."

"Unh-hunh." I have no idea what he means.

"My last morning to wake up undisgusted. Tonight's Ladies' Night. Means the so-called ladies will be packed in cheek to jowl, all boozed up on half-price drinks, throwing themselves at anything in pants. They ought to call it Whores' Night." He makes the word sound like the beer: "Hoors."

I wonder once again why Ralph works a job he hates so much. Why he's so annoyed with the mating dance that plays out nightly on the other side of his beer-stained bar or why he's stuck with it for close to thirty years.

Ralph shakes his head as another group of tanned babes appears on the beach, their little navel rings flashing in the sun.

"Shit, remember when there wasn't even a beach here?"

"When was that?" asks Ceepak.

"In the early '80s. It was deserted over this way. Then they put in the fucking jetties. Stopped the erosion. Built the beach back up. That's when the sluts returned, too."

"Were you here then, sir?"

"Fucking-a. Stuck behind that goddamn bar. Every goddamn summer since 1977. Maybe I shoulda gone back to college. . . ."

I hear sirens approaching. Our backup has finally arrived.

"What's going down?" Ralph asks, using the lingo he's heard on too many cop shows.

"Sand Castle Competition," I say. "We're bringing in extra security. For the backhoes."

"Fucking sand castles. Whose fucking idea was that? Means we'll be super fucking crowded tonight." He mutters while he works his way through five paper matches that sputter out before he can light up. "Fucking wind." He slaps at the greenhead nipping at his neck. "Shit. Fucking flies. Catch you later, Danny Boy."

"Yeah. Later, Ralph."

Finally, he walks away. Up and over the dune, down to where the wind won't blow out the last of his paper matches.

"Bitter man," says Ceepak when Ralph is gone.

"Yeah."

Ceepak pulls out his notebook and jots something down.

I believe the belligerent bartender just made Ceepak's suspect list.

TWENTY-NINE

We need to put up some screens. I want this whole area sealed off."

The first unit responding to our backup request?

Santucci and Malloy.

Santucci is all of a sudden acting like he's in charge because he has extra stripes on his sleeve. Ceepak, you have to understand, never bothered to take the sergeant's exam last winter. Santucci took it five years ago. Passed it two years later.

"Where's Tray?" Santucci snaps.

"Tray?" Malloy screams at this young kid in navy blue shorts and a baseball cap.

"Here, sir."

Tray is Keith Barent Johnson III, the son of a local hotel owner. It's a nickname, something to with his being KBJ Number Three. Either that or he used to work in a cafeteria. Anyhow, Tray is a summer cop like I used to be. Only I worked with Ceepak. He's been dealt Santucci and Malloy.

"Tray," Santucci says, sounding a lot like one of those mean drill sergeants in military movies, "I want you working with the guys from the municipal garage."

"You got that, son?" echoes Malloy.

"Yes, sir," says Tray. He salutes, too. Either that or he can't see because the sun is in his eyes and he's using his hand as a makeshift visor.

I see Ceepak checking his watch. Again. Still no word from Diego.

Santucci points toward the competition site. "I want crash curtains everywhere. Establish the perimeter, then seal it off. Understood?"

Malloy leans in, shouts in the kid's ear. "Do you understand?"

"Yes, sir." Tray looks confused. "I mean, no. What are crash curtains, sir?'

"Jesus," growls Santucci. "Just how stupid are you?"

"Answer the sergeant's question," adds Malloy. "How stupid are you, son?"

Now Tray looks like he might cry, which is never a good choice when you're on the job. Trust me. Nobody wants to see their law enforcement personnel being *that* sensitive. Kind of ruins the whole cop image if you're dressed in blue but boo-hooing like most guys only weep when they watch *Brian's Song*, or maybe *Dead Poets Society* (even though they'd never admit it).

Ceepak steps forward, tries to get between the kid and his two tormentors.

"Crash curtains are seven-foot-tall green tarpaulins that the State Police use to shield accident scenes from motorists in an attempt to reduce rubbernecking delays."

Tray straightens up. "I see. Thank you, Mr. Ceepak. I didn't know."

"Take it easy son," says Ceepak. "It's all good."

Santucci turns to face Ceepak.

"All good? All *good*? No, it is not. It isn't *good* at all. You're interfering here, Ceepak. Subverting the chain of command. Auxiliary Officer Johnson reports to me, not you. Is that clear?" Santucci's wearing his mirrored sunglasses, looking like Smoky or the Bandit— I forget which one of those two dorks wore the silver shades. "Do we understand each other?"

Ceepak grins. "Completely, Sergeant."

Santucci works his gum. Snaps an air pocket between his molars. He leans in close so Ceepak can smell his fresh, minty breath.

"You know, this used to be a quiet little town until you showed up."

"Excuse me?"

Santucci points at the holes in the sand.

"This skull crap. We didn't have problems like this until you joined the force."

"Actually," says Ceepak, "according to the evidence recovered thus far, these particular incidents took place in the early 1980s. I was in junior high school at the time. In Ohio."

"Yeah? Well this is Jersey, okay? You got a problem with that?"

I have no idea what Santucci's talking about. Maybe he's trying to invent his own Code. Either that or he's working on a new state slogan, something to put on the license plates, since nobody ever bought that whole "Garden State" deal.

Santucci's partner, Malloy, is staring at the four holes Ceepak and I dug in the sand. He moves his head. Back and forth, back and forth. Real slow. It's hard for Malloy to shake his head because his neck muscles are so thick his noggin is basically a golf ball teed up on a stump.

"Look at all these holes," he says. "It looks like that Disney movie. You know—the one with all the holes in it. What was that one called?"

"*Holes*?" I say.

Santucci turns. I see my smiling face reflected back in his mirrored glasses. Yeah. He's right. I definitely look like a smart ass.

The radio on Santucci's utility belt squawks. He whips down the hand mike clipped to the top of his left shoulder.

"This is Sergeant Santucci. Go."

"Dom. Chief Baines. What's your 10-38?"

"We are on-site, sir. Oak Beach. Situation is well in hand."

"Is Ceepak there?"

"10-4."

"Good. I want you and Malloy to take over Sand Castle security. Ceepak should continue to gather evidence but should do so without drawing unwanted attention to his activities. Copy?"

Ceepak nods. This means two things. The chief's still not calling the FBI or the State Police, and Ceepak and I are still in charge of excavating the treasure chests—but we have to do it in a way that doesn't let anybody on the beach know what we're digging up.

"10-4, Chief," says Santucci. "I'll give Ceepak his marching orders."

"I think I just did," the chief snaps back. "I also gave you yours."

We don't do any more digging.

As soon as Santucci, Malloy and Tray traipsed down to the contest site and started setting up stanchions for their crash curtains, Denise Diego radioed us with the results of her search.

"I found it," she says. "The book of Ezekiel. Chapter twenty-three."

"Read it back," says Ceepak.

"It's kind of a weird passage."

"Hold on."

We move away from the crowds. Walk further up the sloping sand, up to the sea grass and fencing again. Ceepak depresses the button on his handy-talkie. "Go ahead, Officer Diego."

"Okay, I'll cut to the chase. These are verses twenty-five to twenty-seven. . . ."

We hear her clear her throat. Take a deep breath. She starts reading from the Bible: "'And I will set my jealousy against thee, and they shall deal furiously with thee: they shall take away thy nose and thine ears; and thy remnant shall fall by the sword. They shall take thy sons and thy daughters; and thy residue shall be devoured by the fire. They shall also strip thee out of thy clothes, and take away thy fair jewels. Thus will I make thy lewdness to cease.'"

They shall take away thy nose and thine ears.

Nothing too bizarre here.

Just some freaky psycho going around town doing exactly what God and Ezekiel told him to do.

THIRTY

Sea Haven's Department of Municipal Maintenance must have a ton of tarps.

Santucci and his team have completely fenced in about ten thousand square feet. The whole First Annual Sand Castle Competition area, plus the plot where Ceepak and I found the skulls. Everybody on the beach—and there's thousands of them now—thinks the giant green screens are part of some mysterious big unveiling to take place Thursday afternoon when the sand sculpture exhibition is officially opened to the public. The current buzz is that the drapes will be majestically pulled down during a big ribbon cutting ceremony.

Chief Baines looks pleased.

He's on-site inspecting the situation: hands on hips, chest swelling with salty sea air. The chief doesn't wear a uniform anymore. These days he prefers a natty tailored suit. I think he buys them in bulk from the Men's Wearhouse. His gold badge shines on his hip, clipped over his belt. I think he might also have strapped on one of those ankle holsters. Either that or he's retaining water something fierce. His right ankle looks humongous, like it's wrapped with an Ace bandage over a sheet of bubble wrap.

The chief and Santucci stare at the billowing sheets.

"Excellent job, Dom."

"Thank you, sir."

"Terrific response to the situation. Well done. I've talked to the mayor. The C of C. They're all on board. Think the tarps will help build suspense for the grand opening. Good job, guys."

"We're not postponing the event?" Ceepak asks.

The chief gives him a tight, bright smile. "No way."

"But. . . ."

The chief walks away. Down to the beach to personally greet some of our "guests." The paying visitors he doesn't want to scare off the island.

Santucci stations himself in front of the entrance to the Sand Castle Kingdom. If any civilian sunbathers attempt to sneak a peak at what's going on behind the curtains, he'll most likely bayonet them away.

Just kidding. But old Dom is standing tough. Looking fierce. Probably always wanted to be a bouncer when he grew up.

The chief prowls the sand like a politician, moving among the sun umbrellas, stopping to greet families spread out on cheerful towels, surrounded by their brightly colored beach gear. He pumps hands and laughs and encourages everyone to *"Have a Sunny, Funderful day."*

That's the official slogan in Sea Haven, even though it officially sucks.

Ceepak and I pull open a flap in the tarp surrounding our pock-marked section of sand. The fabric is hot and has that oily scent of a tent pitched in the sun too long. It's time to go back to work.

Time to continue our treasure hunt.

Ceepak goes to Hole Number Four. He takes a miniature compass out of his cargo pants and holds it flat in the palm of his hand.

"Due east," he says, and strides across the sand, heading toward the ocean. Only I can't see the sea—just the tarp wall separating our designated quadrant from the Sand Castle construction site. To my left, I see dancing shadows of kids flinging Frisbees. To my right, more shadows. A volleyball game. Ceepak and I are alone inside our walled-off little world. Alone except for whatever we find buried in Hole Number Five.

Ceepak walks seven steps, kneels on the sand.

"Danny?"

I start digging.

"Slow and steady," says Ceepak.

"Right."

I slow down. Shovel the sand into a little mound off to the left of the hole. When I get three feet down, there's sweat stinging my eyes and I hear the all-too-familiar sound of metal tapping plastic.

Ceepak motions for me to stop.

"Photograph."

"Right."

I take out the camera. Snap a shot.

"I'll continue the dig," says Ceepak. "You record the evidence as we uncover it."

"Right."

He digs. I do the pictures. In about two minutes, we've unearthed yet another plastic bin. This one is more squarish. The sides are milky white. The top, black.

"Removing container from hole," Ceepak narrates.

The plastic box is heavy. He sets it down near the hole's rim. I see him squint.

He doesn't want to open the lid just yet because he already knows what's inside.

So do I.

Ceepak takes a breath, finds an edge, and pries it open.

"Jesus," I moan.

It's more of the same. Another skull, the flesh long gone, rotted away.

I have a feeling we're going to need more grocery sacks before this day is done. I wouldn't mind one of those airsickness bags, either.

• • •

"John, it's a cold case. Heck, it's so cold, it's frigid."

Chief Baines has joined us inside our tarp fortress behind the green privacy screens.

We have most of the evidence from Hole Number Five lined up in a neat row in front of the sand crater. The skull. The newspaper wrapping. The baggie with the index card and treasure map. And something new: a twist the killer must've added when he got bored of doing the same-old, same-old on the first four holes.

Ceepak's holding the new stuff. Two snapshots we found taped to the bottom of the plastic box. Polaroids. Before and After pictures.

We haven't shown these to the chief yet.

"We should drop this thing for now," he says. "You guys can pick it up again later. I'm thinking after Labor Day, when the tourist season is over."

"That will be too late, sir," says Ceepak.

"Too late? Come on, John. We're talking about crimes allegedly committed back in the 1980s. When was this one. . . ." He searches for a good way to say it. "You know—decapitated?"

Ceepak doesn't need to look at the index card. He has it memorized.

"August 25. 1981. A Monday."

"Okay. Good. That's what? Over twenty-five years ago? Nobody ever reported this girl missing, did they?"

"We don't know that. We should check with the CJIS."

"Hmm?"

"The FBI's Criminal Justice Information Service."

The chief just grunts.

"Her name is Esther," says Ceepak. "She had auburn hair."

Baines eyes the white skull baking in the sun. "You found a strand of hair?" he asks. "Where? In the bin? The baggie?"

"She had bangs that parted in the center and brushed across her eyebrows. Came to the beach in a polka-dot bikini."

"Really?"

"Yes, sir."

"You got all that from this?" He points at the naked skull and empty plastic container

"No, sir."

It's time to show the chief the first Polaroid.

The Before shot.

"That her?"

"Yes, sir."

"Okay. I see. Attractive girl. That's how you knew about the hairdo and bikini."

"Yes, sir. This is her as well." Ceepak flips the Chief the second shot. The After.

"Aw, Jesus, Ceepak."

I hope the Chief doesn't puke. His shirt with the cuff links looks pretty expensive. Be a shame to stain it with regurgitated orange juice and waffles or whatever he had for breakfast.

The After shot shows Esther with her head halfway sawed off. It's heavy, so it droops to one side. You can see fleshy tubes worming their way through her neck meat. You can also see the buckets of blood that gushed out of her carotid artery and poured down her chest, making her bikini top lose its pink polka dots and go jet black. You can see the cardboard sign the killer hung around the sawed-off stub of guts that used to be a pretty girl's neck: WHORE.

At least she still has her ears and nose. The killer must've chopped those off later. Ceepak found more cut marks on either side of her skull and up near the nasal bone. He said the cuts were more precise than those detected on the first four skulls. Less nicking and chipping of bone matter.

The chief burps. Puts a fist to his sternum. Burps again. Now he smoothes out his shirt.

"Very dramatic, John. Nice. You almost made me hurl."

"Not my intention, sir."

The chief puts his hands on his hips.

"No? Okay, tell me—what exactly is it you want?"

"To call in the Federal Bureau of Investigation."

Baines shakes his head. "No. I will not jeopardize every business on this island in a misguided quest to solve an ancient mystery."

"At least let us keep following this trail until we find its end."

Ceepak now shows the chief the two maps we found in Hole Number Five's baggie.

"*Two* maps?" the chief says.

"Roger that. One is a Resort Map. The streets and main tourist attractions in Sea Haven circa 1981."

"That's when The Sand Bar was still called Poppa John Dory's," I say, pointing to the intersection where it's situated today. A cartoon of a green fish holding a mug of beer and smoking an ash-tipped cigar indicates the old nightclub in the same location. When Ceepak and I work a case, I'm typically the one in charge of Sea Haven Watering Hole History.

"For whatever reason, for his next kill, our perpetrator was already planning on relocating his burial ground." Ceepak taps a red-circled area on the Resort Map, down near the southern tip of the island.

"There's nothing but houses down there," Baines says. "Expensive homes. Private beaches."

"Not back then," I say. "That's all new development. Beach Crest Heights didn't go in until 1990-something."

Beach Crest Heights is the gold coast of our barrier island. The streets are paved with moola and named after the ones in Beverly Hills. We have our own Rodeo Drive.

The chief frowns. "So you want to go down to Beach Crest and dig up backyards? You want to rip out the gardens of this town's richest citizens?"

"Just this one," says Ceepak. He shows the chief the second map. It's hand-drawn, with a spot marked by an X. If I have my bearings correct, the X would be on the beach just off a street now named Palm Drive.

Our fearless leader sighs.

"Okay, Ceepak. Tell me why this can't wait until sometime in October?"

"The ears and nose."

"Excuse me?"

"The jars we found, sir. The killer is putting his trophies on display to taunt us. To let us know he's restless and ready to strike again. Are you familiar with the BTK serial killer in Kansas City?"

"Of course."

Even I know this one. They called him BTK because he used to Bind, Torture, then Kill his victims. He teased the police. Sent them letters. His crimes, mostly committed in the 1970s, remained unsolved for nearly three decades.

"BTK kept silent for twenty-five years, sir," Ceepak says. "The police assumed he had died or disappeared. Maybe he had just burned out. Then something snapped. He sent the police a new piece of evidence. He couldn't resist the urge to reclaim the limelight. I believe we are currently facing a similar situation with Ezekiel."

The chief looks confused. "Ezekiel?"

"It is the handle I have given the Sea Haven Serial Killer," Ceepak explains.

"On account of the Bible quote," I chip in. "It comes from Ezekiel."

The chief stares at me. Probably wonders when I all of a sudden became a Scripture scholar.

"I believe," says Ceepak, "that, by placing his cherished souvenirs where we were absolutely certain to find them, our killer is sending us a signal. I fear Ezekiel is poised to strike again."

The chief stares at the two maps. I can see he's working his jaw, trying to find some moisture for his mouth.

"In fact," Ceepak continues, "it is quite common for serial killers to go through a period of depression and dormancy then. . . ."

There's a rustle of fabric. The tarp separating us from the Sand Castle site flaps open. It's Santucci.

"Chief?" he says, his voice sounding shaky. "One of the bulldozers over here, one of 'em just dug something up. . . ."

"What is it, sergeant?" the chief snaps.

Santucci sort of points at Ceepak.

"Another of Ceepak's goddamn skulls."

THIRTY-ONE

Mary Guarneri.

The girl who once wore a charm bracelet with a tiny church dangling off it. The girl who went to the World's Fair in New Orleans with her mother. The girl who ran away from Erie, Pennsylvania, then changed her name to Ruth when the Reverend Billy Trumble dunked her in the ocean and washed away all her sins.

That's whose head it looks like the backhoe just dug up.

"Her name was Ruth," Santucci says. "Says so right here on the Polaroid. See? He wrote the name. 'Ruth.'"

"It's Mary Guarneri," Ceepak says softly.

"Sorry, Sherlock. You're wrong."

Santucci waggles one of the photographs he and Malloy found in the bottom of another plastic salad bowl. I can see the picture over Ceepak's shoulder.

It's the After shot.

I recognize Mary's face from the side of that milk carton Cap'n Pete dug up. Only in the Polaroid there's no smile and her whole head is tilted to one side, like it toppled off the neck. The head is barely attached to the rest of the girl's body by a few stringy tendons. Her eyes are wide and wild with terror. The neck looks like a bloody stump someone tore through with a chain saw.

The chief is burping again. Trying to force down whatever it is that wants to sneak up.

Ceepak looks away from the Polaroid.

"Her name is Mary Guarneri."

"Jesus, Ceepak," Santucci scoffs. "What? You can't fucking read? Her name is *Ruth!*"

The chief finds his voice. "Stand down, Santucci. Ceepak? Do you know something about this girl? Why the hell do you keep calling her Mary?"

"Mary Guarneri changed her name to Ruth when she was baptized by the Reverend Billy Trumble."

Santucci whips off his shades. "Says who?"

"Is this the girl who had the church charm on her bracelet?" the chief asks. "The girl from the milk carton?"

"Roger that."

"I see. Okay. You should've said so. Okay. We're making connections. Filling in the missing pieces. When was she murdered?"

"Well, sir," says Santucci, hiking up his belt, "my best guesstimate is sometime on or about July 3, 1985." He points to the newspaper he found the skull bone wrapped up in. "Lots of Fourth of July ads and whatnot in the newspaper there. So, we figure, she had to be, you know, dead before the Fourth."

Malloy muscles in with his two cents. "Also, sir—we picked up a pretty solid clue right here." He holds up the other Polaroid. The Before.

Ceepak cringes. Not because the picture is gruesome. It isn't. It just shows a young girl in a lacy black bustier with a big crucifix dangling down between her breasts—the kind of stuff Madonna used to wear back in the '80s when she was still singing on MTV about being a virgin.

No, Ceepak's cringing, I think, because our esteemed colleague is holding the evidence with his greasy, just-ate-a-melty-Snickers-bar fingers. No gloves. No evidence bag. Just his chocolate-covered thumb and forefinger.

"See there, Chief?" Malloy says. "The killer wrote a date on the Polaroid! July 3, 1985."

Ceepak shakes his head.

"You got some problem with our detective work here, Officer Ceepak?" Santucci snarls.

"Yes, Sergeant Santucci. You've taken us out of sequence."

"Come again?" says the chief.

"Danny and I were proceeding in an orderly, chronological fashion. The bowl containing the skull labeled DELILAH was, apparently, the killer's first. It was dated 1979. The map uncovered in that hole led us to another skull, dated 1980."

Santucci sniggers. "Wait a second, Ceepak. How do you know there ain't a 1978 head buried someplace else? Hunh? How can you be certain this Delilah was the first?"

"We can't," Ceepak admits.

"See? Jesus. I don't know why everybody says you're such hot shit."

"All right, Santucci," the chief says. "Enough. We're all on the same team here."

"Yes, sir. But Malloy and I want to follow up this lead."

Santucci waves what looks like another Resort Map in our collective face. Malloy pulls a second map out of his back pocket. It's the hand-drawn sketch, the one with the X marking the spot, and it's also smeared with chocolate from whatever he had for his mid-morning power snack.

"According to these maps," says Santucci, "we'll find something buried up north near the lighthouse. Request permission to go dig it up, sir. Tray can handle things here."

The chief looks confused. "Who the hell is Tray?"

"Summer cop. Tray can maintain security. Keep the looky-lous away from the skull holes. Maybe Officer Boyle can assist. He was pretty good helping old ladies cross the street last summer—before he hooked up with Ceepak." Santucci shoots me a look that says I should still be working crossguard duty.

"I need Officer Boyle," says Ceepak. "He knows the beaches on the South End."

The chief shakes his head. "North End. South End. This guy is sending half the department off on a scavenger hunt. . . ."

"One team will wind up back here," says Ceepak. "Most likely Danny and I. We are following clues that predate the 1985 slaying of Mary a.k.a. Ruth. Of more importance, however, will be any evidence pertaining to killings which took place post-1985. . . ."

Santucci jumps in. "Those are ours!"

Ceepak shakes his head. I know what he's thinking: we're trying to track down a serial killer. Santucci wants to play "first dibs."

The chief plucks at his mustache. That's what he does whenever he's stressed.

"Ceepak?"

"Sir?"

"You and Boyle head south."

Ceepak was in the military for fourteen years. He knows how to follow orders.

"Yes, sir."

"Sergeant Santucci?"

"Sir?" He says it louder than Ceepak did. Wants to look like an even better soldier.

"You and Malloy head north. Have your auxiliary officer maintain security here. Did you show the backhoe people what you found?"

Santucci blinks. Tries to think. Come up with the right answer.

"They, uh, unearthed it, so to speak. So, naturally, they were somewhat curious as to its contents."

"So you showed them?"

"I wouldn't say we 'showed' them, sir."

Malloy tries to help out. "It was more like they watched us, you know, pull the skull out of the bowl and all."

The chief presses his clenched fist against his gassy gut again.

"Okay. I'll call in more personnel. Cancel vacations. We can't have rumors running up and down the beach. We need to lock this down. Fast. Swear everybody inside the tent to secrecy. If they don't cooperate, we'll react accordingly. Jesus. Today's what?"

Santucci answers fast because he wants more brownie points. "July 17, sir."

The chief shakes his head some more.

"Well, at least we had half a summer of peace and quiet."

THIRTY-TWO

We spent the next two hours racing up and down the island like we're one of the treasure-hunting tribes on *Survivor*, hoping we don't get voted off.

Down south, we found our sixth skull. We did it without attracting any attention. The rich people whose beach we dug up weren't home. It's only Tuesday, so I figure they're up in the city working to pay the mortgage on their mansion.

The skull was labeled ZEBUDAH. Probably not the name her parents gave her. Her decomposed head came complete with the whole kit. The Bible quote, the date, the Before and After headshots, the maps to guide us to the next location.

And so we took off for Cherry Street, back up toward the center of the island. Our next X marked a spot near the public pier, close to The Rusty Scupper, where Aubrey Hamilton—the girl I might date sometime this century, when work slows down—waitresses.

When we arrived on scene and marked off the paces indicated, we realized something: this seventh chest was buried underneath the dock.

Fortunately, it was near a piling sunk into the dirt on shore, not permanently underwater. I didn't bring a change of clothes to work today. We dug up a big, mucky plastic box, some kind of watertight storage tub like they sell at Home Depot to stow tools in. It had a rubber gasket around its lip to seal the latched lid and keep the contents dry.

All the evidence inside, another complete set, had survived high tides for over two decades.

"Hey, Ceepak. What you guys doin' down there?"

Ceepak closes the box. We crabwalk out from under the dock.

It's Gus Davis. This is the pier where our retired desk sergeant parks his boat.

"Retrieving evidence."

Ceepak and I climb up to the dock.

"What kind of freaking evidence you find down there? Barnacles?"

Ceepak flashes a smile.

"How are you, Gus?"

"Can't complain. You still looking for that runaway from back in 1980-whatever?"

"Not really," says Ceepak. He doesn't add, *"We already found her. Part of her, that is."* He just stands there, waits for Gus to say something.

Gus tugs on the brim of his fishing cap. "Good," he says. "You know why?"

"No. Why?"

"You ain't gonna find her down there!" Gus wheezes a laugh.

I notice he's carrying a tackle box. I also notice that the tackle box looks a lot like the plastic container we just pulled out of the dirt underneath the dock. The one big difference? Ours is black, his is yellow.

I glance at Ceepak. He nods. He sees it too.

"That your tackle box?" Ceepak asks.

"Yep. Kind of dinged up, hunh?"

"I'm sure it's seen a great deal of use."

"Ain't that the truth? Used to keep it in my trunk, in case I ever caught a minute or two to hit the pier after my shift. Now, all I got is time, you know what I'm saying?"

"You earned it, Gus," says Ceepak.

Gus adjusts his hat again. He gazes out at all the boats lined up along the pier. It's a little after two and the sun is starting its slow slink toward the west.

"You know," he says, "you have too much free time, you maybe think too much, too."

"I suppose so."

"That's what I've been doing. Thinking. Ruminating, so to speak. Ever since you two mamelukes came by my boat and started giving me the third degree. . . ."

"What's on your mind?" Ceepak steps sort of sideways so he's blocking the slanting sun and Gus's view of our muddy box.

"That girl you were hassling me about. The runaway. What was her name again?"

"Mary Guarneri."

"Yeah. I've been thinking that if this Mary Guarneri got herself in trouble or whatever, maybe it was her own fault."

"How so?"

"You've been here, what? A year?"

Ceepak nods.

"You meet any of these girls? These runaways?"

"A few."

"Then you know what I know. They're tramps. Whores. There. I said it. These girls come down here looking for a good time. You gotta figure one or two of 'em are gonna wind up partying with the wrong type of individual."

Ceepak's eyes narrow.

Gus doesn't notice. "So all I'm saying is—don't come around here blaming me. This girl got in trouble? Chances are, trouble is exactly what she came looking for in the first place."

Ceepak stays silent.

"Nice bumping into you guys," says Gus. "See you 'round. I got fish to catch."

He shuffles up the dock, raises his fishing rod hand to signal goodbye.

"Do you think?" I whisper.

"It's a possibility," says Ceepak. "Hopefully remote."

"Yeah."

"Let's take this box back to the car. Catalog the evidence."

"Yeah."

We don't want to scare the people on the dining deck outside The Rusty Scupper. The food the Scupper serves is already scary enough.

Secure behind the tinted windows of our patrol car, we re-open the box.

It's Lisa DeFranco. Killed in the summer of 1983. When I look at her Before Polaroid, I can see the LISA earring sparkling in her left ear lobe.

"It's the end of our line," says Ceepak. He's been studying the map. "It leads us back to Oak Beach and the spot where the backhoe unearthed Mary Guarneri."

"So now where do we go?"

"The Sonny Days Inn. We need to talk to Reverend Trumble again. ASAP."

The Ezekiel quote. The biblical names. The Polaroids of girls with a placard draped around their necks proclaiming their sin of whoredom. The kindly preacher man they might have confessed their sins to *has to be* a prime suspect.

"What about the surgeon? The jerk from Princeton. He used to come here back in the 1980s."

"He's on the list, too. As is your bartender friend. I believe he was in town during the 1980s as well."

"Yeah."

In my mind, I see Ralph slicing and dicing lime wedges like the guy in the Ginzu commercials. He does it with a couple quick flicks of his wrist.

"Let's roll," I say, juiced to be doing something besides digging up buried skulls all over the island. As soon as I slap the transmission into drive, the radio crackles with static.

"Ceepak? Come in. Over."

It's the chief.

Ceepak reaches for the radio mike mounted on the dash.

"This is Ceepak. Over."

"We need you on the North End. Now. Meet me at the pier behind the former location of The Palace Hotel. Copy?"

"10-4." Ceepak gestures for me to make the appropriate course correction. I hang a U-turn in the middle of Bayside Boulevard. Burn a little rubber.

Ceepak grabs an overhead grip and steadies himself so he can continue his chat with the chief.

"What's the situation, sir?"

"Santucci and Malloy worked the North End. Dug up six more boxes. Followed the trail. Found the final hole."

"Come again?"

"We found the final hole. It was empty. Except for a photograph tucked inside a plastic sheet protector."

"A photograph?"

"Yeah. The Before shot. You were right, Ceepak. This guy's getting ready to kill again. He's already picked out his next victim."

"Do you recognize her?"

"No. Doesn't look to be a local."

Ceepak waits a beat, stares out the front window. Then he brings the microphone back up to his mouth.

"Is the photograph dated, sir?"

"Yeah."

"And?"

"It's today."

THIRTY-THREE

We're speeding up Ocean Avenue, flashers topside twirling.

I'm not using the siren. Don't really need to. Folks see all those police lights in their rearview mirror, they usually move out of my way.

One of Ceepak's cell phones blurts out an odd ring tone. A synthesized samba. Ceepak pulls the phone from its plastic holster, checks the caller ID, flips it open.

"Hello?"

Must be his personal line. He never says "Hello" when fielding official calls. He says "Ceepak" or "Go." Brusque walkie-talkie stuff like that.

"We're just running around the island," he says. "Looks like it could be another long night."

He's right. If the killer really wants to slay his next victim today, he's only got ten hours left to do it. Coincidentally, we've only got ten hours left to stop him. Even if the chief decides it's finally okay to call in the FBI, no way will they get here in time to do us much good.

"I'd appreciate it," says Ceepak. "So would he. Thank you."

I figure it's Rita.

"You know where I keep his dry food? Right. That's under the sink, too."

Yeah. It's Rita. She'll be taking care of Barkley again tonight. Ceepak and I will, most likely, be busy—trying to save some young girl's life. Trying to stop Ezekiel from playing another round of Mrs. Potato Head.

"Enjoy your night off." His expression softens. "Me, too," he whispers into the phone.

I figure Rita just told the big lug that she loves him, but he's way too macho to let me hear him say it back so he goes with the ol' "me, too."

"Thanks again," he says. "Right. Don't worry."

Telling her not to worry isn't exactly a lie; more like wishful thinking.

Ceepak presses a button to power down his phone. He's officially switching off his personal life until we collar Ezekiel and stop him from causing another young girl's lewdness to cease.

There's nothing left of the old Palace Hotel on the north end of the island but a flat field of charred bricks. It burned down last summer. I know because I was here when it caught fire. So was Ceepak.

Beyond the rubble and burnt brick, I see the chief's black Expedition and Santucci's cruiser. They're both parked near the dilapidated old pier that used to be the hotel's private marina.

I drive over that way, parking our cruiser alongside Santucci's.

Ceepak and I climb out.

The chief is standing next to a three-foot-deep hole in the sand, hands on hips, head swinging back and forth like he can't believe how beyond-bad this situation has become.

"John," he says to Ceepak, "fill me in."

"Sir?"

"We need to know everything you know. We need to know it now."

Santucci and Malloy flank the chief. The three of them look like all of this is Ceepak's fault.

Ceepak tilts his head toward the sand hole. "Might I see the evidence you uncovered?"

"Later," says the chief.

"Time is of the essence."

"Tell me something I don't know!"

Santucci smiles smugly—a quick change from the scowl on his puss when he greeted us.

"I need all available units working the case," the chief continues. "I can't afford any Lone Rangers on this one, John. We all need to know everything you know. Immediately."

Ceepak keeps his cool.

"Might I suggest, once again, that we contact the FBI?" he says. "We should have the NCAVC enter it into the Profiler computer."

"There's no time to call in NCAVC!"

Santucci looks confused. So does Malloy. They stand on either side of the chief, squinching up their faces.

Ceepak helps them out. "National Center for the Analysis of Violent Crime. The FBI Profiler computer could help us ID the perp."

Santucci snorts. "Yeah? Well, you heard the chief. We don't have time for all that FBI crap. Not on this one, Ceepak."

"We have a deadline, John," the chief starts in again. "According to the evidence Santucci and Malloy uncovered, your killer has selected his next victim and is poised to strike before midnight tonight!"

Your killer?

All of a sudden this serial sicko works for Ceepak?

"So tell us what you know! Now!"

Ceepak pulls out his spiral notebook.

"We are dealing with an organized serial killer who plans his murders and escapes with utmost care. As Vronsky states in *Serial Killers: The Method and Madness of Monsters.* . . ."

I see Santucci grimace. He's probably only read one book since high school: *The Sergeant's Test Study Guide for Dummies.* I'll bet he moves his lips when he reads the phone book.

Ceepak continues. "Our killer scrupulously targets his victims and stalks them for as long as necessary. This is often referred to as the 'trolling phase'. . . ."

"You troll when you fish," says Santucci, like he knows everything Ceepak knows. "You spread out your net where you figure there's a whole bunch of fish to catch. That's what we call 'trolling,' Chief."

"After he's seized his victim," says Ceepak, "the killer typically takes her to another, more secure location. There he disposes of the body in a manner meant to insure it will never be found."

"We found the skulls!" says Malloy.

"Only because he wanted us to. In fact, he literally drew us a map. It's what led you here."

"Go on," says the chief.

Ceepak closes up his notebook. He has it all memorized.

"The organized serial killer is difficult to track. He is, typically, socially competent and gainfully employed. He is often married. He follows reports of his crimes in the media. He is intelligent, cunning, and controlled. He brings his own weapons and restraints. . . ."

The chief holds up his hand.

"Okay. Enough. What do you know about *our* guy?"

"I suspect he is a local."

"On account of the newspapers," says Santucci. "He uses a local newspaper."

"Which a tourist could easily purchase from numerous curbside vending machines," says Ceepak. "No, I suspect he is local because of his intimate knowledge of the island's topography. He knows where he can safely bury his treasures and not be detected doing so."

"What else?"

"Our killer is also something of a missionary who, most likely, thinks he is doing society a favor. If he is offended by the young women he stalks, if he considers them to be 'whores,' then in his mind the people around him must feel the same way. That they don't act on their disgust simply means that he is more powerful, more righteous than any one else in his community."

The chief nods agreement. "Understandable. He's going after runaways. Maybe hookers. His vics are society's losers and leeches."

Ceepak grimaces.

I figure he's seeing Antwoine James's face again. The poor black kid who got blown up over in Iraq and nobody back home seemed to give a damn. The kid who was somehow less dead because he was one of civilized society's so-called losers and leeches.

Ceepak narrows his eyes. He's not happy. When he speaks again, it's in that tone he uses when he's pissed. "Our killer clings rigidly to religious doctrine as spelled out by Ezekiel in the Old Testament. I further suspect he is familiar with, or was at one time a member of, Reverend Billy Trumble's congregation. It appears that the majority of our victims passed through the boardwalk ministry and the community it feeds."

"So you think Reverend Trumble knows who did this?" asks the chief.

"I believe he and the killer may have met. That's all I can surmise at this juncture."

The chief checks the time.

"Okay. It's two forty-five. Ceepak, you and Boyle talk to Trumble. Santucci?"

"Sir?"

"You and Malloy scour the island, find the girl in the picture."

"We're on it, sir."

"May I ask a question?" says Ceepak.

The chief checks his watch to see if it's changed any since he checked it ten seconds ago.

"What?"

"The penultimate hole," says Ceepak. "The one before this, the clues that led you here. Who was the victim? What was the date?"

The chief shoots a look to Santucci.

"Girl named Orpah," Santucci says reluctantly. "You know like Oprah, only spelled wrong."

"Actually," says Ceepak, "Oprah's name is the misspelled one. Orpah is a biblical character who. . . ."

"Save it for Sunday School! We've got work to do."

"What was the date?"

"July. 1992."

"Interesting," says Ceepak. "The killer has been dormant for a full fifteen years."

"Well, he's awake now," says the chief. "That's why we're in a hurry. There's not a minute to waste."

"He's got his next girl all picked out," adds Malloy. "From the look of things, I figure she's a prostitute from down in Atlantic City bringing her act up here, you know what I mean?"

"No," says Ceepak. "May I see the photograph?"

Baines looks at Santucci, who reluctantly pulls something from his back pocket.

The suspense is killing me.

What Ceepak takes from Dom isn't a Polaroid, like all the other photographs we found in all the other holes. It's a folded sheet of regular typing paper.

"Computer printout," says Ceepak.

"Yeah. I guess," says Santucci. "Probably. Off a printer."

Ceepak nods. "Inkjet, not laser. We need to check all local office supply stores. Track residents and visitors who may have purchased color ink cartridges. We should also ask if anyone has special-ordered ribbons for an antiquated IBM Selectric typewriter. I'm assuming the index card found in this hole had typography similar to that found on. . . ."

"John?" The chief rolls his eyes. "We don't have time for any of that."

"Understood." Ceepak stares at the photo. "He's definitely gone digital. He's using a camera with an impressive zoom ratio."

The chief cuts him off. "And guess what? We also don't have time to go see who bought digital cameras at Best Buy and Circuit City!"

"Agreed."

Ceepak studies the photo of the killer's next intended victim. The Bride of Ezekiel. How can this be happening in Sea Haven? The big event this week was supposed to be the Sand Castle Competition, not the beheading of a beach babe.

Now he hands the paper to me.

It's a snapshot of a girl hitchhiking near the causeway bridge.

Stacey.

The redhead who recently dyed her hair green.

It's a good thing the photographer didn't zoom out, didn't capture more of the scene.

My Jeep might be in the picture.

THIRTY-FOUR

Santucci, Malloy, and the chief take off.

They're heading back to headquarters to work up anything they can on the redhead. See if she's on file in Atlantic City. Check with the State Police over in Trenton. See if Stacey is a "person of interest" to them, as Malloy so eloquently assumed when he called her a hooker. At the same time, they need to call in every off-duty cop on the SHPD roster and start a hard target search—the beach, the boardwalk, the motels, the works.

I'm left wondering if Stacey is her real name. Maybe that's just what she tells suckers like me who can't stop staring at her cleavage when she climbs into their cars.

"I'll drive," says Ceepak.

I have a feeling we're going to fly down to The Sonny Days Inn for our second interrogation of Reverend Billy, like avenging angels flapping wings at warp speed. Ceepak clutches the steering wheel with one hand, works the radio mike with the other.

"Helen?" he says to the dispatcher. "Please ask Officer Bright to go into the evidence room and examine the guest book from The

Howland House Whaling Museum. Tell her we're looking for the following male names on the guest list: Billy Trumble. Ralph. . . ."

He looks at me.

"Uh. . . ."

I realize I don't know Ralph the bartender's last name. He's always
just been "Hey, Ralph" or "Catch you later, Ralph," so the only
answer I can give is a shoulder shrug.

"Any and all Ralphs," Ceepak says. "The one we're interested in
works as a bartender at The Sand Bar. . . ."

"Ralph. Bartender. Got it," says Helen. "Who else?"

Ceepak lets go of the button, slides us into the center lane so we
can do ninety instead of just eighty.

"Danny? That surgeon. Do you recall his name?"

I rattle around some brain cells. Knock some useless stuff, like the
meaning of the "33" on a Rolling Rock beer bottle, off my mental
shelf. Strain to remember. Oh, right. He gave me a business card!

"Teddy. Teddy Winston."

Ceepak depresses the red button again. "Dr. Theodore Winston."

"Theodore Winston. Got it. Keep going."

"10-4. Gus Davis."

"Gus?"

"Right."

"Our Gus?"

"Yes, Helen."

"He likes whales?"

"Perhaps."

"Well, I know he likes to fish . . . never knew he was into whales."

"Helen?"

"Yes?"

"Tell Jane we need this information, stat."

"Will do. But the chief has her running through mug shots right
now, trying to match them to some picture Sergeant Santucci found."

"Understood."

Ceepak can't overrule the chief's commands or reset the boss's priorities. We'll have to wait a little longer to see if any of our suspects were cocky enough to sign the museum guest book.

I decide it's time.

Time to turn the front seat of the Ford into a rolling confessional booth.

Forgive me, Ceepak, for I have sinned. It's been at least eleven months since my last confession. . . .

"Ceepak?" I say.

"Yes?" He's only half-listening. He's also half-driving like a maniac, racing around this cute little Honda with a surfboard sticking out its open hatchback. Any other day, Miss Honda would have earned herself a ticket or at least a stern lecture about the dangers of unsecured objects in automobiles becoming unguided missiles in rapid braking situations.

"That girl?" I say. "In the picture?"

"Yes?" Now we weave past a pickup truck with a whole row of burlap-balled hedges bouncing around in its bed. Louie the Landscaper, taking his foliage out for a ride.

"I met her."

"Come again?"

"I picked her up. Hitchhiking. She was wearing the exact same clothes she had on in the picture."

"When?"

"Sunday."

"Two days ago?"

"Yeah. I was on my way home after dropping you off to meet Rita at the animal shelter and I saw her thumbing near the causeway. Just like in the picture."

Ceepak cuts a sharp left turn. We tilt sideways, like we're riding a corkscrewing roller coaster, the kind that sends you upside down into a spinning barrel roll. We swerve into a rubber-squealing, tail-skidding U-turn.

"We need to re-examine the area surrounding Santucci's final hole."

"Okay." I'm confused. Plus, my stomach has been involuntarily relocated to my rib cage.

"It's possible Ezekiel only recently selected his next victim. If the photograph shows her as you saw her two days ago. . . ."

"He probably just buried the picture yesterday or maybe today!"

"Affirmative. We may find trace evidence at the scene. Some clue as to who he is. Good work, Danny!"

I decide to get it all off my chest.

"She was also at Reverend Billy's."

"The motel?"

"Yeah."

"When?"

"This morning."

Ceepak's brows pinch together to puzzle over my remark. "Danny, I specifically requested that we both be on the lookout for. . . ."

"She dyed her hair. It was green."

He turns, shoots me a look.

Shit.

Yes, technically I obeyed The Code. I did not lie, cheat, or steal. This morning, he asked me if I saw a redhead. I did not. I saw a girl with *green* hair. Therefore, I did not actually tell him a lie—I just totally screwed up.

"I'm sorry," I say. "I should've . . . you know . . . said something."

Ceepak nods. Looks glum. No. Heartbroken. I have so totally let him down.

"I should have. . . ."

He presses his foot down hard on the accelerator. I can see his thigh muscles twitching under the cargo pants. He keeps applying this much pressure, he might break the gas pedal off its post. The engine is rattling, the whole hood rocking. I don't think we've ever asked our friendly Ford to do over 100 before.

"I know I should've said something," I say—loudly, so Ceepak can hear me over the engine. "I didn't. I'm sorry. I guess I was embarrassed. Didn't want you to think I'm out on the street picking up girls. I should've told you!"

Our speed eases. We're back down in the 90s.

"I'm sorry. I should've known better."

We dip under 85. When we hit 75, Ceepak finally speaks.

"Danny, don't 'should' all over yourself. We are where we are. You had no way of knowing the significance of your omission. We'll deal with it."

"Okay."

"However, in the future, I hope you will be more forthcoming with any and all information you may possess. No matter the personal embarrassment it may entail."

"Sure. No problem." I let it all come tumbling out. "She was also with the surgeon. I saw them outside The Sand Bar. Saw them head off to Smuggler's Cove together. You think he's already killed her?"

He shakes his head. "No."

Duh. Of course not. She was alive when I saw her *this morning!* I should probably engage my brain before I speak.

"Whoever placed the girl's photograph in that final hole is goading us, Danny. First, he revels over his past triumphs by placing his souvenirs on public display. Then, he sends us all on a treasure hunt up and down the island—rubs our nose in the murders he has committed for decades without arousing any suspicion. Now he is daring us to catch him before he strikes again."

Ceepak presses the pedal to the metal again.

If anybody can catch Ezekiel before he kills another girl, it's John Ceepak.

THIRTY-FIVE

We park where we parked before.

Ceepak kneels down beside the hole. He shakes his head. The sand is dimpled with footprints. Mostly the kind made by big, clunky cop shoes.

"I'm afraid we won't find any evidence of significance here."

"Yeah. Unless we want to frame Sergeant Santucci."

Ceepak actually smiles. "Don't tempt me," he says.

I smile back. We're a team again.

Ceepak stands up. Scans the horizon. Mumbles.

"There are *'Lives on the line where dreams are found and lost.'"*

He's quoting Bruce again—still doing "Darkness on the Edge of Town."

He keeps looking around. Keeps mumbling.

"'I'll be there on time and I'll pay the cost, for wanting things that can only be found . . . .'"

He doesn't finish. So I do. Silently: *"In the darkness on the edge of town.'"*

Hey, seeing how we're on the top edge of the island contemplating the apocalyptic darkness dreamed up by some kind of sick demon who thinks he's doing what God told him to do, it seems pretty appropriate.

"Tell me what you know about this doctor," Ceepak suddenly asks.

"Well, he was at The Sand Bar. Sunday and Monday."

"Did you two talk?"

"Yeah. Some. Actually, I listened. He talked. He's pretty full of himself. Likes to hear his own voice even though he sort of sounds kind of prissy. You know—like rich guys always do. And, of course, he's cheating on his wife. . . ."

"Would you say he's charming?"

"I guess. Yeah. He uses big words. Sounds smooth and sophisticated. Almost has a fake British accent. Some girls like that."

Ceepak rotates. Looks south, out across the charred remains of the hotel.

"If Ezekiel drove up here to dig his hole, we might find tire treads. However, it appears as if heavy machinery has been working the site."

The rocky lot is rutted with deep, dried-in tread tracks. No way for us to isolate the ones belonging to a killer's vehicle.

"Dr. Winston likes to fish," I say. "He took a charter on Cap'n Pete's boat but his wife got seasick. He said he usually rents a boat and goes out on his own."

"The photograph," Ceepak says, sounding like he's in a trance. "It was looking up. Toward the bridge. A profile shot. Taken from below. Meaning he was either down near the water's edge. . . ."

"Or on a boat! In the bay—pointing his camera up toward the bridge!"

Ceepak rotates another 180 degrees. Looks north. Out to the rotting dock, the dilapidated pier that looks mostly like telephone poles holding up one of those rickety swing bridges forever dangling over caverns of molten lava in video games.

Ceepak starts walking toward the water.

I follow him.

He picks up his pace.

I do the same.

"See it?" he says.

"No. What?"

"Something shiny. There." He points to the spot where the dock meets dry land.

I see the glint.

We quick-time it to the pier. Ceepak holds up his right hand to halt our charge. He points at a shattered board in the dock decking.

"Note the hole. In the planks."

I see one of the rotting planks has a gaping circle at its center. A foot hole.

"Perhaps he came here on a boat," Ceepak thinks out loud. "Docked. Moved too rapidly down the deck. Fell when the rotting floor boards gave way. . . ."

"And something flew out of his pocket."

"Or his hand."

Ceepak moves closer.

"Footprints," he says. "We should plaster-cast them."

We will, too. I know it. We have this stuff called dental stone in the car. You pour it on a footprint and when it hardens, you can take the shoe impression home with you. We could also use it to make Christmas tree ornaments out of seashells or Barkley's paw prints if we weren't so busy chasing a serial killer.

Now Ceepak crouches. Pulls the tweezers out of his left thigh pocket.

"It's a key. Appears to be an antique or an imitation thereof."

He pincers the key and shows it to me. It's one of those old-fashioned ones with a big, ornate handle. Like a scrolled skeleton key from a haunted house, the kind that slides into a black metal keyhole.

Ceepak rotates the key so I can read its curlicue engraving.

"C."

"Could be the unit in a motel," says Ceepak. "Room C. Most likely from one of the local bed-and-breakfast establishments. Hence the antique effect."

"Winston was staying at Chesterfield's!" I say. "Kept moaning about B&Bs and how much he hated them."

"C. Chesterfield's. Good work, Danny. We need to radio this in. Put out an APB for Dr. Theodore Winston."

"You think he's our guy?"

"I'm not certain. However, I'll feel better knowing he's off the streets for the remainder of the day."

"Yeah."

It's almost three-thirty P.M. and July 17 has less than nine hours left. That may be all the time Stacey, the serial killer's next intended victim, has left, too.

Ceepak's cell phone rings. The black one. The one he uses on the job.

"Ceepak," he says when he flips it open. "Right. I see. Okay. Thanks, Jane."

He closes the phone calmly.

"The plaster casts will have to wait."

"Did Jane find a name in the guest book?"

"Roger that."

"Dr. Teddy Winston?"

"No. His wife. Mrs. T. A. Winston."

I drive. Ceepak works the radio.

"This is Unit Twelve. We are en route to Chesterfield's. Elm Street off Ocean. We will 10-31 Dr. Theodore Winston and bring him in for questioning."

We're 10-40ing it.

That means we're on a silent run, no lights or siren, just plenty of speed. I'm pegging ninety just like Ceepak did. I think the Ford is going to need a crankcase worth of fresh oil tomorrow. Maybe a new crankcase.

10-31 means we plan to pick up Dr. Teddy Winston and haul him into headquarters for a little one-on-one conversation. Ceepak will handle the interrogation. He's a pro. He can tell if you're lying by which way you look when you answer a question—whether your eyes dart right or flash left. It's called the DEA eye test.

It seems everybody has a logical side and a creative side. So first you ask a question your suspect shouldn't have to think about—maybe you ask him to confirm the ZIP code on his driver's license or something. Then you watch his eye movement. He glances to whichever side and offers an answer without any creative embellishment. Now you know which way he looks when he's telling you the truth. Left or right. You've established his pattern. When you ask your next question, maybe the one to do with the crime, if he glances the other way, you know he's fibbing.

Ceepak can actually do this.

Me? I think I lack the necessary powers of concentration.

I tried it once on my buddy Jess. We were at The Sand Bar and I did the ZIP code bit but forgot to look at his eyeballs. Then I asked him about this ten bucks I think he borrowed from me back when we were in high school. I studied his eyeballs in the mirror behind all the whiskey bottles. Since it was a reflection, the eyes were, you know, backward.

Ceepak is tapping the Mobile Data Terminal.

"No wants or warrants," he says. "Except for several outstanding parking tickets, Dr. Winston's slate is clean."

"But you said these serial killers are smart. Know how to avoid police detection."

Ceepak nods. "Indeed. They typically study police investigative techniques. In fact, in twenty percent of cases, the killer participates to some degree in the police investigation of his own crime."

"No way."

Before Ceepak can say, "Way," the radio crackles back at us.

"This is Unit Six." The voice gasping out of the tinny speaker sounds agitated. Winded. "We caught Ceepak's call. We are already at Ocean and Elm."

It's Santucci.

"We will apprehend suspect. Request backup. Consider suspect armed and dangerous."

"Danny?"

I jam down on the gas pedal.

We need to be at Chesterfield's like ten minutes ago.

THIRTY-SIX

We scream up to the curb in front of the old-fashioned gingerbread house that's now doing duty as a boarding house for romantic yuppies.

It's a little before four P.M.: high-tea time at Chesterfield's B&B.

That's why, when we hop out of the car, we're surrounded by about a dozen smartly-dressed but panicky people milling around on the sidewalk, nervously clattering cups and saucers—the kind of china my mom keeps locked in the hutch so nobody will use it.

"Don't shoot!" shouts one guest. He has a pencil-thin mustache and it's twitching like an over-caffeinated caterpillar. "Those other two police officers! They waved their weapons at us! They're inside!"

"The responding officers drew their sidearms?" Ceepak asks.

"Yes!" This from an angry-looking woman in a long blue dress and lacy black gloves up to her elbows. I think it's a costume. Either that or she stopped shopping for new clothes sometime after the Civil War.

"Are you the owner here?"

"I am." She looks at Ceepak warily.

"Were any shots fired?"

"No," she admits. "However, I still consider this an open-and-shut case of police harassment! I intend on speaking to my lawyers."

"Please remain here on the sidewalk. We are attempting to apprehend a suspect in connection with an ongoing investigation. Danny?"

We march up the steps, past the wicker furniture and potted ferns, and enter the foyer.

Knocked-over knickknacks lie scattered across the oriental carpet. Even the silver tea-service stuff is lying on its side, staining the rug brown.

"Santucci," mutters Ceepak.

The bull in the china shop. Who got here just in time for the Lipton. Now he shouts it: "Santucci?"

"We're clear!" Santucci screams from a room upstairs.

"Clear!" Malloy seconds him.

Ceepak shakes his head and we pound up the steps to the second floor.

"We're in here," says Santucci. "Rose Room."

We hike down the hall.

Santucci and Malloy are hovering over a woman hunched up in the corner of a wingback sofa. She's rocking slightly and has wrapped a bed quilt around her shoulders to keep warm—even though it's still 90-some degrees outside and the A/C unit in the window is shut off. Her eyes are sad. Her chin rests heavy in her hand.

She looks worse than when I saw her in The Bagel Lagoon on Sunday morning.

"Meet Mrs. Winston," says Santucci as he snaps his holster shut. Guess he's done waving his Glock in people's faces. Ceepak and I never pulled ours out.

"Are you all right?" Ceepak asks.

Mrs. Winston stops staring off into space long enough to glare up at Ceepak through sad, sleepy eyes.

"Peachy," she says. Now she reaches under the quilt and pulls out a cigarette and a Bic lighter.

"Douse it, lady," says Santucci. "This is a non-smoking room."

"So?" she answers once she's all stoked up. "Arrest me." She reaches over to a coffee table and grabs the crystal OJ goblet she's been using since breakfast for her ashtray. "I didn't ask for a non-smoking room. These fuckers just put me in one."

"I believe they permit smoking on the front porch," says Ceepak. "I noted decorative ash urns."

Mrs. Winston blows out a stream of tar and nicotine. "You think I want to go sit on the fucking porch? Down where everybody can laugh at me? They all know about Teddy."

"Is your husband here?" Ceepak asks.

"Negative," says Santucci. "Apparently, Dr. Winston took off before we arrived on scene."

"These jerks," she laughs, spitting out a couple puffs of smoke. "They race up the street, sirens wailing. Teddy's downstairs in the tea-room. Hitting on the college girl who hands out the cookies and crumpets. I saw them. Saw them from the top of the staircase. Bastard."

"Why did he run when he heard the police?" asks Ceepak.

"Who knows? Perhaps he assumed one of these gentlemen was the young girl's father."

She reaches for a brown prescription bottle on the table near her ash glass.

"Fucking childproof caps."

She works the bottle open by biting at it sideways with her teeth. She pries off the lid, palm-chucks a little blue pill into her mouth. I figure it's not the day's first. I also figure it's some kind of antidepressant. The kind that almost make you sleepy enough to forget how sad you feel.

"You and Boyle stay here," Santucci says to Ceepak. "Take her statement. We'll nab Winston. He can't have run too far."

"What about the girl in the photograph?" asks Ceepak.

"Don't worry. We got other people on the street looking for her. Jesus, Ceepak—you think you're the only one who knows how to do this job?"

Ceepak turns to the couch. "Does your husband carry a weapon, Mrs. Winston?"

She shoots us a smoky spurt of a laugh. "Just the thing in his pants. He pulls that one out constantly."

Ceepak turns back to Santucci. "I don't think your pursuit of this suspect warrants armed intrusions into. . . ."

"Ceepak?"

"Yes?"

"Don't you even *try* to tell me how to do my job, okay?"

I see Ceepak's jaw popping in and out near his ear. Guess that stops him from telling Santucci to fuck off, which is what I'd do.

"Malloy?" says Santucci. "Let's roll."

They saunter out, leaving the sour smell of testosterone in their wake. Sea Haven's Finest.

On the couch, Mrs. Winston turns toward the bay window. The vinyl blinds have been rolled all the way down to keep the sun out, the darkness in.

Ceepak takes a step toward the sofa. The floorboards squeak.

"Can you believe I'm the one who suggested this vacation?" she says to the window. She gives a snort. Laughing at herself. "Beautiful, sunny Sea Haven. Historic home of my husband's infamous frat-boy conquests. His glory days."

Oh, man — if *she* starts quoting Springsteen, *I* might need to borrow some of those antidepressants.

"Now Teddy's picking up girls in the same house where he keeps his tired old hag of a wife locked up in her room. Typically he has the decency to carry out his vacation liaisons in some remote motel. I often find odd keys in the laundry bag when we unpack. Twisted up in his pants pockets."

"Did he recently lose his key to this room?"

She turns to Ceepak. Smiles.

"Oh. You know about that?"

Ceepak shows her the key we found at the Palace pier. It's in a sealed plastic bag.

"Where'd he lose this one?"

"Ma'am?"

"He drops his drawers so often, he's forever dropping his keys as well. Two—no three—so far this week. He just pays the fee at the front desk and asks for a new one. He loses cash, too. Or so he says. In truth, I suspect he sometimes pays the young ladies for services rendered. That's why he never carries his wallet." She cocks her head toward a bedside table. "Doesn't want his 'dates' taking his credit cards, too."

Ceepak slips on a pair of evidence gloves and flips the wallet open. Flashes me the driver's license. I see Dr. Ted's DMV portrait. That'll help.

"Mrs. Winston, we noted your name in the guest book of The Howland House Whaling Museum."

"So?"

"Were you there yesterday?"

"What can I say, Officer? I was bored out of my fucking gourd."

"Did your husband go with you?"

She almost gags on a smoky chuckle. "Teddy?"

"Yes, ma'am. Was he with you at the museum?"

"Of course not. All he wants to do on our one vacation together all year is fish. First, he drags me on this charter boat with an imbecilic clown of a captain . . . "

That would be Pete.

" . . . then, when I tell him how much I hate it, he drops me off at the dock and rents a dinghy for the day. Probably rented a first mate, too. In a bikini."

Ceepak folds up the wallet, tucks it into a plastic bag.

"We need to take this with us," he says. "We will return it as soon as possible."

Mrs. Winston waves her cigarette around in the air. She could care less.

"What make and model of car does your husband drive?" asks Ceepak.

"Down here?"

"Yes, ma'am."

"Porsche Boxster. The girls *love* his little hot rod. Until later, of course—when they discover what it is he's compensating for."

The woman could write an antimarriage manual. It's like Springsteen says in that "Tunnel of Love" song: *"Man meets woman and they fall in love. But the house is haunted and the ride gets rough."* I figure the Winstons' ride ran off the rails ages ago.

"He collects their panties," she says out of the blue. "Sometimes earrings. I found them. At home. In the basement. He has all his souvenirs lined up in a footlocker, sorted and stored in little plastic bags. He even labels them. Name. Date. Score. I believe five stars is his highest rating."

"These labels," says Ceepak. "Does he type them?"

"I don't recall. As you might suspect, I didn't spend all that much time admiring his collection. One fleeting glance was enough." She grinds her cigarette out in the juice glass. I hear it sizzle when it finds liquid. She pulls a fresh smoke out of the pack.

"Do you have any idea where your husband has gone?"

"You mean now?"

"Yes, ma'am."

She sends a jet of butane flame up to the tip of her cigarette. Sucks in to get it going. Blows out.

"Well, let's see. Your fellow police officers probably scared off his tea-cart tart downstairs. Therefore, I can only assume Teddy is once again on the prowl, hunting for fresh, young meat."

Unexpectedly, she focuses on me. Gives me this lewd leer. Ceepak is watching her but she's zeroed in on the sidekick. So now he's watching her watch me. Meanwhile, I'm wishing I were somewhere— or someone—else.

"How about you, young man?" she says almost flirtatiously, flicking her tongue at the white stuff caked in the corner of her dry lips. "Where do you go to meet eager and willing young girls?"

I don't answer.

Suddenly, the idea of ever meeting another girl, for any reason whatsoever, is totally grossing me out.

In fact, it's downright frightening.

THIRTY-SEVEN

We swing by the station house to drop off Dr. Winston's driver's license.

Denise Diego scans it into her computer and in ten seconds flat, Dr. Theodore A. Winston's headshot is displayed on Mobile Data Terminals inside cop cars up and down the island and over on the mainland.

"Handsome dude," Diego says, wiping Dorito grease off her fingers and onto her pants.

"Stay away from this one, Dee," I say. "He's trouble."

"Roger that," says Ceepak.

"A bad boy, hunh?"

"Yes, ma'am."

"Sometimes those are the most fun."

We leave our colleague to her dirty daydreams and head out of the computer room, into the open bullpen around the front desk.

"Ceepak? Boyle?"

It's Chief Baines, lurking in the doorway to his office.

"Sir?"

"Santucci's back on task," he says. "I told him to concentrate on finding the girl."

Ceepak nods. It's not what he wants to hear, but he has to live with it for the moment.

"Did the wife know where Dr. Winston went?"

"Negative," says Ceepak.

"He's probably our doer. Why else would he run?"

"It's a possibility, sir."

"The guilty ones always bolt."

"So do the frightened ones, sir."

"Yeah, well, I say he's guilty. Where do you think he's hiding out?"

"No telling. He's pretty familiar with the island. He's vacationed here a number of summers over the years."

"He was here back in the 1980s? When those other girls were killed?"

"Yes, sir. Our intelligence suggests as much."

I smile a little. I'm "our intelligence" because I let the jerk talk my ear off one night in a bar.

The chief doesn't know this, however. I think he thinks *he*'s the one who just figured it all out. "He's our man, John. Go nab him."

"Yes, sir." Ceepak says it without any of the gung-ho enthusiasm I suspect the chief was looking for.

Ceepak just said it so the chief would shut up and let us go do our job.

"Where now?" I ask.

"Reverend Trumble's," says Ceepak. "I suspect Life Under the Son is where our killer first met his victims. Perhaps his face is even captured in one of those photographs hanging on the Reverend's office wall."

"Those surf baptisms? The ones with the crowds?"

Ceepak nods. "The killer may have heard the girls confess their so-called sins and then, his head filled with the Reverend's fire and brimstone, become something of a vigilante, enforcing a rigid code of justice as outlined in the writings of Ezekiel — a code he may have first learned from the Reverend himself."

We head over to Beach Lane and travel north to The Sonny Days Inn.

"Let's see if the good Reverend is in."

We head toward the office. On the walk across the parking lot, my stomach growls because it's after five and I can smell Italian sausage, onions, and sweet peppers wafting on the breeze. We're that close to the boardwalk. I can even *see* the sausage booth. The curly fries shop. The funnel cakes wagon. It's hard to resist the siren call of indigestion.

But I do.

I pull open the squeaky aluminum storm door and we enter the motel office. In here it smells wholesome. Like air-conditioned lemonade and sugar cookies and crisp apples.

The young girl behind the counter is definitely a devoted member of the Trumble flock. I can tell by the tight green T-shirt hugging her ample chest. It says, NO TRESPASSING. MY FATHER IS WATCHING. Clever. Disappointing, but clever.

"We need to see Reverend Trumble," says Ceepak.

"Do you have an appointment?"

"We need to see him now."

"I understand, but. . . ."

There is the sound of a door opening.

"Hello, Officers."

We turn around. Smiling at us, the Reverend Billy waves off his anxious, T-shirted minion and beckons us into his private chambers.

"Are you familiar with Ezekiel Twenty-three, verses twenty-five to twenty-seven?" asks Ceepak.

"Of course. 'And I will set my jealousy against thee, and they shall deal furiously with thee: they shall take away thy nose and thine ears; and thy remnant shall fall by the sword!'"

He recites it like he's Charlton Heston in that movie about Moses. He points a finger toward the ceiling, up where God is, I guess. In a room on the second floor. Maybe higher.

"'They shall take thy sons and thy daughters; and thy residue shall be devoured by the fire. They shall also strip thee out of thy clothes, and take away thy fair jewels. Thus will I make thy lewdness to cease from thee, and thy whoredom brought from the land of Egypt!'"

He looks at us when he finishes.

"I believe I quoted it correctly."

"Have you preached on this text?"

"Certainly."

"Often?"

"Indeed. For it describes the punishment God promises all promiscuous women."

"Really?" says Ceepak. "I always thought it was more of a metaphor."

Another smile. "Officer, there are no 'metaphors' in the Bible. It is, quite simply, God's Holy Word." He picks up the Bible conveniently perched on his desk. "I, sir, believe in the *whole* Bible. I don't throw out the unpopular parts, the verses that make so many so-called Christians squeamish. For instance, I firmly believe that, as is stated in First Corinthians, all those who engage in premarital sex are automatically damned to Hell."

He says it to Ceepak like he knows about Rita. Then he points his finger upstairs to God's room again.

"'Neither fornicators, nor idolaters, nor adulterers, nor abusers of themselves shall inherit the kingdom of God.'"

Now I think he's talking about me.

Ceepak edges closer to the preacher's big desk.

"Tell me, sir, exactly how many ears and noses have you personally cut off?" Ceepak points to the framed pictures lining the walls. "These girls. The ones you baptized after they confessed their sins. Some of them had been promiscuous?"

"Indeed. It is a common transgression."

"Then I'll ask you again, how many noses and ears did you take away? Or did you ask someone else do it for you?"

Ceepak pulls out a copy of Teddy Winston's driver's license photo.

"Was this one of your disciples?"

Trumble studies the picture.

"Doubtful. He looks far too old."

"What about twenty-eight years ago? 1979. Was he here the same summer as Delilah?"

"I have no way of. . . ."

"What about 1980? Was he here with Miriam and Rebecca?"

"As I stated. . . ."

"Maybe 1981. That's the summer Esther and Deborah had their ears and noses cut off. The summer one of your followers amputated their heads. Mutilated their faces. Did exactly what you and Ezekiel told them to do!"

The preacher looks shocked. He's finally figured out that Ceepak and I didn't come here for Tuesday evening Bible class.

"Someone actually . . . ?"

"A dozen times we know of."

"Oh my God."

"I'll ask you one more time: is this man in any of those photos?"

"I . . . I. . . ."

"Was Theodore A. Winston one of your disciples?"

Trumble is fresh out of smiles.

"Many youngsters who heard my words chose to take up the road to redemption. . . ."

"And one chose to do exactly what you told him to do. Remember, there are no metaphors."

The Reverend holds on to the armrests of his chair; he's a shriveled balloon all out of hot air.

"Please believe me, Officer," he says weakly. "I never thought any one would . . . never, ever believed. . . ."

His voice fades into silence.

"Danny?"

"Yes, sir?"

"Take the photographs off the wall. All of them." Ceepak leans on the desk. "Sir, do you have a box we might use?"

"Hmm?"

"A box."

"Yes." Billy Trumble has lost his radio voice. He sounds like a sad old man. "Take whatever you need. . . ."

"Use that one," says Ceepak, pointing at an empty carton on the floor. Probably left over after somebody made a food donation. I don't think Reverend Billy would ever let his flock down a whole case of Captain Morgan Rum.

"Take down the photos, Danny."

I yank the framed photographs off the wall. They're all from the '80s and early '90s. Strange hairdos. Bushy sideburns. College-aged kids lined up along the beach, watching the Reverend dunk another sinner in the surf. I scan their faces, looking for a younger version of Teddy Winston. Did he crash the scene on the beach? Was this his happy hunting ground?

In one picture, I see a girl on the shore I think might be Ceepak's Rita, only younger, her hair wilder.

"Let's roll, Danny."

Reverend Billy Trumble sits slumped in his chair—probably wondering what he's going to tell God the next time the two of them chat.

We hit the parking lot.

"We need to rush these pictures back to HQ," says Ceepak. "Find someone to examine them more closely, check for a younger Dr. Winston. Meanwhile, we will remain mobile and continue field pursuit of our prime suspect."

"Right."

I pull open the cargo bay to stow the cardboard carton. I take one last look at the boardwalk to bid a fond farewell to the sausage-and-pepper sandwich I know I won't be eating any time soon.

Suddenly, I see her. Strolling up the boardwalk near The Frog Bog.

The redheaded girl.

The one with the green hair.

THIRTY-EIGHT

Stacey still looks as sexy as I remember.

She has on a new bikini top. I can see the red-and-white sunburn lines from the other bathing suit, the one she was wearing Sunday. Today's is even skimpier.

Now she turns and bends. Her tiny Catholic schoolgirl miniskirt rides up high on her thighs and reveals a bikini bottom that looks more like a pair of white panties.

I watch her fingers dip into the back pocket of the guy in front of her at The Frog Bog, who's paying no attention to what's happening behind him. He's too busy smacking his mallet down on a tiny seesaw to send a rubber frog flopping up into the air, aiming to land it on a floating lily pad too small to actually hold the fake amphibian.

"Ceepak!" I yell. "Girl." I point. "Girl!"

Ceepak's momentarily confused, trying to figure out what the hell I'm yelling about.

"Redhead! Boardwalk. Green hair!"

He pivots. Sees her. Makes the connection. He rips the Motorola mike off his shoulder.

"This is Ceepak. Request all available backup. Boardwalk area near Sonny Days Inn."

"The Frog Bog!" I try to help out.

"Frog Bog. We have made visual contact with target. Repeat. We have spotted the girl from the photograph."

Ceepak has good breath support. He's able to say all that stuff while we run across Reverend Billy's parking lot. A chest-high chain-link fence is fast approaching. It separates the motel property from the boardwalk. I figure we'll be scaling it soon.

"Girl is approximately 5'5"," Ceepak continues. "She is wearing a white bikini top, short plaid skirt, yellow sandals. Her hair is green. Repeat. Hair is currently dyed green."

We reach the fence.

Ceepak braces the top bar, swings his legs sideways, does an Olympic-style vault, and flies over. I need to jam my toes into the chain gaps and climb it like a ladder. When I reach the top, I sort of haul myself up and over in stages. The fence shakes, rattles, and pings.

The girl hears the metallic racket. She turns. Sees us.

She kicks off her flip-flops and runs.

Man, she's fast. Like one of those Olympic sprinters who train up in the mountains of Kenya. Her bare feet barely touch the boardwalk. At least she won't have to worry about splinters.

We take off after her.

She has a head start and a better idea of where she might be going.

Up ahead, I see Water Blast, Lord of the Rings Toss, Peach Bucket Ball, and Crabby's Race Track, where you squirt a water pistol at a target to make your crab race up this track against everybody else's crab—and if you win, you get a stuffed Nemo.

"Danny?"

"Yeah?" I huff. He runs every day. Five miles. The only exercise I get is playing beer pong.

"Swing right," he says. "I'll swing left."

We're in a stretch of the boardwalk that's like a mall—booths and shops lined up on both sides.

"If we run behind the stalls, she may think she lost us."

"Got it."

"Reconnoiter at the Whack-A-Mole." He does one of his three-finger hand chops toward the horizon. About a block ahead, I see a gap in the booths—an open square at the next street entrance to the boardwalk. I also see the blinking chaser lights screaming WHACK-A-MOLE in yellow, green, and red.

"We'll surround her."

"Got it."

"Go!"

We split up.

He scoots through an alley alongside a zeppole kiosk. I dash down this narrow strip between Splash Down and Looney Ladders.

Behind me I hear a grunt and thud.

I stop, check over my shoulder.

Ceepak's on his butt.

"You okay?"

"Slipped," he says, hoisting himself back up.

Guess that's where the zeppole folks change their fry grease once a month.

"Go, Danny!"

I don't answer. I just run.

I turn right and I'm behind all the booths, zooming along this tight little path as fast as I can. I have to leap over a tall stack of cardboard boxes. Then I almost trip on a tangle of air hoses and electrical cords behind the Balloon Pop. But the clearing, the opening onto Whack-A-Mole Square, the rendezvous point, is just up ahead. I can hear bells ringing. Kids squealing. Fuzzy hammers hitting furry heads.

I make the right. Race into the square. Ceepak is already standing there.

He's looking left, looking right. Looking like we lost her.

I meet him in the middle. Kids licking lollipops the size of steering wheels surround us. I see tattooed slackers lugging gigantic plush toys they wish they hadn't just won for their girlfriends because now they have to haul them up and down the boardwalk all night long.

The sun is sinking lower so half the booths, the ones to my west, are in deep shadows. The kind of shadows that make good hiding places.

"Do you see her, Danny?"

"No."

I crane my neck. I see this other girl, about nine. She is whacking the bejesus out of the moles that keep popping up in the five holes in front of her. The digital counter clicks over every time she whacks a mole back into its hole. She grips her hammer with both fists. The hammer head is huge, resembling a forty-eight-ounce can of stewed tomatoes wrapped with grey foam. Lights flash. Whistles whoop. Little Miss Mallet is very close to going home with a stuffed gopher.

But she isn't our girl.

"We've lost her," says Ceepak, his eyes sweeping the scene.

"Yeah. But she couldn't have gone far."

"Roger that. Where are we, Danny?"

Ceepak knows of my misspent youth. He knows I know this boardwalk better than Bruno Mazzilli, the guy who owns most of it.

"About a quarter mile down," I say and point at the ramp to our west, sweeping down to Beach Lane. "This is the Dolphin Street entrance."

Ceepak nods, works his handy-talkie.

"This is Ceepak. The target has fled. She was last seen in the vicinity of the Dolphin Street entrance to the boardwalk."

While Ceepak calls it in, I check out the game booth directly in front of us.

There's an Asian-looking dude behind the counter, a clothesline of yellow Tweety Birds strung up over his head. The booth is called Machine Gun Fun. Behind the guy is a row of targets. Sort of like the ones they have at the police academy shooting range, only the targets here look more like the mobsters on *The Sopranos*.

I aced the firing range when I did my nineteen weeks at the academy. Mostly because I spent my formative years playing *Halo* on my Xbox, blasting Grunts, Jackals, and Drones. In Jersey, you need an 80 on the standard shooting test to become firearm-certified. I scored a 96. And my mother used to tell me I was wasting my time pointing my plastic pistol at the TV set!

Now I notice the Asian guy is wearing a head mike but he's not saying anything to hustle up a fresh crowd of suckers. All the barkers manning the other games of chance are into their raps, telling every-body how they can be a winner and take home a Tweety for their Sweetie. But this guy directly across from us is, for some reason, keeping mum about his clothesline full of Tweeties.

I also notice he's standing extremely close to his front shelf. His belt buckle is pressed up tight against the plywood.

There are no shooters. No customers.

But the guy is wearing a goofy, dreamy grin.

He slumps down some. Maybe an inch. Now the counter cuts him off above the waist. He wobbles a little. Closes his eyes.

Okay. I know where Stacey is.

"Ceepak?"

"What've you got, Danny?"

I nod toward the booth.

"I think our suspect is over there . . . under the counter. I think she's, you know, giving that guy a. . . ."

Ceepak nods. I need say no more.

We walk slowly, so as not to draw the guy's attention. Not to worry. His attention is currently fixated somewhere near his zipper.

"Oh, shit!" cries this angry voice behind us.

It's the little cutie on the Whack-A-Mole game. She's smashing her mallet against the glass panel that shows her score.

"Shit, fuck, shit, fuck, shit!"

She has a 95. Guess you need a 100 to win. Guess you learn those words when you're nine years old these days.

"Fucking piece of fucking shit!"

The glass pane isn't shattering. Her mallet is mostly sponge.

Her colorful choice of words, however, has snapped the guy at Machine Gun Fun out of his trance.

He sees us.

Two cops strolling over to tell him his fly is open.

His hands drop from his hips and fumble under the counter.

His row of toy machine-guns shakes. One pops off its pedestal. The countertop is being bumped from below.

Ceepak starts to trot. So do I.

The Asian guy falls backward like a tight end just chop-blocked his shins. I see a flash of green hair as Stacey bobs up and heads for the rear wall. She pushes and shoves against the stuffed purple bears hanging there. Only it's not a wall. It's a door—a swinging panel. She knocks it open and, once again, flees.

We dart up the boardwalk. Now she's the one working the narrow alley behind the booths.

I see flashes of green hair every time we cross a crack where one booth stops and another starts. Past Splash Down. Skee Ball Bob's. Rat-A-Tat Tattoo. Past this place that sells really good water ices.

"There she is," yells Ceepak as we near the blinking lights of another zeppole stand. We race to the end of what is basically a parked food trailer and come upon a cluster of picnic tables, where people sit stuffing clumps of sugar-powdered, deep-fried dough into their faces. I wish I could join them.

We stop. Wait. No girl pops out from behind the food cart.

"She must've doubled back!" I yell. "We should. . . ."

Ceepak holds up his left hand. Gives me the halt sign.

He sees something.

"Is your sidearm loaded?" he whispers.

I swallow hard. "Yes, sir."

"Cover me."

My hand is shaking, but it finds my holster and unfastens the strap that cradles the Glock in place. My thumb finds the trigger. Caresses it.

Ceepak makes an almost imperceptible tilt of his head to the right.

To one of the picnic tables.

To where Dr. Theodore Winston sits biting into the butt end of his hot dog.

"I'm on point." Ceepak moves toward the table.

My hand hovers over my Glock.

Ceepak is the one who suggested I go with the .40 caliber Glock 27 instead of the 23; he said with the 23 my hand would be bigger than the gun. All I know is, right now my hand is sweaty. The pistol might be the right size, but it could slip out of my wet grip.

Teddy Winston is alone. He crumples up the tissue paper from his hot dog, wads it into a ball, and tosses it toward an overflowing trash barrel. He misses by a mile.

"Dr. Theodore Winston?" Ceepak says in his most heart-stopping cop voice.

"Yes?" He squints. He has to. The sun's behind Ceepak's head. I'm certain my partner planned it that way. Gives him the tactical advantage.

"Sir, please stand up and place your hands behind your back."

Ceepak finds a pair of plastic FlexiCuffs on his utility belt. He does so without breaking eye contact with Dr. Winston.

"Am I under arrest?"

"Yes, sir."

"That's preposterous. What, pray tell, is the charge?"

Ceepak nods toward the crumpled hot dog wrapper lying on the boardwalk.

"First-degree littering."

THIRTY-NINE

D r. Teddy Winston doesn't like it when his fingers get rolled across the inkpad back in the booking room.

The surgeon doesn't seem to think the big man in charge, Sergeant Pender, is treating his delicate digits with the proper respect.

"These hands are insured, you know," he says.

"Who you with?" asks Pender. "Chubb? I signed up with Chubb to insure my feet. I'm on my feet all day so I figured, you know, I better make sure they're covered. They gave me a bunion rider."

"I want to call my wife."

Pender cocks a sly smile. "You sure about that, Doc? From what I hear, Mrs. Winston isn't all that thrilled with your recent choice of recreational activities."

"She'll call my lawyer."

"She'll call her divorce lawyer is my guess."

Ceepak tilts his head to suggest that he and I leave Winston and Pender alone in the tiny fingerprinting room. That way, we can pull the ol' bad cop, good cop routine. We'll let Pender continue to piss the doctor off. Later, Ceepak and I can waltz into the interrogation room, offer Teddy a cup of coffee, maybe a nice cold Coke, and become his best buddies in the whole wide world.

We close the door and head up the hall leading to the bullpen. We pass the framed pictures of former chiefs and retired cops lining the walls. Years ago, a couple of these guys busted me and my buddies for drinking beer on the beach.

When we reach the lobby, our most recent retiree is waiting for us. Gus Davis. He's out in front of the short railing that separates Us from Them: the public servants from the public.

Gus looks upset.

"Good evening, Gus," says Ceepak.

"Can it, Ceepak."

His face is red. Retirement doesn't seem to be agreeing with him at the moment. Any second now, he could go postal on us.

"Why the hell did you send Santucci over to bust my chops?"

"Come again?"

"Don't play dumb with me, smart ass. He says you gave a list of names to Jane Bright. Wanted to see if I went to some kind of freaking whale museum."

"Would you like a cup of coffee, Gus?" Ceepak asks. "It's still as bad as. . . ."

"No, I don't want a goddamn cup of coffee!"

Several night-shift guys are strolling in the front door, ready to do the seven-thirty P.M. roll call and pass-on. They take their time heading to the locker room. Seems they prefer to hang out here and catch the floor show.

"Let's step into an office," says Ceepak.

"Forget it, you prick. Santucci said you're trying to make me for a string of murders that went down in the 1980s."

Ceepak doesn't reply.

Gus moves a step forward, braces the bar, and gets in Ceepak's face.

"Just because I didn't track down that tramp when her mother called. Screw that noise. We were busy! I didn't have time to go search under every bed in town for some two-bit slut!"

Ceepak holds up his hand.

"You don't want to say these things to me, Gus. Not now. Not without your lawyer present."

Gus backpedals a step or two.

"My lawyer? I don't have a freaking lawyer. Never needed one until you sent Santucci over to bust my hump."

"Perhaps you should retain one now."

"What? You think you can arrest me? I still got friends in this town. More friends than you, that's for damn sure. You know why? Because you annoy people, Ceepak. You act all superior and sanctimonious. Like you're some kind of freaking Boy Scout altar boy. Well, who the hell died and made you pope?"

"No one."

"You got that right. No one! And don't you ever forget it!"

"Go home, Gus. We'll talk about this tomorrow."

By tossing in the "tomorrow," I'm pretty sure Ceepak just handed our old friend a huge hint: he is not really a prime suspect. If he were, we'd be talking to him *tonight.* We'd be talking to him right now.

"Fuck you," says Gus, flipping Ceepak the finger. Way mature. In fact, the bird never looks all that menacing when extended upward on a sixty-five-year-old hand. Too many liver spots. Wrinkles. Bony knuckles.

"Fuck you, too, Boyle!"

Guess he read my mind.

"Go home to Fran, Gus." Helen, the dispatcher has come out of her cubicle to join the audience.

"Fuck you, Helen!" Now Gus sees the crowd of cops staring at him. Knows he's made a fool of himself. "Fuck you all," he mutters. "Every blue bastard one of you!"

His hands tremble into his pockets and his shoulders sag.

No one says a word. Heads drop all around the room. Nobody wants to watch the show anymore. This thing stopped being funny a while ago.

Gus turns, the crowd parts, and he makes his way out the door.

"I only spent one night with the girl."

All of a sudden, Dr. Teddy Winston doesn't want to wait for his lawyer. He wants to talk. It's almost seven-thirty P.M. I figure he must have another hot date lined up for later tonight.

"You were there," he says, fluttering his fingers in my general direction. "Remember? You were at The Sand Bar and told me where I might procure a six-pack to go."

I sink down in my chair an inch or two.

We're in the interrogation room. Like most such spaces, it's got one of those one-way-mirror window deals. Chief Baines is currently on the other side watching us, and now the suspect is describing how I aided and abetted his bedding of the underage girl we've all been hunting for by pointing him toward Fritzie's Package Store.

I figure I could crawl under the table but that might make me look even worse.

"She's the one you ought to arrest," says Winston. "The girl."

"Why's that?" asks Ceepak.

"For prostitution."

"Did you pay her?"

"No. She robbed me."

"When?"

"You know. After. She took one hundred dollars. Cash."

"Did she take the key to your room at Chesterfield's as well?"

"No. I simply lost it."

"When?"

"Which time are you talking about? I've lost it a few times this week."

"Tell me about them all."

"Heavens—I don't know. I don't really pay much attention to such things. Fine. I confess to being absentminded, but the folks at the front desk don't seem to care. In fact, they have been quite accommodating. Surely it's no crime to lose one's room key. And this ridiculous littering charge. . . ."

Ceepak flashes open the wallet we retrieved from the B&B.

"Is this your driver's license?"

"Yes."

"Is 08540 your current ZIP code?"

"Yes."

Ceepak's watching his eyeballs. Now he knows which way Teddy's eyes will swing when he flings us a fib.

"Do you come to Sea Haven often?"

"Not recently. Not in ten, maybe fifteen years."

"What about in the past—specifically the 1980s?"

"Yes. When I was in college. I came down here quite a bit. So did a lot of people. The beaches, as I recall, were always quite crowded."

I think he's trying to be sarcastic.

Ceepak keeps going. "During these visits, did you ever attend religious services at Life Under the Son?"

"*Church* services?" The doctor is indignant. "Do you seriously imagine attending worship services was ever my idea of a fun weekend?"

Ceepak arches an eyebrow. I think Teddy just looked the wrong way.

"Are you certain?"

Teddy leans back in his chair. Ruminates.

"Life Under the Son?" He's acting up a storm. Scrunching up his face. Thinking. He'll probably rub his chin pretty soon. Yup, there he goes. "Is that down by the boardwalk?"

Ceepak nods.

"They used to put on some sort of show out in the surf. Baptisms, I believe."

Ceepak gives him another nod.

"Okay. Yes. Now that you mention it . . . once or twice I may have stopped by. This was decades ago. . . ."

"I know."

"I remember the girls involved were always quite attractive. College girls. Sexy. All lined up along the shore in their bathing suits. Several of the young ladies weren't quite ready for heaven, as I recall. They were still eager to raise a little hell."

"Did you spend time with any of these girls?"

"Perhaps."

"It's a simple question. I'm looking for just a yes or no."

"Yes."

"How many?"

"One or two. Maybe more. After all, they'd already displayed their willingness to . . . uh . . . sin."

"Did you hurt any of them?"

"The girls?"

"The girls you picked up at the church."

Teddy smiles. "Not that I recall. However, I am rather, how shall I put this, rather well endowed."

Left. That's the liar side. That's where he just looked.

"Did you kill any of them?"

"Excuse me?"

"How many of these girls did you kill?"

"What?"

"It's a simple question, sir."

"I . . . I. . . ."

The eyeballs are staring straight ahead now.

"Did you cut off their heads?"

Ceepak flops one of the After shots down on the table. Teddy looks down and his face loses all its tan.

There's a knock at the door. The chief swings it open.

"Ceepak?"

"Sir?"

"Need you out front. You too, Boyle."

"What is it?" Ceepak asks the chief when the three of us are in his office.

The chief holds up a plastic bag.

Inside I can see a THANK YOU note—the kind my mother used to make me send to all my aunts and uncles before I could spend any of my Christmas money. The front flap is decorated with a sketch of a watering can stuffed with flowers. Ceepak and I screw up our eyes, trying to decipher the snatch of verse printed in blue ink against the blue sky.

Chief Baines reads it to us: "'Just at the right time, the Lord will send showers of blessings. Ezekiel 34:26.'"

Ezekiel.

Now he holds up another baggie. Inside, there's a hot-pink envelope.

"I think it's addressed to you, John."

There are two initials typed on the front flap: J. C.

"Your serial killer is sending you fan mail."

FORTY

H elen found it when she stepped outside for a smoke."

The chief sets the two bags down on his desk.

"Where was it?" asks Ceepak.

"Stuck in the gravel. Poking up near the curb."

The grounds around police headquarters are landscaped with pea pebbles instead of grass. Crushed rock requires little in the way of maintenance, irrigation, or a green thumb.

"Did she see who placed it there?" asks Ceepak.

"No," says the chief.

"Were any vehicles in the vicinity?"

"I don't think so."

"Pedestrians?"

"No. She just saw the envelope."

"Was it Gus?" I ask. "You think he put it there before he came in?"

"It's a possibility," says Ceepak.

Our old pal just worked his way back onto the suspect list.

Ceepak finds another sterile pair of gloves in his cargo pants.

"This message," he says, "as well as the initials J. C. typed on the front of the envelope, was done on an IBM Selectric typewriter."

The chief nods. "Just like the cards we found buried in all the holes. We should check the office supply stores in town. Office Depot over on the mainland. Staples. See who's been buying ribbons for antique typewriters."

Ceepak stops his study of the card long enough to shoot me the slightest little look, because the chief just said exactly what he had said earlier. Back then, our boy Baines told us there wasn't enough time for such niceties.

Ceepak goes back to work. Guess we'll gloat or scream later. It seems our serial killer has climbed out of his mole hole and, after years of silence, wants to communicate with the police.

"'Thank you for arresting the doctor,'" Ceepak reads. "'He is an odious fornicator.'"

"See?" says the chief. "He's been following us! Knows what we've been doing, knows we brought in Dr. Winston."

Ceepak is unsurprised. "Fits the profile."

"We might as well cut Dr. Winston loose," the chief says.

"Agreed," says Ceepak. "Perhaps we can prevail upon him to show us where he met the girl. It might be a location she frequents."

"That's what I was thinking," says the chief even though I doubt he was thinking anything like that.

"I'll put Kiger on it," he announces. "Have him drive Dr. Winston around town."

Ceepak reads on.

"'I have come forth to complete God's work. To finish the task he hath placed in my hands. She is a whoring harlot defiling all good men who cross her path. Therefore, her lewdness shalt be made to cease as I continue to live my life under the Son. Do not dare judge me for, in the end, He, the Son, the true J. C., shalt find me steadfast, loyal, and true. Thou shalt not stay my hand nor prevent His will from being done on earth as it is in heaven. Amen.'"

Ceepak puts the card back into its plastic bag. Similarly, he places the pink envelope back in its bag. With the evidence secured, he takes off his gloves.

"I need to talk to Rita," he says.

The chief looks confused. "Your lady friend?" He twists his wrist to check his watch. "Jesus, John—I was sort of hoping you guys would stick with this thing . . . see it through."

"Rita Lapczynski knows someone who was part of Reverend Trumble's community during the time period when the serial killer was most active. Perhaps her contact will remember something that everyone else has forgotten."

The chief shakes his head. "You still worked up about Reverend Billy? Do me a favor, John—give it a rest. The guy's already called the mayor who, of course, called me. Trumble claims you're harassing him, infringing on his freedom of religion, yadda-yadda-yadda."

"Be that as it may, I sense Life Under the Son is the key to all of this."

"Why? Because the nut job's mash note had a few 'shalts' and 'thous' in it?"

Chief, were you even listening? I want to say. *He spelled it out, right there in the middle of his THANK YOU card! He lives his life under the Son? Duh. Buy a vowel, big guy.*

But I don't say any of this because I've become sort of accustomed to receiving a paycheck on a regular basis. Besides, Ceepak will say it better than I ever could. He knows how to remain professional in all circumstances. Even on days when the boss forgets to pack his brains.

"Sir—were you listening to what I just read?"

Okay. Maybe Ceepak's had enough, too. Who could blame him?

The chief slants down one eyebrow, squints up the eye underneath it.

"Come again, John?" Hey, I think he's miffed.

"Sir, the note writer clearly states, 'I continue to live my life *under the Son.*' An odd choice of words unless, of course, he is referring to Reverend Trumble's ministry. A group that, as I have said, I believe our killer has had some prior association with."

"Maybe," says Baines. "However, you might also consider. . . ."

"Danny?" Ceepak heads for the door.

I follow.

"Where do you two think you're going?"

Ceepak stops. Turns.

"To catch a killer. We haven't much time. Less than five hours."

We walk out the door.

Behind us I hear the chief say, "Dismissed."

Guess it makes him feel better.

FORTY-ONE

The Bagel Lagoon at 102 Ocean Avenue is closed.

Nobody's in the mood for ethnic doughnuts at seven-thirty P.M. The sun has pretty much slipped down in the west, out over the bay. If I were at The Sand Bar, I'd be out on the deck settling in with a cold brewski and a basket of peel-and-eat shrimp, all set for another spectacular show. Sunset. Happens every night but never at the same time. Keeps things interesting.

I'm parked on Ocean Avenue, right in front of a fire hydrant. My buddies on the volunteer fire squad tell me that's how they know where to find a hydrant: just look for where the cop cars are parked.

Ceepak went upstairs to his apartment to talk to Rita. We didn't actually discuss it, but we both silently decided it would be better if he went up there alone.

I was sort of surprised that we came to Ceepak's place to find Rita. I don't think they're living together but I guess they planned a whole bunch of overnight adult activities for the week her son is up in NYC.

I wonder what's keeping Ceepak. He's been upstairs a while.

Guess he's still explaining our situation. Rita will definitely tell him the name of the friend who looked out for her when she was pregnant and scared and all alone at Reverend Billy's. This person who is now one of our town's most prominent citizens and probably doesn't want anybody else to know she once did time at a boardwalk sanctuary for unwed mothers.

Rita will reveal the name to Ceepak because she promised she would—if and when we really needed to know it. Rita always keeps her word. She's like Ceepak that way.

I crank up the radio. The one with the FM dial, not the official one straddling the drive hump. That radio's powered on and squawking but I'm not really paying attention to cop chatter because WAVY is spinning a live version of Springsteen's "The Promised Land."

We're almost at the chorus. The part with the *sha-la-la*'s I do so well.

I let Bruce handle my intro, set me up:

"Mister, I ain't a boy, no I'm a man. And I believe in a Promised Land."

Then he goes on about how he's done his best to live the right way, how he gets up every morning and goes to work each day. I can relate.

Okay.

Here we go.

Sing-along time.

"All units. 10-49."

It's the other radio. The Motorola Spectra police radio.

"Repeat. 10-49. Shots fired. 10-50. Corner of Oak and Ocean. The Seafood Market. . . ."

10-49 means *urgent*. 10-50? *Use caution.*

Oak and Ocean is where Mama Shucker's is located. I know it well. It's this huge, open-air steam bar and seafood market.

"Request all units respond. Officer Malloy is reporting more shots fired. . . ."

Malloy. His partner Santucci is probably the one doing the shooting.

We need to roll. Ceepak needs to be down here. Now.

I lean on the horn.

I flip on the siren.

I hit the horn again.

Here comes Ceepak. He's moving fast. He's taking the steps two at a time like a man running down an up escalator. He probably wishes he had installed a Batpole outside his kitchen window for emergency situations such as this.

I see Rita with the dog, standing outside the door up on the second-story landing. Barkley is living up to his name. Barking like mad. Guess he thinks I'm making too much noise. I lay off the horn.

I lean across the front seat and yank open the passenger side door to save Ceepak a second or two.

"10-49," I yell to him. "10-50! Shots fired!"

Ceepak nods. "Got it."

He hops into the passenger seat, practically rips the seat belt off its pulley tugging it down.

"Let's roll."

I flick on the light bar. The siren keeps screaming.

"It's Santucci and Malloy," I say. "Seafood Market. Mama Shucker's. Ocean and Oak."

Ceepak nods. I see him pull his pistol out of its holster. Pop out the magazine. Check his ammunition. Slap it back in.

I stomp on the accelerator and jerk the Ford into the middle of Ocean Avenue. Traffic moves out of my way. The Ford is shimmying. I swerve and weave between lanes.

We pass The Pancake Palace. Pudgy's Fudgery. We reach Jacaranda Street. The roads in this part of town are named after trees and go in alphabetical order. Kumquat will come next. Oak is four after that. We pass Santa's Sea Shanty.

"That's her store," says Ceepak.

"Who?"

"Sarah Byrne. The woman who took care of Rita. The one from Life Under the Son."

But we can't stop now. Sarah Byrne will have to wait. As much as we'd like to talk to her, we can't go see Santa until after we see Santucci.

And Santucci has a gun.

FORTY-TWO

Mama Shucker's usually has a message scribbled on the white marker board where they post the daily specials. Today it's BE NICE. WE'RE NOT ON VACATION.

Sergeant Santucci must not have read it.

When we arrive on the scene, though it's gotten dark, we can see in our headlights Santucci crouched behind his cruiser. He's using the car's hood to steady his grip on his weapon. I pull in alongside his vehicle. Without bothering to even bob up and aim, Santucci squeezes off another blind round at the Seafood Market.

I hear glass shatter. Water splash. Gallons of it. It sounds like the tail end of a good log-flume ride. I think Santucci just took out a lobster tank.

Another shot is fired. I flinch. Almost duck down. I figure it's the bad guy returning fire.

It isn't.

It's Santucci again. I see him poking up his pistol with both hands and firing wildly.

My eyes flick back and forth trying to trace the random burst of bullets, try to see what the hell it is that Santucci's shooting at.

But all I can see are impacts and ricochets.

One bullet nails an igloo of chipped ice and sends up a cloud of pink shrimp shrapnel.

Another hits a column of breadcrumb canisters.

One takes out a light fixture.

Three shots shatter assorted bottles of Louisiana hot sauce lined up like clay pigeons on top of the deli case.

Santucci is a lousy shot.

"Cease fire!" Ceepak yells as he jumps out of our car and attempts to assess the scene. I pull open my door, hit the ground, scramble over to Santucci and Malloy's Chevy Caprice. I take cover behind the trunk and flip up the Velcro flap locking down my own sidearm.

"Cease fire!" I hear Ceepak scream again when he reaches Santucci up near the front tire.

"Fuck you, Ceepak!" Santucci sticks his gun up over the hood again, waves it around back and forth, and lets fly another couple rounds.

This time he takes out the glass case displaying Mama Shucker's famous clams casino. They're good. Better without the tiny shards Santucci just added to the recipe.

"Lower your weapon, Sergeant!" Ceepak orders.

Santucci squeezes the trigger one more time.

Fortunately, all I hear is a click. He's empty. Apparently, he unloaded a full magazine into the seafood shop. Sixteen bullets. Enough to make fish and lead chips for the whole family.

Ceepak looks ready to rip the pistol out of this idiot's hand. I hunker up against the rear wheel well. Behind me, from inside the cruiser, I hear Deadeye Dom's partner.

"We're taking fire! Suspect is armed and dangerous. Repeat, armed and dangerous!"

Malloy must be lying on the floor, working the radio.

"Are you hit, sergeant?" Ceepak asks Santucci. "Sergeant? Have you taken fire?" He sounds like he's trying to shake Santucci awake.

I look over at the two of them.

Santucci is having trouble finding a fresh magazine of ammo on his utility belt because his hand is too jumpy. The fingers fumble, can't work open any pouch snaps.

Now his knee starts thumping up and down. The heel of his heavy shoe is twitching, spiking a ditch into the gravel underneath it. A drop more adrenaline and I guarantee Santucci will officially be having a heart attack.

"Dom—who is your target? Dom? Talk to me. Who's in there?"

"Your suspect."

"Come again?"

"Your suspect. Ralph Connor. The bartender. From The Sand Bar."

"Who said this bartender is a suspect in our investigation?"

Santucci takes a breath. Fills his chest with enough oxygen to make him an asshole again.

"Cut the shit, Ceepak. Jane Bright told me. Said some bartender named Ralph was on your list with Gus and the doctor. Only you guys couldn't even nail this Ralph character's last name so Malloy and me had to step up to the plate, do your job for you. We nosed around. Asked the right people the right questions. Got the name. Then we spotted him down on Oak Beach."

"Was he with the girl?"

"What girl?"

"The one in the photograph. The one we're looking for."

"Hell, no. He was alone like these psycho killers always are. We tailed him up here. When I pulled out my sidearm, he grabbed a hostage. Hustled her into the back."

"Who?"

"Some old broad."

Great. Ralph the angry bartender has taken a senior citizen hostage. I hope Medicare covers it.

"What happened to your pursuit of the girl?" Ceepak asks. He's worried about the dwindling hours in the killer's schedule. Especially since we're wasting time here watching Santucci shoot at oyster-cracker boxes when he was supposed to be apprehending the girl and putting her into protective custody.

"Don't worry," Santucci says. "She's long gone. She skipped town."

"Are you certain? Did you witness her departure?"

"No, Ceepak. I just used my head, okay? Applied some fucking common sense to the situation." Yelling at Ceepak seems to have calmed Santucci down some. His hand has stopped trying to jump off his arm. He resumes his search for ammunition. "After you two bozos chased her up and down the boardwalk, you gotta figure she's moved on to greener pastures. Probably halfway down the Parkway to Cape May by now."

"Who's the hostage? Inside?"

"Like I said—this old lady. She works behind the fish counter."

"Where are they?" Ceepak asks.

"Inside."

"Where? Which sector of the market?"

"Back there!" Santucci points backward over his head, to the general vicinity of the other side of his cop car, so our situational intel at this point basically blows. No problem. Ceepak is used to being sent into battle with faulty intelligence. It's the only kind they had back in Iraq.

"Give me some ammo," Santucci says. "I'm out. Need to reload."

"Stay where you are."

"Gimme a clip!"

Ceepak ignores Santucci, turns to me. "Danny?"

"Yeah?"

"I'm going in."

"Okay," I say. "Me, too."

"Negative. You will remain stationed here with Sergeant Santucci."

"Give me your bullets, Boyle!"

"Forget it," I say. "Come on, Ceepak. I know this guy. Ralph and I talk all the time. You need me in there with you. I can help."

Ceepak gives me a doubtful look. It may not be the time for *talking*. This isn't Happy Hour.

"Hey," I say, "the state of New Jersey gave me a gun, remember?" As a visual aid I pull out my Glock, wiggle it around some.

"Give that to me, Boyle!" Santucci tries one more time.

"No way. You've done enough damage for one day, okay? You already knocked down all the Tabasco bottles, so you win any stuffed animal you want—but you don't get to shoot again, okay?"

Santucci sulks. Ceepak, I see, is holding back a grin.

"I'm a pretty decent shot," I remind him.

"Roger that," he says with the hint of a proud-poppa smile creeping across his face. "If memory serves, you scored a 96 on the range."

"Yes, sir. Tops in my class. Master of disaster."

Ceepak nods, turns to Santucci.

"Secure the perimeter, Sergeant. Officer Boyle and I are going in."

FORTY-THREE

I check my pistol.

Ceepak gives Santucci further instructions.

"Keep those civilians back and out of harm's way." He points across the street to the crowd of curious and terrified spectators. Of course, Santucci's fireworks display has drawn quite an audience. "When backup arrives, have a team lock down traffic on Ocean Avenue. Both directions. We don't want anybody caught in the potential line of fire. Understood, Sergeant?"

"Yeah. Fine. Whatever."

"Understood?"

"10-4," Santucci snaps. "Okay? I fucking got it, GI Joe. Back off."

Ceepak hesitates a second. I figure he's contemplating avenging the lobsters by knocking Santucci unconscious with a quick jab to the jaw. Would make our lives easier, too.

Instead he sidles up along the car and raps against the driver side door.

"Officer Malloy?"

"Yeah?" comes the muffled reply from inside. I figure Malloy is face down, kissing carpet.

"Please remain on radio and advise all units that officer Boyle and I are going inside to talk to Mr. Connor. Ask all responding officers to hold their fire. We no longer consider our person of interest to be armed or dangerous. Please further advise all units to withhold any and all ammunition from Sergeant Santucci."

"Who the hell are you to. . . ."

Ceepak ignores Santucci, plows ahead with his orders for Malloy.

"We hope to negotiate Mr. Connor's immediate surrender. Meanwhile, keep all citizens safe and all officers out of the building until we complete said mission. Okay, Mark?"

"Yes, sir," says Malloy. "Sorry about . . . you know . . . this . . . situation."

Situation? Cluster-fuck is more like it. But Ceepak takes the high road.

"Don't worry, Mark," he says. "It's all good."

We work our way into the building using the picnic tables at the south entrance as cover.

Judging from where Santucci was shooting—more or less where he pointed his pistol—Ralph the bartender is most likely holed up somewhere in the northeast corner of the fish market. Probably splayed out on the floor. Probably down there hiding from Santucci's blizzard of bullets.

But what if he's been shot? What about the hostage?

Ceepak takes the lead and, hunkered down, we move through the market. It's slow going. My thighs throb. I need to add squat thrusts to my physical training routine if, you know, I ever actually start exercising.

We creep along, using the fish cases for cover. Several of them are leaking, spewing out oily water. It splashes on the floor. Slick puddles are everywhere. My socks and the hem of my pants are soaked. Every now and then, we crunch across shrimp shells or slip on melting ice.

Ceepak holds up his hand.

He taps his eyes, does a two-finger point to the front.

I assume he sees Ralph.

I touch my lips. I don't know the official Army hand signals—they didn't teach us those at the Academy—so I hope Ceepak gets what I'm trying to communicate.

He nods.

Giving me permission to speak.

"Ralph?" I call out. "Ralph? It's me. Danny. Danny Boyle. From The Sand Bar? Ralph? Are you okay, man? Sorry about. . . ."

"What the fuck is going on? This is insane! Why is that moron shooting at us? Do you see what the fuck he's done?"

The silence, at long last, is broken.

"Listen. He had a reason. He says you have a hostage. A woman."

"What?"

"Sergeant Santucci says you grabbed a hostage when you saw he was a cop."

"Fuck that shit!" says this other voice. Female. Old. Angry. Angrier than Ralph, which I would've thought to be impossible. "Fucking cop came into the store, pointed his fucking gun at us. Scared off my fucking customers!"

"Danny?" Ralph cuts in. "This is my mother."

I'm still more or less crouched down, my back pressed up against a refrigerator case, but I remember my manners.

"Oh. Hey, there, Mrs. Connor. Nice to meet you. Ralph and I have known each other for what? Six, seven years?"

"Yeah," says Ralph. "Something like that. Six, seven years. . . ."

Ceepak slouches. Shakes his head. Tries not to laugh.

"So why the hell is that goddamn idiot shooting up my shop?" Mrs. Connor screams.

"Easy, mom."

"Don't you 'easy, mom' me! That asshole out there must've given every single lobster a fucking conniption fit!"

"You got insurance."

"Not against asshole cops!"

I don't blame her but I need to break this up.

"Ralph?" I call out. "I'm going to stand up now, you guys okay with that?"

"Sure. No problem."

"How about you, Mrs. Connor?"

"You got a goddamn gun?"

I lay my Glock on the floor.

"No, ma'am."

"Good."

I stand up. I can see Ralph and his mom. She's short and looks like she's tired of getting up at four every morning to haul heavy slabs of fresh fish off the docks.

I try a smile. She gives me a toothy snarl. Like a Rottweiler.

"Mrs. Connor, this is my partner. John Ceepak." I point. Ceepak stands. His gun is snug in its holster. "Ralph, you met Ceepak on the beach this morning. Remember?"

"Oh, yeah. Sure. How's it going?"

"Fine. Thank you for inquiring."

Ceepak now takes his radio mike off his shoulder, calls in our status.

"Situation is secure," he says. "All units stand down."

"We're coming in!" I hear Santucci say back over the radio.

"Not necessary, Sergeant. As I stated, situation is secure. The woman with Mr. Connor is his mother. I believe this is her establishment."

"That's right, pal!" she yells loud enough for Santucci to hear without needing his radio. "My lawyers are gonna sue your ass six ways to Sunday, you fucking putz!"

Ceepak grins. Puts the radio to his mouth.

"At some point, Dom, I'm certain Mrs. Connor would indeed like to talk to you and the chief about the damages done to her perishable goods and store fixtures."

"Tell her to wait," says Santucci. "We're busy out here. Traffic. Crowd control."

"Roger that."

Ceepak clips the mike back to his shoulder and we move forward.

Ralph and his mom were hiding in the prep area where they gut the catch of the day.

The floor is covered with those honeycombed rubber tiles that are easy to hose down. Behind Mrs. Connor, I see a big cutting board sitting atop a stainless-steel counter. The chopping block looks like it used to be white but now it's stained a permanent pink with decades of fish blood. On the cinderblock wall near to the slop sink, I see a rack full of knives. About six, all different lengths, shapes, and sizes. Filleting knives, curved boning knives. There's a sharpening rod hanging up there, too—so I know the blades are wicked sharp. A rusty hacksaw hangs off a hook near the knife rack.

Hmmm.

Every serious fisherman probably has the same sort of tools stowed on his boat—especially a guy like Gus Davis who loves to catch and clean his dinner every day. You don't think of this gear as dangerous when you think of a guy heading out to fish the day away. Fishing's a peaceful sport.

But now, when I close my eyes, all I can see is one those hacksaws working its way through a neck bone.

FORTY-FOUR

I t's nearly nine P.M. by the time we pull into a parking space in front of Santa's Sea Shanty on Ocean Avenue at Locust Street.

"What about Gus?" I ask again.

I shared my fisherman theory with Ceepak back at Mama Shucker's but he insisted we come see Santa Claus first. Me? I'm not in what you might call a festive holiday mood.

"It's gotta be Gus!"

"I don't think so," says Ceepak.

"Okay. If not Gus, who?"

"That's what I hope Ms. Byrne will help us determine."

"What if she tells us that Gus used to hang out at Life Under the Son?"

"Seems highly doubtful."

"But if he did, then can we arrest him?"

"He'll certainly warrant further attention. However, at this point, although I find your theory sound, I do not think Gus Davis is our man. I doubt he would have had the time or temperament to become a member of a youth-oriented church group operating out of a converted motel."

Ceepak is probably right. Gus would rather be fishing. Says so on the bumper of his car. But what if he was fishing for victims? *Trolling?* That's the term Ceepak used when talking about serial killers and how they hunt down their victims.

"Let's roll, Danny," says Ceepak. "We don't have much time."

I nod and open my door. He's right. The sun is long gone. There's only three hours left to July 17.

The twinkle lights that illuminate Santa's Sea Shanty are still sparkling bright. Must be a billion tiny bulbs in the fake evergreen garlands wrapped around the building and buried in the even faker fiberglass snow banks surrounding the window display's miniature Victorian Village. Santa is still on duty.

We open the door. Sleigh bells ring. Of course.

"May I help you officers?" asks a chubby lady in reading glasses behind the cash register. She's got the apple cheeks. The button nose. Put a little bun in her hair bubble and she could be Mrs. Claus.

"I was just closing up. Is there some problem?"

"Are you Ms. Sarah Byrne?"

"That's right. Have we met?"

"No, ma'am. I don't believe so. I'm John Ceepak. Rita Lapczynski is a friend of mine."

"Is that so? How is Rita?" She smiles. "Is she still working over at Morgan's? Haven't been by there in ages. Store keeps me busy. It's Christmas three hundred and sixty-five days a year in here."

Ceepak moves closer to the counter. He's so tall his head scrapes against the plastic mistletoe suspended from the ceiling.

"Ms. Byrne," he says gently, "we need to ask you some questions about the time you spent at Reverend Trumble's mission. We need to know about Life Under the Son."

She looks up at Ceepak. The sugarplum twinkle is gone from her eyes.

"Rita told you?" she says. She looks surprised.

"Only because you might be able to help us in a matter of utmost urgency."

"I see."

"Ms. Byrne," says Ceepak, "lives are at stake."

She probably heard him but doesn't act like it. Instead, she fiddles with the felt hat on top of a papier-maché caroler's head.

"I assure you, Ms. Byrne, anything you tell us will be held in the strictest confidence."

She finally looks up. Stares into Ceepak's eyes. Sees what she needs to see. Then she looks at me.

"Young man? Could you kindly lock the front door?"

"Sure."

I throw the deadbolt. Flip over the CLOSED—FEEDING THE REINDEER sign.

Ms. Byrne moves out from behind the cash register to stand near an aluminum tree loaded down with seashells and sequined tropical fish.

"What do you gentlemen need to know?"

"You joined the community run by the Life Under the Son ministry?"

"Yes. I had run away from home. My stepfather. . . ."

She doesn't finish. She doesn't have to. Ceepak only wants information that's pertinent to our investigation.

"This was in the 1980s?" he asks.

"That's right. 1985."

"Did Reverend Trumble baptize you?"

"Yes. We walked out to where the waves break. He dunked me under; I swallowed a mouthful of saltwater. When I came up I was Joanna—a biblical name that means *God is gracious*. Reverend Billy chose it for me."

"How long did you room at his mission?"

"I was there through September. Until I miscarried."

Ceepak nods solemnly. "Yes, ma'am."

"Rita told you about that as well, I take it?"

"We needed to know."

"I see." She looks lost. Lost to us, at any rate. I figure she's thinking about the past.

We wait patiently.

Even though we're in a huge hurry.

The clock is ticking, but Ceepak's giving her all the time she needs. I just hope she doesn't need too much more.

Finally, the respectful silence is broken when Ms. Byrne clears her throat and says, "But how is it I can help you, Officers? I'm sure Rita must have thought I could or she wouldn't have sent you over here, would she?"

Ceepak reaches into his shirt pocket, pulls out a copy of the missing-person milk carton photo Cap'n Pete found buried in the sand.

"You say you were at the mission in 1985?"

"That's right."

"Do you remember this girl?"

He hands her the picture. She adjusts her glasses.

"Yes. She was my friend. Her name was Mary. Mary . . . something. Italian. Rhymed with Mary. . . ."

"Guarneri?"

"Yes. Mary Guarneri. That's it. We shared a room at the motel."

"She was also a runaway," says Ceepak.

"That's right. Her mother didn't like the boys she'd been fooling around with back home in Pennsylvania. So, she came down here to fool around with ours."

"Was she pregnant?"

"No. Merely promiscuous. She had no intention of 'washing away her sins,' as Reverend Billy liked to say. She just needed the free room and board."

"Do you remember what happened to Mary?"

"Not really. I know she pretended to be baptized."

"Pretended?"

"She played along. Said all the right words. Before you could be born again, you had to stand up in front of everybody, the whole congregation, and confess your sins. Reverend Trumble always insisted that we be very specific. I think he liked hearing the intimate details."

Ceepak nods.

"Well, let me tell you, gentlemen—Miss Mary Guarneri did not disappoint. No, sir. She regaled us all with lurid tales of wild sex on the beach, in the back seat of Buicks, under the boardwalk. I don't know how much she made up, how much was true, but the day after her X-rated admissions, Reverend Billy dragged her out into the ocean, dunked her under a breaker, and Mary became Ruth."

"Do you remember when she was baptized?"

"Not really. Sometime in July. Before my miscarriage."

"And she remained at the mission?"

"For a while. She put on quite a show. Even took to acting like the true believers. The zombies. She called herself Ruth. Called everybody else brother and sister. Sent out the postcards like Reverend Billy told her to. Even sent one to her mother and pretended to make amends."

"Do you know what happened to Mary a.k.a. Ruth?"

"No. Mary, or Ruth, simply disappeared. It was hot and muggy here that summer. Awful. There was no air conditioning at the motel in those days. I always assumed she ran away to someplace cooler. Maybe up to Canada." She stares at the milk carton panel. "Was someone searching for her?"

Ceepak nods. "Her mother."

"Did she find her?"

"No, ma'am. Mary Guarneri never came home."

"I'm sorry to hear that."

"Do you remember any of the young men who might have been at the mission that same summer?"

"No. Not really. The boys drifted in and out. Not many took rooms. They came for the food, a hot shower, and, if you ask me, to meet girls who had already proven themselves to be . . . readily available."

My turn to butt in: "Were any of those guys police officers?"

"Police?"

Ceepak tries to clear things up: "Ms. Byrne, did you know Sergeant Gus Davis when he was with the SHPD?"

"Sure." She smiles for the first time since we strolled through her door. "Everybody knows Gus. He stops in here all the time. Buys every fishing Santa I stock. Gus loves Christmas. Under that gruff exterior, I suspect he's a sentimental softy."

"Do you remember seeing Gus at Life Under the Son during the summer of 1985?"

"Gus? No. Never."

"Are you certain?"

"As certain as I can be, I suppose. It was such a long time ago. I've tried to move forward and forget all that."

"Are you sure he wasn't there?" I ask.

"I'm sorry. I wish I could be of more help. But I simply don't recall many details." She turns to Ceepak. "Perhaps you should talk to Pete."

"Pete?"

"Peter Paul Mullen," says Ms. Byrne. "Do you know him?"

"Yes, ma'am. Captain Pete."

"That's right. Well, back then, before he was married, he was one of those young men I was telling you about. His mother wouldn't let him go out on dates. So Pete was a good boy and spent his weekends with the boardwalk ministry. He never did anything, mind you. Never hit on anybody. Never even flirted. I remember he always hung out in the back. Kept quiet, kept to himself. . . ."

Ceepak turns to me.

"Danny, it seems your theory may be correct."

Yeah.

I just had the wrong fisherman.

FORTY-FIVE

We're hauling ass up Ocean Avenue.

Ceepak is tapping on the Mobile Data Terminal keyboard, looking up Peter Paul Mullen's home address, running a search through state and national crime databases for anything they have.

"He lives up north. 14th Street in Cedar City."

That's like seven miles away.

"Let's swing by his dock first," Ceepak decides.

That's two blocks up Ocean, three over to the bay.

"Lights and siren?" I ask.

"Negative. If he is there with the girl we don't want to spook him."

"Roger that," I say and hang a sharp left on Gardenia Street.

"Should we call for backup? Alert the chief?"

Ceepak leans back in his seat. Checks his ammo again. I see him glance over to the rearview mirror. I know he's thinking about Santucci—back there at Mama Shucker's, directing traffic and steering rubberneckers away from the mess he made.

"Negative," he says.

"Right," I crack, "the chief might give Santucci fresh ammo."

"Roger that," says Ceepak.

He isn't joking.

At Ceepak's suggestion, I park at the corner of Gardenia and Bayside. We're about one hundred yards from Cap'n Pete's Pier. In the distance, I can see a string of carnival lights swinging in the breeze.

Ceepak taps his chest. Points toward the darkened office.

We're going in.

I see the double-door ice machine. The picnic table. I figure I can use those for cover if this thing goes hot.

Ceepak pulls out his pistol. I do the same. My palm is clammy, so I slip my gun back into the holster for a split second so I can dry my hand across the seat of my pants. Then I take it out again. Hold it with both hands. Hold it out in front of my face.

Ceepak zigs and zags in a crouch across the parking lot. I do the same. He uses light poles and parked cars and a telephone booth to make certain we're not sitting ducks or fish in a barrel.

I do the same.

We reach the ice machine and he raises his right hand. We halt. He points down to something on the deck in front of the office door.

It's Pete's stupid talking parrot.

Somebody ripped it off its hook and tossed it to the ground. Looks like they stomped on it, too. There's a deep dent cracked into its bright yellow belly. I wonder if that annoying voice chip recorded something Cap'n Pete didn't want anybody else to hear. Maybe a girl's screams.

"Looks like a possible 10-36," Ceepak whispers.

Vandalism.

We now have probable cause to search the premises.

Ceepak raises his pistol skyward. I keep mine aimed straight ahead. He'll do the door. I'll deal with whatever's on the other side once he swings clear.

He nods. I nod back.

His left hand twists the metal knob on the screen door. It's unlocked. Also rusty. He pulls it open. Slow. The door squeaks.

Ceepak peers through the window at the top of door number two, the fiberglass storm behind the screen.

"Clear," he whispers. He tries the second door. "Unlocked."

You'd think you'd lock your doors if you were inside sawing someone's head off.

"Going in."

Ceepak speaks in quiet, terse bursts. I nod. I know what I'm supposed to do: cover his ass. He is putting himself in the most vulnerable position, making himself the first target. My job is to shoot anybody who shoots at him.

He raises his right leg. This door will be kicked open so he can keep his gun in front of his chest. He's done this before. Lots of times. They were always knocking down doors back in Baghdad. Busting up apartments doubling as bomb factories.

He kicks.

The cheap storm door nearly flies off its hinges. It swings open so fast it hits an interior wall and bounces right back. Ceepak kicks at it again, softer this time. Gives it more toe, less heel.

"Clear!" he shouts.

We storm into the front room.

"Clear," I shout back because I need to shout something.

The room looks like it did when Cap'n Pete was showing us his shoebox full of treasures. No wonder the worst treasure hunter in Ceepak's club was finally able to actually find something: it was all stuff he had buried himself so he knew where to dig.

Ceepak points to the curtained partition separating the public space of the office from the private back room. The storage room. The room where, I've heard, Cap'n Pete keeps a cot for those late nights when he's been out on the continental shelf in his boat, fishing for blues, and doesn't return to dock until three or four in the morning. The same cot he probably slept on back in the '80s, after those long nights of strenuous mutilation in the service of the Lord.

Ceepak snags my attention.

He's going into the back room.

I'm aiming my Glock forward again.

I nod.

He nods.

He takes in a deep breath, shoves the heavy blanket aside. It slides away like a wool shower curtain.

We step into the darkness. The room has no windows. No lights. Our eyes adjust.

When the shadows start to take on shapes that make sense, we see that the side walls are lined with industrial shelving. Metal racks with exposed nuts and bolts and diagonal slats like you'd use in your garage. The shelves are crammed with neatly arranged plastic storage bins stacked on top of each other. At the far wall, ten feet in front of us, I make out the shape of a small rollaway bed.

Ceepak flicks on his Maglite, swings the flashlight beam over to the bed.

Stacey is lying spread-eagled on the mattress. I can see her dyed hair but not her face.

She is lying on her stomach.

FORTY-SIX

There are no sheets or blankets on the bed.

Stacey's face is buried in the lumpy crevices of the stained mattress. Her arms and legs are anchored to the bedposts with plastic FlexiCuffs strapped around her ankles and wrists.

Ceepak dashes over to her.

I twist around, aim my pistol back at the curtain. I don't want Pete sneaking up behind us with his hacksaw.

"She's been drugged," says Ceepak. "I suspect trichloromethane. Chloroform."

I back up so I can keep one eye on the door, the other on Ceepak and the girl. When I bump against the shelf unit behind me, I hear the unmistakable rattle of glass jars.

I think we've discovered the Cap'n's private museum. The place where he keeps his favorite trophies and souvenirs.

Ceepak pulls out his Swiss Army knife and uses the scissor tool to snip through the four FlexiCuffs. Then, he gently rolls Stacey over. He wants to put her on her back, wants to check out her face.

I turn away. Focus on the curtained entryway. Raise my gun higher and aim it at nothing.

I don't want to see Stacey's nose and ears or what Cap'n Pete might've already done with his knives. I assume he cuts up his victims here in this dark chamber but maybe he takes them out back and uses that plastic fish-cleaning table mounted on the dock. That's where he keeps his crate of old newspapers. He could wrap up Stacey's skull in Friday's local Sports section, then hose everything down, wash all the evidence down the drain, and watch it trickle off the dock, out into the bay, disappearing into the Atlantic Ocean.

"We need to call an ambulance," says Ceepak.

"Is she . . . did he . . . ?"

"She's unconscious but uninjured."

I decide it's okay to look.

Stacey still has her nose, which I now notice she's currently using to snort out some room-rumbling snores. Ceepak takes off his windbreaker and drapes it over her. For the first time since I met her over near the causeway, Stacey looks like what she probably is: a high-school kid who needs a nap.

"This is Unit Twelve," Ceepak says into his radio.

"Go ahead Twelve."

"Request ambulance at Cap'n Pete's Pier House. Bayside Boulevard and Gardenia Street."

"Status of injured party?"

"The prognosis is optimistic. We assume she was the victim of foul play, an abduction involving chloroform. Please advise the chief that we have located and secured the girl, the subject of Sergeant Santucci's recent search."

"Is she the one who needs the ambulance?"

"Roger that. We also need to issue an APB. Please alert all units to be on the lookout for one Peter Paul Mullen."

"Cap'n Pete?" The dispatcher sounds surprised.

"Suspect should be considered extremely dangerous," Ceepak continues. "Please send a unit to his house at 32 West 14th Street in Cedar City."

"He and his wife go to my church. His sons are. . . ."

"Send the car to his house immediately. Officer Boyle and I will continue our search here at his Pier House and dock."

"10-4."

Ceepak clips the mike back to his shoulder.

"Should we check out these boxes? On the shelves?" I ask.

"Not now. We can surmise what they contain. Doubtful they will give us clues as to our suspect's current whereabouts."

Stacey moans. Squirms. Flutters her heavy eyelids.

Ceepak moves back to the bed.

"Keep an eye on the entryway, Danny. I suspect Mullen will soon return to finish what he was preparing to start."

"On it," I say. I move closer to the curtains. A drop of sweat trickles out from under my cop cap. Stings my eye. I squint. Great. If Cap'n Pete busts in now, I'll have to take him down with one eye clamped shut.

"Ma'am?" I hear Ceepak say behind me. "Ma'am?" Now I hear a rattling of springs. He must be rocking the bed, shaking her awake.

"Oh, shit," I hear her mumble. "Where the fuck. . . ."

I sneak a peek. She's trying to sit up.

"Stay still, ma'am. . . ."

"You . . . you're the asshole cop who was chasing me. . . ."

"Yes, ma'am."

"Him, too!"

Guess she recognized me.

"We need to take you into protective custody," says Ceepak.

"What?"

"The man who brought you here. . . ."

"Stupid fucker tricked me."

"Ma'am?"

"He told me his ankle was twisted. Said he did it playing Skee Ball and needed help carrying his stupid stuffed panda to his car."

"Panda?"

"Yeah. Huge fucking thing. A black-and-white teddy bear that was like five feet tall. Guess he won it somewheres." The more she talks, the more alert she sounds. "So I grab the stupid panda and sort of use it as a shield to hide behind so you two assholes can't see me anymore. And this fucking bear? It's old and ugly and its fur is all matted and dirty and it stinks like a can of tuna."

"Yes, ma'am."

"I figured some arcade must've scammed him, gave the guy a used prize—some secondhand piece of shit they stole from the Salvation Army or something."

Or maybe, cagey Pete brought his prop with him. Maybe he picked it up back in the 1980s when those Chinese Pandas Ling Ling and Ding Dong were all the rage. Maybe he's used the stuffed panda ploy before.

"Where is he now?" Ceepak asks.

"The guy who tricked me?"

"Yes, ma'am."

"I don't know. See, he's hobbling along and I tell him I need a ride out of town. He says no problem. If I help him carry the damn bear, he'll take me wherever I want to go. But when we finally get to his car, he jumps me. Puts some kind of cloth over my face. I have to breathe this gross chemical shit while he shoves me into the back seat."

"Do you remember anything else?"

She thinks, then shakes her head.

I hear a siren approaching.

"Could be the ambulance," I say.

"Or Santucci," says Ceepak. "Stay with the girl, Danny."

Right. Santucci. Maybe he heard Ceepak radio in our location. Maybe he wants in on the action again. We may find ourselves needing to dodge bullets. Stacey, too. And she's not dressed for it.

Ceepak heads outside.

I look at Stacey. Smile.

She pulls a face. Half sneer, half wince.

"I suppose you want your fucking twenty dollars back?"

"Nah. That's okay. We're cool."

She unwraps Ceepak's jacket from her chest so she can slip her arms into the sleeves. I look away. There's too much flesh-stretching and bikini-top-tugging going on in the cot district. Need to maintain my professional demeanor. Need to not stare.

So I peer past the curtains to the front door, which is still wide open. Moths are fluttering inside to check out the light bulbs and Cap'n Pete's charter prices. Outside, in the parking lot, I can see the paramedics hopping out of the ambulance. They open up the back, drag out their gurney.

But I don't see Ceepak.

I look harder. Try to make visual contact with my partner, make sure he's okay.

The ambulance's strobing roofbar sends some light out to where the parking lot meets the street. Finally, in the distance, I see Ceepak.

He's bending down. Petting a tail-wagging dog. His dog.

Barkley.

The dog's dragging his own leash.

FORTY-SEVEN

The paramedics take over inside.

I dash out the door.

Barkley looks worried. You know how dogs get. Their tails go droopy, their ears arch up into question marks, their eyes go wide and sad, and then they whimper.

"What's up?" I ask, winded from my sprint.

"Barkley," says Ceepak. He points to the dog's leash. I can see where it's wet and dirty from being pulled through puddles and gutters. "He's . . . she . . . he was. . . ."

I glance over at him. I have never seen the man look like this before.

I have never seen John Ceepak look scared.

He blinks. Purses up his lips. Pulls a cell phone off his belt. It's the one he uses for personal calls.

He thumbs the power button, presses a speed dial number, raises the handset to his ear. Waits.

"No answer. Just the message."

Waits some more.

"Rita?" I ask.

He nods. Closes up the phone.

"She takes her cell phone with her when she walks the dog. . . ."

I grab the leash. "Come on. Let's roll."

"Where?" he asks.

"Your place," I say. His apartment is close. "We'll run by The Bagel Lagoon. See if she's upstairs. Maybe her phone's not charged or something. Maybe Barkley slipped out the door, took himself for a walk, and got lost."

Ceepak turns away. Faces the dock.

"Mullen's boat," he says, hollowly.

I see what Ceepak sees: The *Reel Fun*'s berth is empty. Maybe Pete knew we were coming to get him.

I see the back of Ceepak's rib cage swell under his shirt. He's taking in two big balloons of air. Pulling himself together. When he swivels around, his eyes are filled with the steely determination I'm used to seeing there.

"Danny?" he says, clipped and efficient. "We need to contact the Coast Guard. Immediately. Advise them to send out their rapid response vessel. Employ any and all air assets at their disposal."

"Right."

"We'll alert the chief. Have him contact the State Police over in Tuckerton. They can deploy marine units."

"Okay. Yeah."

Ceepak scoops up Barkley, cradles him against his chest.

"We need to hustle," he says.

Then he starts jogging toward our parked car.

Once again, I'm right behind him, bringing up the rear. I huff and puff, and I'm not the runner lugging a sixty-pound dog.

Ceepak's mind is racing. "Perhaps we can borrow the Mosquito Control Commission's helicopter again," he shouts over his shoulder.

We did that last October when we had those floods. Rescued some folks off rooftops. October is a slow month for mosquitoes. The helicopter was available.

We reach the car and Ceepak places Barkley in the back seat.

"You drive," he says. "I'll work the radio, call it all in."

"Right. Where to?"

"Home."

The Bagel Lagoon is a straight shot down Gardenia Street to Ocean Avenue.

Ceepak lives only three cross-town blocks from Cap'n Pete's Pier. I think about the THANK YOU note we received. The J. C. typed on the front envelope flap. I'm wondering if maybe our resident psycho has been baiting Ceepak all along. Maybe after a fifteen-year hiatus he wasn't just trolling for his next victim, some runaway girl nobody would care about. Maybe he crawled out of his mole hole seeking the thrill of a true challenge: taking on John Ceepak, Sea Haven's one-and-only supercop. Maybe Pete planted that high-school ring on Oak Beach where he knew Ceepak was sure to find it just to get the game started.

Ceepak uses the radio and the short hop up Gardenia Street to put out the APB. I expect to see the French Foreign Legion and a couple aircraft carriers show up any second now.

"Secure the dog," Ceepak says, leaping out before I've technically brought the car to a complete stop. He bounds up the steps to his apartment.

"C'mon boy," I say to Barkley.

He won't budge. Who knew the back seat of a police vehicle could be so comfy? I tug on his leash. I tug some more.

"Barkley! Come!" It's Ceepak. Apparently, he's swept the apartment. Now he's up on the landing, calling his dog.

Barkley's ears perk up. He snaps to attention and leaps out of the car. When he hits the ground, he barks three short, sharp blasts up to Ceepak. I believe the pooch just gave Ceepak a "Roger that," in response to his "Come" command.

Anyway, Barkley scampers up the steps. Ceepak ushers him through the door. Locks it.

"Stay!"

Ceepak comes pounding down the stairs.

"Rita is not here. There's no note."

The emotion or fear I detected earlier is long gone. He's set to *Search and Rescue.*

"Did you try her cell again?"

"Affirmative. No answer. Voice mail."

"Did you leave a message?"

I don't know why I asked it, but Ceepak answers: "Roger that. I told Rita we were on our way."

FORTY-EIGHT

Do you know what freaking time it is?"

Ceepak glances at his watch. "Twenty-two forty-five."

Our old desk sergeant, Gus Davis, shakes his head, pulls on his I'M RETIRED, DO IT YOURSELF baseball cap.

"Let's roll," he says.

The three of us hustle down the front steps of Gus's tidy little house and hit the concrete pathway out to the driveway and our car. Our light bar's still spinning, streaking the front of Gus's house with flares of red light.

"You guys woke up my wife with your freaking cherry top."

"Sorry about that," I say.

"Yeah, well. Whatever." Gus turns to Ceepak. "I take it I'm no longer a suspect?"

Ceepak stands near the Ford's rear door.

"Gus. I'm sorry. I truly am. I made a mistake. . . ."

"Yeah, yeah. Isn't that why your pencil has that freaking eraser sticking out its ass?"

For the first time in about an hour, I see Ceepak almost smile.

"Roger that," he says.

"Yeah, well, don't worry about it," says Gus, pulling open a passenger door and sliding in. "I would've done the same thing. Hell, Ceepak—I probably would've arrested me. Come on, you two. Enough with the yakking. Let's go nail this nut."

Gus Davis keeps his boat, *Lady Fran*, docked at the public pier.

I help him haul in the lines, run the pumps, get the engines going. Ceepak hails from Ohio. They don't have oceans in Ohio. Just that river. Maybe a lake. He's not much help on deck, so he's up in what we sometimes call the "tuna tower"—the canopied cockpit situated atop the main cabin. He's up there in the command and control center, working the ship's radio, checking up on the air and sea assets currently being deployed up and down the Jersey coastline. Off in the distance, over the ocean, I hear a helicopter. I hope it's one of ours.

"When did Cap'n Pete shove off?" Gus yells up to Ceepak as the motors start to thrum under our feet.

Ceepak leans over the bridge's aft safety rail to answer.

"Uncertain. However, we know he abducted the girl on the boardwalk soon after our own encounter with her in the same general vicinity."

"Okay. So when were you two knuckleheads chasing after this girl?"

"Right before you dropped by the house."

Ceepak omits the detail about Gus telling us both to go fuck ourselves.

"Jesus," says Gus. "That was what? Seven? Maybe seven-thirty?"

Ceepak nods. "Giving him a three-hour head start."

Gus hauls in the last line.

"He could be anywhere. It's a huge freaking ocean. Come on, Danny. Take us out."

"Right."

I scale the ladder up to the flying bridge and take the helm. Gus climbs behind me.

"The Coast Guard Auxiliary Flotilla over in Avalon is sending out their swiftest boat," says Ceepak. "It can do thirty-five knots."

"That'll work," I say, and start manipulating the port and starboard throttles, working the wheel.

"Cap'n Pete can only do about twenty-five knots in the *Reel Fun*," says Gus.

"That's like thirty miles per hour," I say as we back out of the berth, reverse engines, and make for the channel.

"Given his head start," says Ceepak, "our search area therefore becomes a one-hundred-mile circle radiating out from this point."

One hundred miles. He could be far enough out to open a casino. Maybe start up his own country.

We come out of the inlet, parallel to the jetty, and head out of the bay into the ocean. Waves crash against the seawall rocks, the white foam visible in the moonlight. We're in a narrow lane marked by blinking buoys to the right and left. The *Lady Fran* is in fine shape. I figure this is because Gus spends his days tweaking the engine, lubing and oiling the shafts—having himself a whale of a time.

"You're familiar with Mullen's vessel?" Ceepak asks Gus over the roar of the engines.

"Yeah. We're old fishing buddies."

"How so?"

"We share information. Good fishing spots. Dead zones. We swap coordinates."

Gus flicks a switch on a screen mounted atop the control console. The color pixels zip to life, revealing a split image. On one side is a real-time ocean chart showing our current position with a blinking triangle. On the other side is a sonar image detailing ocean floor depth and filling with colorful streaks whenever fish pass under our hull.

"That's the Matrix 97 Fish Finder GPS Combo," says Gus. "Gave it to myself for Christmas last year."

"And how fast can we travel?" asks Ceepak.

"If you push her?" Gus affectionately pats the compass globe bumping up on the control panel. "She'll give you thirty knots before she starts rocking and rolling."

"Should I push her?" I ask.

"Hell yeah, Danny. See if she can do thirty-five. See if she can join the freaking Coast Guard."

I jam both throttles all the way up. The good lady responds nicely. Sure, there's some shudder, but we're speeding up, bumping across waves, bobbing over swells and moguls, churning up a foamy wake. We're out of the channel. Heading due east.

I look out toward the horizon. The ocean is jet black. So's the sky. It's hard to find the line where one begins and the other ends. Higher up, the night sky is filled with stars and just enough moon to give a sheen to the rippling water, to make it look like an ocean of rolling trash bags, the black ones they use on construction sites.

"You think Pete took Rita with him?" Gus asks Ceepak.

Ceepak stares out at the black ocean.

"It's a possibility," he says. "Perhaps as a hostage to facilitate his escape."

And that's the best-case scenario.

I press the heel of my hand against the two throttles, try to nudge the levers a little higher in their slots even though I know it's physically impossible. I glance down at the digital speedometer. Thirty-one knots and climbing. *Lady Fran* must be reading my mind.

"What heading should I make for?" I ask, figuring it's time we decided in which part of the haystack known as the Atlantic Ocean we're going to go search for our needle named Rita.

"Fire up the radar, Danny," says Gus. He points to another instrument box. "Gave that gizmo to myself for Chanukah. It displays close- and long-range views. The more metal in a boat, the bigger the ping."

I push the appropriate buttons. Another split image. I watch the green arm circle around, pick up dots and blots. I feel like I should do the five-day forecast.

"See anything?"

"There's a line of boats heading out to the ridge," I say.

Gus nods. "Night fishing for blues. The commercial guys go out even farther, off the continental shelf, for the scallops . . . stay out all night." He taps the long-range screen. "Most of the captains head out this way."

"What if he's heading to Bermuda?" Ceepak asks. "Maybe the Caribbean?"

"Jeez. He could be heading up to Canada, too. Nova Scotia. You're gonna need a freaking airplane."

"We have two," says Ceepak as he reaches for the ship's radio to check in with the other assets. See if the Coast Guard search planes have spotted anything suspicious.

Then he pauses.

"Gus?"

"Yeah."

"Do you ever communicate with Mullen?"

"Whoa. Hold on, hot shot. I'm not going back on your freaking list again, am I? You making me for some kind of accomplice or something?"

Ceepak shakes his head. "Negative. But, as a fellow fisherman, do you ever chat over your radio with Captain Pete?"

"Sure. We all do it. Pass on tips. Hot spots. Plenty of fish out here for everybody. This, of course, was back before I knew Pete was some kind of freaking whack job."

"But you know how to contact him?"

"Sure. I have his frequency programmed into a preset . . . hey!"

Ceepak holds out the microphone. Its coiled cord goes taut.

"Let's contact him now."

FORTY-NINE

This is *Lady Fran* for *Reel Fun.* Come in *Reel Fun.* This is *Lady Fran.*"

Gus lets go of the thumb switch on the radio's microphone. Shakes his head. Nothing.

Ceepak nods. "Keep heading due east, Danny."

"You got it."

I maintain my bearing of 90 degrees. Heading straight across the Atlantic Ocean for Europe. Maybe Spain. Probably Portugal. It's still Tuesday. We might make it to Lisbon by the weekend.

I check the radar. We're about an hour out. Thirty-some miles. On the long-range screen, to the north and further east, I see clusters of commercial fishing vessels working the Hudson Canyon and the scallop beds. To the south, I'm picking up even bigger ships. Probably oil tankers heading up to Newark to dump their loads and keep the air near the Turnpike smelling like rotten eggs. Here and there I see smaller dots. Fishing boats. Sailboats. Pleasure craft.

I look to my right and see Ceepak checking his cell phones. Both of them.

"No signal," he says.

Gus points to his own cell phone, the one he keeps wrapped up in a tight leather case that reminds me of a steering-wheel cover. His phone is clipped to the control console so it won't fly overboard when the boat bangs across a six-foot swell.

"Cell phones only work about ten miles out," he explains. "After that, no freaking towers. They're not putting 'em on buoys—not yet, anyhow. You know, I thought about getting one of those satellite phones. Maybe next Easter."

"If we were in cell range," says Ceepak, "we might be able to tri-angulate his location—provided, of course, he or Rita are currently carrying their phones."

"Look, I hate to tell you this," Gus says, "but he probably tossed her phone into the drink as soon as he brought his boat out of the bay."

"Agreed."

"The key," I say. Sometimes the hypnotic drone of a boat's motor makes my mind drift.

"Come again?" says Ceepak.

"Dr. Winston's room key. The one we found near the dock on the north shore. He probably lost it on Cap'n Pete's boat when he and his wife went out on that fishing charter . . . probably just slipped out of his pocket while he was working his rod."

Ceepak nods. "Indeed. Mullen then planted the key when he buried the snapshot of the redhead. Both clues were purposely left there to mislead us."

Gus snatches up the radio microphone again.

"This is *Lady Fran* for *Reel Fun.* Come in *Reel Fun.* This is *Lady Fran.* You out there tonight, good buddy? Come back."

We stay silent. Wait for a response. None comes.

I hear the propeller screws churning up water behind us: the con-stant washing-machine *whoosh* of waves and wake, the *flap-slap* sound of antenna poles and jacket fabric buffeted by the sea breeze. Thirty miles out to sea, the world is one gigantic Sharper Image sleep machine, but I'm wide awake.

I look up and make out an airplane's belly lights blinking across the sky.

"Think that's one of ours?" I ask.

"Negative," says Ceepak. "Too high up for Search and Rescue."

He's probably right. Maybe we should've called in more air support. Planes and helicopters cover square miles of water faster than
we can. Maybe we should've called up some of those pilots who buzz
the beach dragging ad banners. Frankly, I don't think the captain and
crew of the S.S. *Lady Fran* have a chance in hell of finding Cap'n Pete.
The ocean is too big, our boat too small.

"I suspect this was his *modus operandi* with the other girls," says
Ceepak.

I figure he's been ruminating on the case. Probably helps him
forget that his girlfriend Rita is apparently an unwilling stowaway on
a ship skippered by Admiral Whackjob.

"He didn't kill the girls at his place," Ceepak continues. "He came
out here, out to his secret fishing spot. Some place where he could
drop anchor undetected, where no one could hear the girls scream.
His boat became his floating torture chamber."

We all let that one soak in for a second.

"The girls would be tied up," Ceepak says in a way that makes you
see it. "Probably down below. In the cabin. He would bring along
provisions, enough for several days. He'd also pack his death kit. Torture tools neatly organized and arranged with excruciating care. He
would derive tremendous pleasure from seeing the girls suffer and
would, therefore, make efforts to prolong their pain. Death would
most likely come at the climax of a final sex act. When he was finished, when he found his release and his fantasy was fulfilled, this
would become his convenient burial ground."

Ceepak waves his hand out at the ocean.

"He'd have his cutting tools on board, of course; the same tools he'd
use on deep-sea fishing expeditions. Knives. Saws. Power equipment.
He would slice up the girls' bodies in the same manner he might a
bucket of bait and chum the water with their flesh, blood, and bones."

Gus and I wince. Like I said, Ceepak has a way of making you see
these things. These awful, awful things.

"Sharks. Carrion birds. They'd help him destroy any forensic evidence. He'd keep the girls' heads. He'd saw them off the spine with the same saw he might use on a ninety-pound swordfish. Then he would take his filleting blade and slice off the noses and ears. He would return to the cabin and preserve his trophies in jars of formaldehyde. His compulsions satisfied, he would chart a course for home, knowing he could safely return to society whenever he chose. No questions would be asked. No suspicions aroused. His profession gave him permission to be out at sea for days at a time, to be bloodstained, and to carry with him at all times the stench of death."

Gus, like me, is disgusted. And angry. He grabs the radio microphone again. Jabs down the thumb button. Hard.

"This is *Lady Fran*. Come in *Reel Fun*. Pete? You out there? This is Gus. What a freaking lousy night. Came out looking for yellowfins, ended up with nothing but a couple tangled lines. Come back."

Nothing.

"Tell you what," Gus practically shouts into the microphone cupped in his hand, "I'm thinking about calling it quits, heading home, saving my bait for another day."

Silence. Then a crackle.

"This is the *Reel Fun*. Come in *Lady Fran*."

It's him.

FIFTY

Hey, Pete. That you?"

"Yes, Gus."

"About time. Thought you might not have your ears on tonight. Over."

"Sorry. I've been busy. Down on deck." Cap'n Pete's voice sounds pinched coming out of the small radio speaker.

"You running a charter tonight?" Gus asks.

"No. Came out for a little R and R. Found a good spot."

"So what's hitting out that way?"

"Mr. Mako took the close line."

"Really?"

"Yes. Forty pound S-fin."

"What'd you use for bait?"

"Mackerel."

"Really? I'll have to remember that one. Mackerel."

"Would you like another tip, Gus?"

"Sure, Pete. What the hey. If you're givin', I'm takin'."

"Stay out of the Hell Hole, my friend. It's deader than dead tonight."

Gus chuckles, even though I can tell it's searing his soul to pretend to be this maniac's buddy. "Ain't that the truth! Deadest spot in the seven freaking seas. . . ."

"Gus?"

"Yeah?"

"We've been friends a long time, right?"

"Sure we have, Pete. We go way back."

"Twenty, thirty years."

"Something like that. Sure."

"You know my wife. Our sons."

"Of course I do. . . ."

"You were a pallbearer at my mother's funeral."

"Yeah. Sad day."

"That was fifteen years ago."

"Was it? Jeez, seems like yesterday."

"Gus?"

"Yeah, Pete?"

"In the coming days, you might hear things about me. Things I'd rather keep from Mary and the boys."

Gus looks to Ceepak.

"What sort of things, Pete?"

"Ugly things. Untruths. Lies. Falsehoods."

"What? Somebody gonna say you're a lousy fisherman? That you couldn't catch a cold running naked in the snow?"

"Worse, Gus. All I ask is that you tell people the truth."

"Whataya mean?"

"Tell people I made my mother proud. Tell them I finally finished my mission."

Gus raises his shoulders to tell us he doesn't know what the hell Pete's talking about. Or what to say next. He dabs some sweat off his forehead with the back of his arm.

"Uh, what's your mission there, Pete? Over."

There's this pause.

"Gus, I will not tolerate sinners. I cannot abide those who defile His laws."

"Hey, I know what you mean, pal. I used to be a cop, remember? Laws should be obeyed. I agree."

"And yet I, myself, did not fully fulfill all His Commandments. My mother told me so. She said I was being selfish."

"When'd she say all this? Before she passed on?"

"About a month ago."

Gus shoots Ceepak a look that says he's hearing the cuckoo clock down in his den counting off midnight.

"Mother told me I was a greedy tub of lard. Always choosing the young girls. Disobeying His Commandments. Violating Ezekiel's law just so I could caress their supple flesh. Flesh already sullied and stained by other men. This is why I never completed my task, Pete. Do you understand?"

Ceepak nods. Suggests Gus continue to play along.

"Sure, pal. Sometimes a pretty girl can turn your head, make you forget your own name."

"These girls were gorgeous on the outside, Gus, but their souls were wretched and ugly. Yet, repulsive as they were, I needed to fondle them. To feel them. And so, I never did all I was meant to do. Do you understand?"

"Sure, pal. Sure."

"I fear, by being selfish, I may have allowed certain sinners to relapse. Is Ceepak with you, Gus?"

Ceepak is about to speak. Gus holds up his hand.

"Ceepak? Nah. He's from freaking Ohio. They don't do deep-sea fishing in Ohio."

"Are you lying to me, Gus?"

"Lying? Me?"

"Gus, did you know that Johnny Ceepak forces himself to tell the truth, no matter how injurious it might be to his own personal well-being?"

"Yeah, I think I heard him say something about that once or twice back when I was. . . ."

"Did you also know that he will not tolerate lies told by others? Did you know that, Gus? Oh, he's quite rigid about that one. But he's the true offender, the foul. . . ."

Ceepak grabs the mike out of Gus's hand.

"This is Ceepak."

"Of course it is. Hello, Johnny. How sweet to hear your voice. Yes, indeedy. Johnny Ceepak. The last honest man on earth. Oh, yes. You would never bear false witness against me, would you, Johnny?"

"Where is Rita?"

"The lovely Miss Lapczynski?"

"Where is she?"

"Did you know she once fornicated with a young man to whom she was not married and then gave birth to his bastard? A child she named T. J."

"Where is she?"

"Reverend Trumble encouraged Miss Lapczynski to renounce her sins and beg God's forgiveness. But Rita left the church and has become something of a backslider. What we call a 'recidivist.'"

"Where is she?"

"Here, Johnny. Here with me. But I suspect you already knew that. Am I right?"

"Did you hurt her?"

"No, Johnny. No. Of course not! Not yet. She needs to repent first. God granted her a new life—free from the stigma of her original sin. Yet she chose to throw it all away, to spit in His holy face, to copulate once again outside the sanctity of marriage. Oh yes, Johnny. I know she has shared your bed on a regular basis. I suspected it for months. Your partner, young Danny, he confirmed it."

Damn. I did. I made that stupid crack about Rita sleeping over at Ceepak's. I said it to Pete that night at his dock.

"Rita is the unrepentant, shameless harlot the Lord has placed in my path as a final test."

"Mullen, if you harm her. . . ."

"If I do so, it will be the Lord's choice, not mine! I am but His hands here on earth! I do but His bidding! Tell him, Miss Lapczynski, tell Johnny why you must be punished!"

The radio cuts out. Cuts back in.

"John?"

It's Rita. Her voice weak. Terrified.

"John?"

"On your knees!" The charter skipper from hell rattles out of our radio. "Beg the Lord for forgiveness! Tell Him how you sinned! How you spread your whoring legs and took this man, this man who is not your husband, this man to whom you are not even betrothed! Confess how you took him inside your loins over and over and over. . . ."

Ceepak is pale, straining to hear.

I hear a tremendous gush of jagged breath rasp out from the radio speaker. Cap'n Pete exhaling or worse.

The radio goes silent.

"Forgive me, gentlemen," Cap'n Pete says finally. "Sorry for that little outburst. It has been quite a long day. I'm certain we're all very tired. And so, we must say good night, gentlemen. His will shall be done. Sleep well, Johnny. Gus. Sleep well, my dear ones. Over and out."

FIFTY-ONE

I don't think the ocean has ever looked so dark.

It's bleak and endless and unrelenting.

"I'm sorry," I say to Ceepak who's standing next to me on the flying bridge, staring straight ahead, his eyes fixed on some distant constellation. "I'm the one who jammed us up inside this hell hole. I never should've said anything about you and Rita in front of Pete."

Ceepak turns to face me. "You had no way of knowing how he would interpret your remarks. Furthermore, *you* cannot be held accountable for *his* actions."

"Yeah, but if I had told you about the redhead. If I had told you earlier that I picked her up hitchhiking. . . ."

"The girl was a distraction, Danny. A red herring meant to throw us off course. If we had apprehended her earlier, some other young woman's Polaroid would have ended up in that final hole. Peter Paul Mullen's primary target was and always has been Rita Lapczynski."

"Still, I feel I'm the one who got us into this. If I had. . . ."

"Danny, I repeat—I do not hold you responsible for our current situation. However, at this juncture, I would appreciate a modicum of silence. We need to concentrate. Focus. Strategize our next move."

He squeezes his eyes shut. Brings a hand up to his head. Massages his temples.

Down below, the engines hum. The waves whoosh. *Lady Fran's* nose plunges up and down.

Ceepak opens his eyes. Stares at me.

"What did you say?" he asks.

I shake my head sideways, hold up my hands, and mime a quick and silent *Nothing*.

"No. Earlier."

"I'm sorry?"

"You mentioned how you felt. You inadvertently echoed a phrase Mullen used in his communiqué."

"Hell hole," says Gus. "They both said 'hell hole.'"

"Yeah," I say. "I feel like I jammed us up—put us in so deep we can't crawl out, in a hell hole."

Ceepak is starting to look more like himself.

"When you two were discussing fishing spots, Mullen advised you to stay clear of the Hell Hole."

Gus nods. "Sure. But he didn't need to bother. Everybody knows it's the worst freaking fishing spot there is. Can't catch nothin' out there but a good nap."

"Where's this dead spot, Gus? If it's a location the local boats know to avoid. . . ."

Gus gets it. "Then it's the perfect spot for Pete to drop anchor with the girls! No one would drift by to bother him."

"Precisely."

"Scoot over, Danny."

I slide sideways, keep both hands clasped on the wheel, keep us heading due east.

Gus hovers over the control panel and starts plunking keys on the GPS monitor. The green screen flashes. The nautical charts change like a quick-flipping slide show.

"I got it stored in the memory here. Patch of most unproductive water in the whole freaking Atlantic . . . maybe it's the spot where they dump the medical waste . . . you know . . . the hypodermics that wash up on the beach . . . maybe the fish faint when they see needles . . . my wife does. . . ."

The chart frame he's searching for finally fills the screen. Gus taps the center with his finger.

"We're in luck, boys. Just need to backtrack a little on a bearing south-by-southwest. Lay in a course, Danny."

I guess I should say "Aye, Captain," like Scotty on *Star Trek*, but I don't. I just twist and tug the wheel, work the throttles, check the compass, and line us up for a quick run down to Hell.

We're plowing through breakers. The *Lady Fran* is doing the Coast Guard one better. She's clipping along at thirty-six knots, plowing up ridges of water in her wake. I wonder what kind of suped-up engines Gus has rigged up under the decking. Somewhere, I suspect, there's a Maserati missing a motor.

"That's gotta be him," Gus says. He's staring at the sweeping circle on the long-range radar screen. A blinking blip is sitting smack dab in the middle of the superimposed chart displaying the Hell Hole. "Radar signature appears to be the right size. We should have visual contact in another five or ten minutes. Hang on. I'll be right back."

Gus scampers over to the ladder and scurries down. The man is spry. He works the railings and rungs like a scrappy rhesus monkey.

Ceepak moves around the control console, hanging on to the rails that pen us in as we slice through the crests tossed up by the tide. He wants to be up front so he can be the first to see Mullen's boat.

Fran is really rocking now. We keep smacking across rollers, the next best thing to a hydroplane.

"Ceepak!"

It's Gus, scaling back up the ladder, lugging a chunky pair of binoculars. Ceepak braces the handrails and works his way back.

"What've you got?"

"Night-vision capability." Gus tosses the binoculars to Ceepak. "Couple years back I helped some DEA boys bust up this drug-smuggling ring coming up the coast from Florida. The guys gave me these as a *thank you*. I use them to watch birds. At night. Their body heat makes the infrared lenses go crazy."

Ceepak nods. Presses the binoculars to his eyes. Scans the horizon.

"See anything?" I ask.

"Negative."

Gus leans in to check the arcing circle on the long-range radar. "He's still too far out for visual. But we're gaining on him, boys. He's definitely dropped anchor. Set up shop for the night. Hasn't moved since we first pinged him."

Ceepak lowers the field glasses, drapes their strap around his neck to free up his hands. He retrieves his little notebook from his front shirt pocket. Flips through a few pages. Reads something.

"Gus," he asks, "do you have a fire extinguisher on board?"

"Yeah. A couple. Down in the cabin."

"We might need them."

"What's up?" I ask.

"I've been contemplating something else Mullen said. About his mission. How he never completely fulfilled the Lord's Commandments."

"What?" I say. "Chopping off their ears and noses wasn't enough?"

"Not if he was attempting to follow a strict and literal interpretation of the Scripture's edict." Ceepak reads from his notebook: "Ezekiel. Chapter twenty-three. Verse twenty-five. 'And I will set my jealousy against thee, and they shall deal furiously with thee: they shall take away thy nose and thine ears; and thy remnant shall fall by the sword: they shall take thy sons and thy daughters; and thy residue shall be devoured by the fire.'"

Gus groans. "Jesus. You think he's gonna go after her son, too? T. J.?"

"Doubtful," says Ceepak. "His narcissistic fantasy is completely focused on females. I suspect, however, he intends to follow through on the final command. To do what he never did before because it would have denied him his trophies, his skulls and fleshy souvenirs."

"He's going to burn her body?" I say.

Ceepak nods. "We should assume that is his plan."

"Jesus. A fire? He'll sink his own freaking boat!" says Gus.

"I believe this man in all his delusions would consider such a lethal conflagration to be a glorious conclusion to what he perceives as his lifelong mission."

"Freaking nut job," Gus mutters. "Freaking, fucking nut."

A flash of green on the radar screen catches the corner of my eye.

"Guys?" I say. "We're here."

FIFTY-TWO

He's showing up on the short-range," I say. "We just pinged him. Bearing seventy-five relative to current course. Range two-point-two nautical miles."

Like a gunner in a tank turret, Ceepak swivels with his field glasses to look where I just told him to look.

Something stings his eyes. He momentarily lowers the binoculars. Blinks to clear his vision.

"Infrared flare," he says.

"Disco birds?" Gus asks. That's what fishermen call the annoying gulls that swoop into the halogen lights off the back of any night-fishing boat while you're cleaning your catch.

"Negative," says Ceepak. He puts the glasses back to his eyes, braced this time for the hot spots. "A burning cross. Two."

Gus peers off toward the horizon. "Like the goddamn Ku Klux Klan?"

Ceepak nods. "Mullen has affixed flaming crossbeams to both out-rigger poles—port and starboard. They must be wrapped with a kerosene-soaked fabric of some sort. . . ."

Great. Cap'n Pete has decorated his ship with holy tiki torches. Next he's going to turn his boat into a luau pit.

"Can you see anything else?" asks Gus. "Do you see Pete? Rita?"

"Negative. No. Wait. Yes. I am reading thermal images of two bodies in the stern cockpit. One stationary and seated. The other mobile." He lowers the glasses. "Danny? Cut back on the engines."

I do.

Ceepak goes back to the night-vision goggles.

"The stationary body is moving. Slightly. Wriggling against apparent restraints."

Good. Rita is still alive.

"Body appears to be tied down in a fighting chair aft of the main cabin," Ceepak continues.

Most fishing boats have these padded chairs you strap yourself into. Makes it easier to tangle with a tuna if your seat belt is securely fastened and you're bolted down to the deck.

"The other body is moving back and forth to the cabin," he continues. "Keeps bringing out heavy objects. Stacking them. Judging from the thermal silhouette, the cold object being carried appears to be round. Doughnut shaped."

I take a wild guess. "Tires?"

"Roger that. S.O.P. Standard Operating Procedure for insurgents. Tires and diesel fuel. Stack 'em up, soak 'em down. Creates an excellent improvised incendiary device. Generates intense heat."

"Freaking psycho," says Gus. "Burning up his own damn boat. Rig for silent running, Danny."

"You want me to kill the motors?"

"Make 'em as quiet as you can. Line up our bow with his foredeck, aim for a spot just off his port. We'll sneak up on him from his blind spot, use his bulkhead for cover."

I turn the wheel, pull down on the throttles.

Ceepak, I notice, is checking his pistol.

"Danny? Lock and load."

"Yes, sir."

"You boys bring along a spare pop-gun?" asks Gus.

"Negative," says Ceepak. "Perhaps you should man the helm from this point on."

"Sure. Make me the freaking chauffeur."

I step aside. Gus takes the wheel, concentrates on maneuvering us into position for our sneak attack. He makes a final twist of the wheel and pulls back on the throttles.

The engines stop whining. Move into a purr. Down into a chug.

"Danny?" Ceepak whispers.

"Sir?"

"I suggest you assume a prone position here on the bridge. It will help steady your aim."

"Yes, sir." I lie down on the deck. Brace my gun against the front-most railing. Line up a shot across our bow.

I hear Ceepak move aft, slide down the ladder, make his way to the bow, and climb out on the harpooning pulpit. He becomes, as always, our forward gunner.

We're drifting.

I can see the *Reel Fun* now.

On it are silhouetted two fiery crosses jutting out on the chrome-fitted outriggers at the stern. They frame both sides of the boat with flame.

Of course, I can't see Rita. She's tied up in the back. We're coming at them from the front.

"One hundred yards and closing," Gus whispers. "Adding speed."

I slide an inch or two forward on my belly, holding my pistol in front of me with both hands. I steady it in a corner where the horizontal railing meets its vertical post.

"Eighty yards."

I peek up and over my gun. Ceepak is crouched in the pulpit that juts forward off the bow. His pistol is pointed straight ahead, too. I wish he had his rifle. Some sort of sniper weapon system. Ceepak can pierce Roosevelt's ear on a dime with a sniper weapon.

"Sixty yards."

Hang on, Rita. The cavalry's coming.

Suddenly, a light goes on at the front of the *Reel Fun.*

A blindingly bright halogen.

It spotlights Ceepak.

"Hello, *Lady Fran.*" Pete's voice crackles over our radio. "You shouldn't be here, Johnny. Not yet, anyway."

I crawl backward. Crab sideways. Move behind the control console. Hug the floor behind Gus's feet.

"You shouldn't be here!"

Ceepak doesn't answer.

"Gus!" Cap'n Pete hollers. "Hello, old friend. Welcome!"

I look up. Above me, I see Gus frozen in a dusty circle of bright light. He reaches down and grabs the radio mike.

"Give it up, Pete," he says. "Over."

I hear Pete's wet, jolly laugh rumble out of the radio speaker. Only it doesn't sound so jolly tonight.

"Johnny," Pete's voice spikes. "I have Rita tied up down below."

I'm guessing Pete is upstairs in his flybridge like Gus—seated at the helm, manning the halogen spotlight, working the radio.

"If you want your whore to live a single moment longer, kindly lower that cannon you're aiming at me. That's the good boy. Now, toss it overboard."

The radio goes quiet. All I hear are the waves slapping the sides of our boat. I stay low, curled up behind the three-foot-wide control console. I'm practically kissing the no-skid strips pasted on the deck.

"Now, Johnny!" Pete screams. "Throw your weapon overboard or Rita dies, do you understand?"

Up front, I hear Ceepak's pistol splash into the water.

Great.

I think I just became the forward gunner.

FIFTY-THREE

'm curled up in a ball, lying undetected on the deck of the flybridge, hidden behind the control console.

However, if Cap'n Pete asks John Ceepak to tell him where I am, I'm totally busted, because Ceepak will not lie, cheat, or steal, nor tolerate those who do—maybe not even when multiple lives are at stake.

The radio crackles with static. "Where's Danny?" asks Pete.

Great. Here we go.

"I'm not certain," says Ceepak.

Okay. Technically, he's telling the truth. He doesn't know if I'm up here, down in the cabin, or hiding with the live bait in the cooler.

"Is he there with you?"

"No."

Again, technically true. I am not standing on the harpooning pulpit *with* Ceepak.

"Probably best that you left the boy at home," says Pete.

Ceepak doesn't answer. Pete forgot to phrase his remark in the form of a question. Blew his chance at becoming a five-time champion on *Jeopardy!*—or at finding my hiding spot.

"Gus, please be so kind as to bring your vessel around to my stern."

"Ceepak?" Gus calls out.

"Do as he says."

"That's the good boy, Johnny. I'll meet you fellows around back. I have work to do."

The radio goes dead.

Gus eases the throttles forward, turns the wheel, brings us around the *Reel Fun*'s port side, pivots our bow left, takes us dead astern to its aft end.

I can't see much. Just the reflection of the flaming crosses dancing on the waxed floorboards on either side of my hiding place.

"Cut your engines!" I hear Pete scream from directly in front of our boat.

"Aye, aye," Gus grumbles.

"Drop your anchor!"

"All right, all right!" Gus moves away from the control console. He goes the long way: to the left and then around the front of the wide podium. He doesn't want to step on me on his way out.

"Hurry up, Gus!" yells Pete. "I'm on a very tight schedule."

I hear Gus clank slowly down the ladder.

"Don't worry, Johnny," says Pete. "Rita is heavily sedated. Won't feel a thing. She was a fighter. Very scrappy. Typically, I like to have my girls wide awake for the cleansing."

Ceepak still doesn't say anything.

I sidle to my right. Peek around the podium.

"I imagined the Coast Guard would spot me first," Cap'n Pete calls out across the span of water separating the butt of his boat from the front of ours. I'm guessing it's only about ten feet. "I assumed they would fly over in one of their search planes or perhaps read the heat signature once my little inferno really starts roiling. But this is better. Much better."

"I want you to untie Rita," says Ceepak.

"Of course you do, Johnny. Tell me—does it pain you to see her like this? To know that I have seen her naked flesh?"

"Please cover her body with a blanket."

"How old is Rita? Thirty? Thirty-five? Still quite attractive. You know, I knew her back in the day. Saw her in a bikini. Firm, full breasts. Still has them, doesn't she? Yes, indeedy. . . ."

"Cover her. Now!"

"No, Johnny. I can't do that. Rita Lapczynski defied the Lord's Commandments. She was promiscuous. She slept with men outside the sanctity of holy matrimony. Not once, but twice. Maybe more often. How many men do you think have had her, Johnny? Did she tell you? Was it a dozen? Two dozen? More?"

"I'll ask you once more, Mullen. Kindly cover her."

"No! I will not obey *your* commands! I only listen to Him! Is that clear? You're like my goddamn mother. Nag, nag, nag. Vicious cunt. She was so disappointed in me, Johnny. So disappointed. Of course, I understand why now. I let her down. I truly did. That's why I have not yet had sex with your girlfriend. Oh, I was tempted. Sorely tested. They all tempted me. Their flesh cold and soft, making me strong and rigid."

I have the Glock in my hand.

I have sixteen bullets. Probably one chance.

"When Mother passed, I thought this was finished. Thought I was done. I no longer felt the urge, Johnny. Not for a full fifteen years. I was content with Mary. Kept my marital vows for a decade and a half. But then, Mother came back to me. Told me I had been selfish. Lustful. Greedy. It's true, of course. I know it. I coveted my souvenirs. I pleasured myself with their flesh. Over and over. Out here. All alone. I did not do as Ezekiel commanded. I admit that, now, Johnny. I confess my sins, here in your presence. And this is why I am so delighted to have you with us tonight. Everyone in town knows Johnny Ceepak cannot and will not tell a lie. You'll tell Reverend Billy and my Mary the truth. You'll tell them all that Peter Paul Mullen kept the Lord's Commandments. He obeyed every single word!"

I hear feet pinging on the ladder rungs again. Gus is climbing back up. I crane my neck, see his head bob into view.

We make eye contact.

He gives me the slightest nod. He hauls himself up and retakes his position behind the wheel.

"Oh, by the way, Johnny," Cap'n Pete chuckles, "please forgive me for misleading you. I buried that snapshot under false pretenses. The redhead was never my intended target."

"I know."

"Of course you do, Johnny. You're very clever that way. Very clever, indeed. But can you forgive me? Please? I know you can not tolerate liars, but surely you understand my need to temporarily distract you."

"Put that down," says Ceepak.

"I can't."

I hear a small electric motor. Chugging.

"We must do this precisely at midnight. Just like the electric chair or the gas chamber."

The motor's purr is coupled with a pulsing click. It reminds me of something.

Thanksgiving.

The electric carving knife.

"You don't need to do that, Mullen," says Ceepak. "Not tonight."

"Oh, but I do, Johnny. It says so in Scripture. Ezekiel's wording is quite explicit. First the ears, then the nose, then the remnant must fall by the sword and the residue must be devoured by fire!"

I spring up into a kneeling stance. Aim.

Cap'n Pete sees me. Looks shocked. Holds a huge electric knife stiffly at his side.

"Daniel?"

Now he glares at Ceepak.

"You lied!"

Gives me time to line up a shot.

"Freeze!" I scream. "Drop the knife! Drop it now!"

He does. I hear it clatter to the deck. The motor keeps running, the blades clicking.

"Put your hands above your head!" shouts Ceepak.

Cap'n Pete does.

Gus guns up the engines. Pushes us forward, tugging against the anchor line. The boat rocks. So do I.

For a second, I lose my line of fire. Stumble forward. Have to reach out with my left hand, brace myself against a railing.

When I look up, I see Cap'n Pete holding a red gas canister.

"Drop it!" I call out, lining up my shot again, aiming for the middle of his chest.

He smiles.

He dips to his right and swings to his left — sending up a liquid line of diesel fuel to the starboard cross.

The vapor explodes into a fireball.

"Take him out, Danny!" Gus screams.

"Now!" yells Ceepak.

I squeeze the trigger.

My first shot misses, thwacks into the gas can, pierces the plastic, sprays flammable liquid everywhere. The fire spreads.

"Ram him!" Ceepak orders.

Gus jams the throttles full speed ahead. We lunge forward, as far as the anchor will allow.

I take a second shot.

My firing stance is shaky but I hit Cap'n Pete in the chest.

I hear a hard smack.

He stumbles backward.

My third shot whacks him in the chest again. Our bow smashes into his stern.

Ceepak leaps off the nose pulpit, boards the *Reel Fun.*

I see Cap'n Pete flip backward over the side rail. Hear the splash.

Gus goes scampering down the ladder. I'm right behind him.

He heads into the cabin to grab one of those fire extinguishers. The right half of the *Reel Fun* is totally engulfed with flames. The stack of tires must be soaked with diesel fuel. They bubble up toxic black fumes.

The fire hasn't reached Rita's chair. Not yet. It licks its way across the deck, picking up speed when the swells rise and tip the boat in her direction. Retreating when it rocks back.

I head up to the bow, race out on the harpoon pulpit. We've drifted back from Cap'n Pete's stern. There's a two-foot gap between the two fishing boats.

Gus, behind me, sprays foam at the fire.

Ceepak uses his knife to cut the restraints off Rita in the portside chair. Her naked skin glistens in the heat of the fire. I see a gutter of flame roll downhill and find Ceepak's shoelace. It burns like a cartoon fuse. Ceepak stomps it out and scoops Rita's slumped body up into his arms.

"Cover me!" Ceepak yells.

The pulpit sways. I point my pistol where I last saw Cap'n Pete. I try to lock my feet. Take a solid stance.

"He's gone!" I yell. "I saw him fall overboard."

Ceepak brings Rita to the railing. Gus shoots more foam at the fire.

I pray to God Rita isn't hurt. I pray to God she isn't dead.

I reach out my left hand to give Ceepak something to grab on to. I keep my right hand, my gun hand, pointed toward the flames. I bet the Coast Guard can spot the fishing boat from the air now. It's sizzling and sparkling like a floating roadside flare.

Ceepak hugs Rita closer to his chest and reaches out for my hand.

Our fingers touch.

I see movement.

I swivel right, let Ceepak slip from my grip. He and Rita topple down. Hit the water. Go under.

Through the flames, I can see Cap'n Pete. He has pulled himself up and over the starboard railing. He must be wearing a bulletproof vest. My shots hit a hard shell of plastic and knocked him backward.

Pete raises some kind of lance or grappling hook or spiked pole. He holds it up over his head like a demented Eskimo spearfishing for polar bears. He tears through the wall of fire, means to use the weapon on Ceepak and Rita, off the side of his boat. Impale them like trapped sharks thrashing in his nets.

I pump the trigger on my Glock. I squeeze off one round, work my way up the target, and squeeze off another—because Cap'n Pete won't fall down. When my third bullet tears through the fleshy double chin cowling around his neck, I hear him drop the metal spike, hear it clank behind him on the deck.

Then he stares at me.

He looks worried. Scared. Hurt. Sad. Like he wants to ask, *"What did I ever do to you, Danny Boyle?"*

But he can't ask anything because he doesn't have a throat anymore, just a big gaping hole in the middle of his neck.

He stumbles sideways.

Takes a step. Maybe two.

His body tumbles over the side of the boat.

This time, I'm pretty certain he's dead.

EPILOGUE

I have the same nightmare again.

I'm a kid. About nine or ten. My Cub Scout pack is deep-sea fishing on Cap'n Pete's charter boat.

"Gather round, laddies," says the skipper. "See young Danny Boyle here? Well, let me tell you, boys—one day he's going to grow up and kill me."

The other kids stare at me. Even my best friend Jess, who's grinning and nodding and giving me two thumbs way up because he thinks it's cool that I'm gonna grow up to become a cold-blooded killer.

Then my Scout pack turns into a bunch of lobsters flailing on the floor in front of a shattered aquarium. And a battery-powered parrot in a puddle starts screeching, "Man overboard! Man overboard!" And a canon fires.

Then Cap'n Pete's neck explodes.

That's usually when I wake up.

I start shivering, no matter the temperature.

Now I know how it feels.

I have killed a man.

• • •

Ceepak and I took a couple days off.

I spent most of that time alone in my apartment listening to this one depressing Springsteen CD over and over: *Darkness on the Edge of Town*. Its tracks are full of sadness and anger and rage all jumbled up together. Songs about badlands and streets on fire, rattlesnake speedways and howling dogs on Main Street, broken hearts and chasing some mirage, living it every day and proving it all night.

"I wanna find one face that ain't looking through me," Springsteen snarls. *"I wanna find one place, I wanna spit in the face of these badlands."*

Lucky for me, Ceepak stopped by the apartment half a dozen times on Wednesday. Ten on Thursday.

He knows what it's like to kill a man.

He brought me food. Told me his stories. Made me tell mine. Over and over. Then, together, we listened to the CD some more. Listened to the Boss scream about a *"twister to blow everything down that ain't got the faith to stand its ground."*

Ceepak nodded every time Bruce sang that line.

Ceepak knows about the twisters.

Thursday night, I nibbled on a Whopper that Ceepak brought me from Burger King. Then I tried to joke about how I dunked him and Rita into the drink that night. How we were lucky Gus's boat didn't catch on fire—even with all that water all around us.

Then I cried.

I think my *Darkness* overdose was bumming me out.

I was definitely caught in a crossfire I couldn't understand: I did good by doing the worst thing a human being can ever possibly do.

Friday, we went back to work.

There's a lot of paperwork to fill out when you shoot somebody. More when you kill them.

Sergeant Santucci was hovering near the front desk when we walked in for roll call, still trying to bust Ceepak's chops.

"Pete Mullen? He wasn't even on your suspect list! Jesus, Ceepak. You call yourself a detective?"

Ceepak ignored him.

Then Santucci was ushered into a little room to talk to the Sea Haven town attorney in order to hash out his personal liability in the settlement deal the township had reached with Mama Shucker's. Sergeant Santucci will probably need to pull some heavy-duty overtime over the next fifty years in order to pay off his portion of the damages.

Retired Sergeant Gus Davis was at the house, too—using our phones to work out his final travel arrangements. He's flying out to Fresno this weekend with a tiny urn filled with the cremated remains—what we have—of Mary Guarneri's body. He'll present the urn to the girl's mother. He'll probably apologize to her, too.

Of course, at roll call, Chief Buzz Baines insisted that everybody keep *hush-hush* about the crazy psycho serial killer who crawled out of his mole hole after hibernating in Sea Haven for fifteen years.

Unfortunately for Buzz, keeping this thing a secret would be totally impossible.

First of all, Ceepak stood up and insisted that we send Cap'n Pete's souvenir collection off to the State Forensics Lab and down to the FBI for DNA analysis. He also demanded that we post all our evidence on the Internet and try to link up with the vast network of missing person sites. Try to give a dozen grieving families some sense of closure.

Second, you have to figure people in town are already talking. Maybe they showed up for their pre-booked fishing charters and discovered that Cap'n Pete and his boat no longer existed. Maybe they went to the Sand Castle Competition and heard rumors about the "buried treasure" the bulldozer guys dug up over near the pirate scene. Maybe Norma told everybody she knows what turned up in the Whaling Museum. Maybe Amy Decosimo let out what strange booty was recently lining the shelves over at The Treasure Chest.

Word will seep out. The truth usually does. All it needs is a tiny little crack. I think that's why Ceepak never lies. As Gus might put it, "What's the freaking point?"

And the hitchhiker—the girl who went from being a redhead to a greenhead (no, not one of the flies)?

Her name is really Elizabeth, not Stacey, and her mother and father are flying in from Pittsburgh to pick her up and take her home. Put her back on her meds. They say she's sixteen and has "issues." In the meantime, she's spending her final nights in Sea Haven as our guest. She has a cot in one of our cozier jail cells. Hey—that's what you get for stealing twenty bucks off a cop.

Seven-thirty P.M., we punch out.

No overtime this Friday. And the chief gave us both the weekend off. I don't think he wants us guarding the Sand Castle Competition. He's got his reasons.

"Are you free this evening?" Ceepak asks as we stroll down the front steps of police headquarters.

"What's up?" I ask.

"T. J. came home from New York this morning. Rita's having a barbecue to celebrate. We'll be grilling burgers and dogs over at my place."

I'm surprised to hear that Ms. Lapczynski is willing to venture anywhere near open flames—propane, charcoal, or otherwise—but I'm in. Burnt meat and cold beer are two of my summertime favorites.

"Sounds cool," I say.

"Good. See you there."

I hop into my Jeep and zip over to the Qwick Pick to grab a couple bags of Ruffles. I figure I should bring something to the picnic table.

I also grab a couple Ring Dings. In case Rita didn't have time to make dessert. And a box of Milk-Bones. For Barkley, the best guard dog ever to shuffle out of the retirement home.

I toss the groceries into the back of my Jeep and head over to Ceepak's.

• • •

"Hey, man. Thanks for saving my mom." It's T. J. He's manning the grill. He puts down his burger flipper and shakes my hand. "Brewski?"

"Thanks."

He pries open the lid on the Igloo; I fish out a frosty longneck Bud. He's sipping a Dr Pepper—he's sixteen.

I twist open my beer and look over at Barkley, who's snoozing in the shade underneath the picnic table.

"I already gave him a couple burgers," says T. J. "Without cheese. Cheese makes him fart."

I nod. "Me too, man."

T. J. nods, too. He can relate.

"Hey, Danny!"

It's Rita. Up at the top of the stairs. She's coming down the steps balancing a big bowl of potato salad and what appears to be a fresh-baked apple pie. Guess I'll save the Ring Dings for a rainy day. Ceepak's right behind her with bags of buns and squeeze bottles of ketchup and mustard.

He sets his stuff down on the picnic table.

"Danny?"

"Yes, sir?"

"Are you free tomorrow evening? Twenty-thirty hours?"

"So far's I know."

"Awesome." Ceepak takes Rita's hand. "We'd like you to be our best man. Will you?"

"Excuse me?"

"At our wedding," says Rita.

"You guys are getting married?"

"Roger that."

"I'm in charge of walking her down the aisle," says T. J. "Barkley's going to be the ring bearer. We'll put 'em in a pouch on his collar."

"Is this a church wedding?" I ask.

If it is, I might need to swing by Sears. Pick up a suit.

"Negative," says Ceepak.

I guess he's had enough organized religion for one week.

"Judge Willoughby will preside," says Rita. "It's a civil ceremony. On the beach at sunset."

"I can't believe this," I say. "This is so cool! Are you guys like registered anywhere? Do you need salad bowls or something?"

"Danny?" says Rita, beaming her impossibly radiant smile straight through my heart, making me feel better than I have in days. "Come on—answer the question! Will you stand up for us? Will you be our best man?"

I smile back.

"Sure. Absolutely."

I say it with great gusto, even though I know it will be an extremely tough act to pull off. Practically impossible.

It's hard for anybody to be the so-called best man when John Ceepak is already standing there.

But I'll give it a shot.

ACKNOWLEDGMENTS

As always, the first person to thank is my wife, J. J. Words cannot describe the gratitude I feel for the joy of having her in my life and by my side. Well, her and the critters — the three cats (Jeanette, Parker, and Tiger Lilly) who keep me company in the writing room and Fred, the dog, who takes me out for long walks so I can figure out what happens next.

J. J. volunteers for an animal rescue group, and I encourage everybody to Do What Ceepak Would Do: adopt your next pet from a shelter. From experience, I can assure you — your new friends will never forget how you saved their lives and they'll show you their appreciation every day.

I want to thank D. P. Lyle, MD, a mystery and thriller writer who runs the Writer's Medical and Forensics Lab and is so unbelievably generous in helping those of us who never made it to med school.

Thanks also to my chief technical advisor, Chief Michael Bradley of the Long Beach Township Police Department, and all the shops, restaurants, and arcades down the Jersey Shore on LBI that serve as inspirations for Sea Haven. Special thanks to Captain Don Mears and *Lady Fran Charters* of Barnegat Light, New Jersey, for taking me out to sea to plot my mystery. I am extremely grateful to have had Michele Slung as my line editor once again (this is our fourth book together), and, as always, I thank Bruce Springsteen for lending me his lyrics — words that give Danny and Ceepak a chance to say more than either one of them could ever say on their own.

To my agent, Eric Myers, and everybody at Carroll & Graf (especially Don, Wendie, Sarah, Will, Michele, Karen, Lisa, Jamie, and Lukas) — thanks!

Thanks from Wisconsin Literacy, Inc., and me to the *real* Sarah Byrne, who contributed so generously to the charity auction at Bouchercon 2006 in Madison for the chance to run Santa's Sea Shanty and be a woman with a shady past.

And, last but not least, thank *you*.

A writer without readers is even lonelier than an abandoned dog named Barkley, Buster, or Fred.

ONE

August 30th is National Toasted Marshmallow Day, so, naturally, we're celebrating.

Sure there's some debate: Is National Toasted Marshmallow Day August 14th or August 30th? We go with the 30th because it's closer to Labor Day. Besides, if you dig a little deeper, you'll discover that August 14th is also National Creamsicle Day, and we firmly believe Creamsicles deserve their own separate day of national recognition.

Five of my longtime buds and I are driving out to Tangerine Beach. Here in Sea Haven, New Jersey, the beaches get named after the streets they're closest to. On the way, we pass Buccaneer Bob's Bagels, Sea Shanty Shoes, and Moby Moo's Ice Cream Cove. In case you can't tell by the waterlogged names, this is your basic down-the-shore resort town: We live for July and August because our visitors go home in September and take their wallets with them.

I'm a part-time summer cop with the Sea Haven Police. That means I wear a navy blue cop cap and help elderly pedestrians navigate the crosswalks. This year I might go full time when summer's over, which is, basically, next week. They usually offer one part-timer a job at the end of the season. The chief gets to pick. We have a new one. We'll see. Anyhow, I put in my application.

Riding up front with me, twiddling her sparkly toes on the dashboard, is Katie Landry. She's a friend who I hope will soon become a "friend." Like the Molson billboard says: "Friends come over for dinner. *Friends* stay for breakfast." So far, Katie and me? We're just doing takeout. Mostly Burger King or Quiznos.

In the second row are Jess Garrett and Olivia Chibbs—a sleepy-eyed surfer dude and an African-American beauty queen slash brainiac. Jess and Olivia are already buttering toast and squeezing orange juice together. She comes home from college every summer to make money to cover the stuff her med school scholarships don't. Jess lives here full time. He paints houses when he's not busy goofing off.

Then there's Becca Adkinson and Harley Mook. Becca's folks run the Mussel Beach Motel, she helps. Mook (we all call him Mook) is short and tubby and loud. He's in the wayback, popping open a bag of Cheetos like it's a balloon. He's just in town for a week or two, which is fine. You can only take so much Mook. He's in grad school, working on his MBA.

According to Jess, that means "Me Big Asshole."

"Hey, Danny . . ." Mook hollers. "What's the biggest crime down here these days? Taffy snatching? Overinflated volleyballs?"

Mook's not funny but he's right: People typically come to our eighteen-mile strip of sand for old-fashioned fun in the sun. It's not the South Bronx. It's not even Newark. But Sea Haven *is* where I saw my first bullet-riddled body sprawled out on a Tilt-A-Whirl over at Sunnyside Playland. I remember that morning. It wasn't much fun.

"Traffic!" Becca says. "That's the worst!"

I'm driving because my current vehicle is a minivan with plenty of room for beer and gear. I bought the van "preowned," my mother being the previous owner. She sold it to me when she and my dad moved out to Arizona. It's a dry heat.

I'd say half the vehicles in front of me are also minivans, all loaded down with beach stuff. Bike racks off the backs, cargo carriers up top.

You can't see inside anybody's rear windows because the folding chairs and inflatable hippopotami are stacked too high. I have plenty of time to make these observations because our main drag, Ocean Avenue, is currently a four-lane parking lot.

"Take Kipper!" This from Mook. Now he's chugging out of a two-liter bottle of grape soda.

"Hello? He can't," says Becca. She points to the big No Left Turn sign.

"Chill, okay?" Katie teaches kindergarten so she knows how to talk to guys like Mook.

"For the love of God, man, take Kipper!" Now Mook's kneeling on the floor, begging me to hang a Louie. For the first time all day, he's actually kind of funny, so I go ahead and make the illegal left.

Oh—the streets in this part of town? They're named after fish. In alphabetical order. Only they couldn't find a fish that starts with a Q so Red Snapper comes right after Prawn.

As soon as I make the turn, a cop steps into the street and raises his palm.

And, of course, it's my partner. John Ceepak. He signals for me to pull over.

There's another cop with him. Buzz Baines. Our brand-new chief of police. Some people thought Ceepak should've taken the top job after what happened here in July. Ceepak wasn't one of them.

I'm not sure if Buzz is Baines's real name or if it's just what everybody calls him because he's really an Arnold or a Clarence or something. Anyhow, Buzz is the guy I hope will give me a full-time job next Tuesday. Today he's going to give me a ticket.

"Danny?" Ceepak is startled to see me behaving in such a criminal fashion.

"Hey."

Ceepak is a cop 24/7. He's 6'2" and a former MP. He still does jumping jacks and pushups—what he calls PT—every morning, like he's still in the army. He also has this code he lives by: "I will not lie, cheat or steal nor tolerate those who do." An illegal left turn? That's cheating. No question, I'm busted.

"Hey, Ceepak!" Becca sticks her head over my shoulder. She loves his muscles. Maybe this is why Becca and I don't date anymore: Where Ceepak's beefcake, I'm kind of angel food.

"Who we got here, John?" Baines hasn't recognized me yet.

"Auxiliary Officer Boyle."

I hear Becca sigh. Ceepak? He's handsome. Buzz Baines? He's handsomer, if that's a word. Sort of like a TV anchorman. You know what I mean, chiseled features with a lantern jaw and this little mustache over a toothpaste-commercial smile.

"Of course. Boyle. You and John cracked the Tilt-A-Whirl case."

"Roger that," says Ceepak. "Officer Boyle played a vital role in that investigation."

"Keep up the good work." Chief Baines winks at me. "And don't break any more laws."

"Yes, sir."

"Call me Buzz."

"Yes, sir. Buzz."

I hear Ceepak rip a citation sheet off his pad. It's all filled in.

"You're writing him up?" Baines asks.

"Yes, sir. The law is the law. It should be applied fairly, without fear or favoritism."

Baines nods.

"John, when you're right, you're right. Sorry, Danny. If you need help with the fifty bucks, come see me. We'll work out a payment schedule."

"Drive safely," says Ceepak.

"Right. See you tomorrow."

"No. Thursday's my day off."

"Oh, yeah. Mine, too."

Ceepak eyes our beer coolers. Marshmallows aren't the only things that get toasted at our annual beach party.

"Then have a cold one for me, partner."

"Roger that."

"But pace yourself. It takes a full hour for the effect of each beer to dissipate."

"Right. See you Friday."

"That'll work." Ceepak smiles. No hard feelings. He even snaps me a crisp "catch you later" salute.

I pull away from the curb, real, real slow. I can't see any signs but I assume 10 m.p.h. is below the posted speed limit.

I can't afford two fifty-dollar tickets in one day.

The late-night guy on the radio is saluting "The Summer of '96," reminding us what idiots we were back then.

"Tickle Me Elmo was under every Christmas tree and Boyz II Men were climbing the charts with Mariah Carey . . ."

Great.

He's going to make us listen to her warble like a bird that just sucked helium.

It's almost midnight. We're the only ones on the beach. Most of the houses beyond the dunes are dark because they're rented to families with kids who wake up at six A.M., watch a couple of cartoons, and are ready for their water wings and boogie boards around six fifteen. The parents need to go to bed early. They probably also need vodka.

I like the beach at night. The black sky blends in with the black ocean and the only way to tell the two apart is to remember that the one on top has the stars and the one below has the white lines of foam that look like soap suds leaking out from underneath a laundry room door.

Katie's sitting with the other girls around our tiny campfire, smooshing marshmallows and gooey Hershey bars between graham crackers. I bet she's the kind of kindergarten teacher who'd let you have s'mores in class on your birthday. She's that sweet, even though she grew up faster than any of us. Her parents died eight or nine years ago. Car wreck.

I need another beer.

I slog up the sand to the cooler. Mook and Jess are hanging there, probably talking baseball, about the only thing they still have in common. Mook wears this floppy old-man bucket hat he thinks makes him look cool. He has one hand jammed in the pocket of his shorts, the other wrapped around a long-neck bottle of Bud, his thumb acting like a bottle cap. The world is his frat house.

"Hey, Danny . . ." Mook shakes the Bud bottle. "Think fast."

He lifts his thumb and sprays me with beer. Now it looks like I just pissed my pants.

Mook's belly jiggles like a Jell-O shot, he's laughing so hard.

"Jesus, Mook." Jess says it for me.

I forgot about Mook's classic spray-you-in-the-crotch gag. One of his favorites. He also used to buy plastic dog poop at the Joke Joint on the boardwalk and stuff it in your hamburger bun when you weren't looking.

"Very mature, Mook." I wipe off my shorts.

"You're not going to arrest me, are you, Detective Danny?"

"No. I'll let you off with a warning. This time."

"You want a beer, Danny?" Jess fishes a long-neck out of the watery ice.

I check my watch.

"What's with the watch?" Mook saw me. "You're actually waiting an hour between brewskis? What a weenie! Your cop pal is a hardass. And that haircut! Who does he think he is? GI Joe?"

If Mook knew Ceepak like I do he'd realize: GI Joe probably plays with a Ceepak Action Figure. The guy's that good. I shake my head, ignore Mook, and mosey away with my beer.

Becca, Olivia, and Katie are sitting in short beach chairs, the kind that put your butt about two inches above the sand. I plop down with them.

"Someone please remind me why we hang out with Mook," I say.

Becca shrugs. "Because we always have?"

I guess that nails it.

On the radio, the deejay's yammering about *"Sea Haven's gigantic Labor Day Beach Party and Boogaloo BBQ. MTV will be broadcasting live. So will we . . ."*

They've been hyping this Labor Day deal all month. Come Monday, the beach will be so crowded, you'll be lucky to find enough sand to spread out a hand towel, maybe a washcloth.

"Here's another hot hit from the sizzling summer of '96!"

The radio throbs with "C'mon 'N Ride It (The Train)"—a bass-thumping dance tune from the Quad City DJs, the same people who gave the world "Whoot, There It Is." The choo-choo song was big in 1996, the summer The Marshmallow Crew first got together and somebody said, "You know what? We should do this again next summer!"

"Hey, let's dance!" Katie pops up, like she's ready to teach us all the hokey-pokey—the adults-only version.

The girls fling off flip-flops, kick up sand. Becca cranks up the volume on the radio, shimmies her blond hair like she's in a shampoo commercial. I attempt to get my groove thing going. Basically, when I dance, I stand still and sway my hips back and forth. Tonight, I also "move my arm up and down" as the singer suggests. Lyrics like that are extremely helpful for those of us who are dance impaired.

"Hey, isn't dancing on the beach against the law?" Mook brays like an annoying ass. Actually, the herky-jerky moves he is currently making should be ruled illegal. "You gonna haul us off to jail, Danny? Get your picture in the paper again?"

Ceepak and I got some press back in July. The wire services and magazines picked up the Tilt-A-Whirl story. I was semifamous for about a week. On top of being obnoxious, Mook sounds jealous.

Fortunately, any thoughts of Harley Mook drift away when Katie sashays over to dance with me instead of the whole group. She opens up her arms, swings her hips, invites me to move closer.

Then I hear these pops.

Pop! Pop! Pop!

Like someone stomping on Dixie cups up on the street.

I'm hit.

My chest explodes in a big splotch of fluorescent yellow.

Katie's hands drop down and fly behind her. She must be hit, too.

Pop!

A paintball hits the radio and sends it backwards. The batteries tumble out. The music dies.

Pop! Snap! Pop!

We're all hit—splattered with this eerie yellow-green paint that shines like a cracked glow stick. My sternum stings where the paint-ball whacked me.

"Danny?" It's Becca. She sounds hurt. "Danny?"

She sinks to her knees and brings a hand up to cover her eye.

It's fluorescent yellow and red.

The paint is mixing with her blood.